D0477193

A PERFECT MOTHER

Born in France of an American mother and a Viennese father, Katri Skala has lived in the United States and across Europe. She has worked as a senior arts administrator, script editor, and literary editor in the field of new writing in Britain and the US for a range of organisations that include Channel 4, BBC, the Manhattan Theatre Club, the Arvon Foundation, the University of East Anglia and the Writers Centre Norwich. She holds undergraduate and graduate degrees in literature and journalism from Vassar (in the US), Cardiff and the University of East Anglia. She has had published short stories and magazine features. *A Perfect Mother* is her first novel. She works as a mentor to writers in all genres and at all stages of their writing life.

Katri Skala

A PERFECT MOTHER

HIKARI
PRESS

First published in 2018
by Hikari Press, London

www.hikaripress.co.uk

Distributed in the UK by
Combined Book Services Limited
Paddock Wood Distribution Centre
Paddock Wood
Tonbridge
Kent TN12 6UU

© Katri Skala 2018

ISBN: 978-0-9956478-4-8

British Library Cataloguing-in-Publication-Data.
A catalogue record of the book is available
from the British Library.

Designed in Albertina by Libanus Press
and printed in England by
Gomer Press

For M.D.

Acknowledgements

For, variously, advice, encouragement, practical help and feedback during the writing and publication of this novel, my deepest thanks go to Rose Baring, Alex Cadell, Alison Fell, Star Gifford, Vesna Goldsworthy, Eileen Horne, Derek Johns, Christopher MacLehose, Mark Macrossan, Magda Russell, Laura Scott, Christopher Skala and Lottie Skala. My grateful thanks also go to my publisher and editor Isabel Brittain, whose generosity and vision have brought this novel to light. Lastly, and mostly, to my companion in life and in love, Jon Cook. Without whom … as the saying goes.

I'd also like to acknowledge the following, whose work informed some of the themes of the novel: the writings of psychoanalysts Estela Welldon and Anna Motz; author Carol Loeb Schloss for her biography about Lucia Joyce; Jan Morris and Joseph Cary for their beautiful books on Trieste. The lyrics on page 80 are from *Lily the Pink* by The Scaffold, 1968.

PART ONE

'And the strangers there were sad and double.'
Roberto Bazlen in Joseph Carey's
Ghosts of Trieste

HE ARRIVED LATE AFTERNOON IN THE MIDDLE OF October. It was his first visit to the city and it had taken him many years to get there.

The imperial facade of the hotel stood high above the lapping waters of the small bay. Delicate mist smudged contours. He had a curious sensation of being in Prague or Vienna, and seemed to himself to be in two different worlds, not quite knowing which was real.

A group of women were gathered in the lobby. They were speaking English, animated and loudly present in the cool interior. He wondered about them. Trieste was not a tourist destination at this time of year.

His room on the second floor had a balcony and sea view. He opened a window. A gentle drizzle was falling. Not much sea visible. Gulls circled and called. The sound of traffic rose from the busy arterial below.

He shivered and turned into the room. Faint sounds came from the corridor: a door opened, another closed, then women's voices tailed off.

He unpacked, and lined up on the desk several books, against which he propped a photograph of his grandfather, taken sometime in the early 1970s shortly before the old man's death. Standing in a garden, he wore a long jacket that hung from a skinny torso in awkward lines; melancholy.

3

Next to the picture, he placed an old postcard from Trieste in the late 1930s, written by his grandad's father, Theodor. Satisfied, he then put on a fresh shirt and returned downstairs for a drink.

———

The bar was airy with a singular shell-shaped ceiling – baroque, he noted, but the design of the room was contemporary. Smooth marble floor like fluid. It put him in mind of a skating rink, and this turned his thoughts momentarily to last Christmas, neither white nor festive, when he had taken his sons to skate at Somerset House in London only weeks after he had left the family home; and in his memory, the pain of encounter slipped into the sharp sensation of cold as his arthritic limbs crashed onto the ice.

At the tall counter he ordered a grappa, the local drink recommended by guidebooks. The women he had seen earlier were now sitting in a corner chatting. He had an uncanny feeling of being watched. He turned to look more closely: on quick glance they ranged in age from early thirties to late middle age; and in their ease of appearance he saw prosperity and confidence. He also noticed one of them was set apart from the rest, seemingly on the alert, looking for someone, or something. She caught his eyes, lingered, and moved on.

The hotel seemed empty of people other than himself and these women. Murmurs of their conversation echoed in the large room. To his left a piano stood in an enclave, its gleaming black lid reflected a single hanging teardrop light. Shadowy bookshelves recessed into darkness. In that moment he felt he might see men in buttoned suits materialise out of the gloom, clutching bound ledgers as they would have done one hundred years ago when the hotel was headquarters of the marine insurance company that dominated the city. Or so he had read. The scene shifted to a memory of rough thick wool, scratchy against his young skin, wool from the jacket worn by his grandfather, a jacket unlike that of his father's or any other grown-up of the time; a jacket from elsewhere, worn with tenacity by the old man, as if it were the only object left to him of a former life. Grandad … the old man appeared to him in his entirety, a ghost in the gloom of this seaside city. Stefan then, not yet Stephen, a young Jewish boy on a jaunt with his businessman father. Long gone.

He drank some more grappa.

'Penny for them.'

He was startled. Standing next to him was the attractive stranger from across the room. He had not noticed her approach. She followed the greeting with a cheerful laugh and an apology. 'I've been watching you,' she said kindly. They introduced themselves. 'Jacob Bedford!' She repeated his name with relish. 'I thought you were English.' She looked at his clothing: a scruffy corduroy jacket and jeans; self-consciously he brushed some faint dust from his lapel. 'Clothes, always a giveaway. Little game of mine when I'm abroad: spot the Brit. The men are never peacocks. Nice quality.'

This observation piqued his vanity and momentarily caused him to want to retreat; however, he responded with an enthusiastic acknowledgement. His infallible courtesy had often given rise to quarrels with his estranged wife. 'You'd be pleasant to a serial killer rather than feel awkward,' she had once said. He extended his hand in greeting.

The stranger's name was Jane Worth. It inspired in him a flirtatious question which he as quickly repressed. He would not have been the first to play with her name. Did it suit her? He smiled inwardly.

She asked the young bartender for a bottle of wine and then turned to him: 'Would you like a drink?'

He had often been picked up by women; a consequence, or so he thought, of a seemingly open manner and average good looks, both a matter of birth, he had reasoned, and as much blessing as curse in his life. Gradually, with the passing of years, the approaches had diminished. And now he was compelled to notice daily how his sparse, ambiguously pale hair exposed the pink of his skull; how from his tightened belt splurged a ring of flesh. How crooked his back and droopy his jaw. How fewer and fewer women looked at him when he walked into a room. His eldest son, Finn, at seventeen, was now taller than he was.

Jane Worth was closer to his own age than he had at first thought. Women can do that: tricks of make-up and light. Across the room had sat a handsome brunette in her thirties with a broad forehead and full mouth. In front of him stood a portrait of elegant maturity nudging fifty. Grey streaks and fine lines; fitted jeans and a green silk blouse. He nodded approvingly.

She sat on the stool next to him and in quick sentences told him she was a forensic therapist from Gloucester here with her book group. She sent the waiter with a bottle of wine over to the women. 'They're colleagues. We take it in turns to organise jaunts of this kind around a read.' And what kind of book had brought a group of professional women involved in prisons and mental health to Trieste? 'Oh,' she chuckled – it was a throaty teasing sound, and he warmed to her – 'you seem like the kind of man who knows about books. I take it you've heard of James Joyce?' He said he had. He pressed her to say more. 'We've just finished a biography of Lucia, his daughter. Do you know about her?'

No, he confessed, he didn't. Lucia, she said, had been born in Trieste and spent her childhood in the city. 'And what about you? Am I close to the mark? Are you the bookish type?' He shrugged and said he was a journalist. Didn't she know that all journalists had at least one book in them?

'Really?' She rummaged in her bag for a pen. A prick of irritation momentarily stirred him.

The waiter poured them two glasses of grappa and she signed the bill. He noted: Room 28. Same corridor as his.

Her sexual appeal was strong. She must know this about herself. She was at home in her body – a very lovely body – and this provoked in him the contradictory sensations of intimacy and isolation.

She turned her attention back to him: 'Is that why you're here?' Her straightforwardness surprised him. He told her he had a commission from a magazine to write about Trieste. He said he was also investigating a family link, a story of a vanished ancestor. He hoped he had not been staring at her too intensely.

'Ah!' she said, 'so *that's* the book in you.'

'Could be.'

She intrigued him. Rarely had he been so directly apprised, and never on first meeting. Usually it was up to him to get people talking – an inevitable element of being a journalist – yet here a strange woman had unearthed his speculative project within minutes of meeting. It was exhilarating. He felt grateful to Jane Worth for bringing him back into the world. He wanted her to say more.

Yet she was distracted. After each snippet of conversation she glanced at the entrance.

'Did Lucia have an interesting life?' He knew little about Joyce's children. He wanted to bring her back to him.

She looked thoughtful. 'Depends on your view of interesting. Do you know much about her father?'

He told her about reading *Portrait* as a teenager and immediately imagining himself as Stephen Dedalus. Then later when he needed to shore up his intellectual credentials as an arts correspondent he sweated over *Ulysses*. 'I can't pretend to have understood it,' he said with a self-deprecatory grin. He did not want Jane to find him pretentious.

'Me neither. Didn't know much at all about any of them until reading the biography. The Joyces lived here till Lucia was nine.

She was put in a mental hospital for the first time in Paris when she was twenty-five and after that she had analysis with Jung but nothing seemed to work. Eventually her mother and brother put her away for life. Sad story.'

Suddenly a large smile broke over her face and she jumped to her feet. He turned and saw approaching a tall slim woman, so bony and pale he thought he was seeing an apparition. Large blue eyes slid over him and stirred in him an acute self-consciousness.

Jane embraced her vigorously.

'Charlotte! So good so see you. Here, meet my new friend, Jacob.'

He saw that Jane was jumpy. She had not struck him as someone who would lose her cool so easily. Quite the reverse. As for the other: a beauty.

He invited them both to sit at the bar. Charlotte looked past him. Jane gathered up her things in a show of fitful energy. 'No, no, I think we'd best be off. They may not hold our table. But thanks Jacob. Perhaps another time.'

He knew this was an excuse. They strode away with hardly a goodbye. A shadow of disappointment swept over him. Such swift turning away. It left him with an uncomfortable sense that he had been found wanting.

———

He had supper in the capacious empty restaurant, returned to his room and sent his two sons messages. Since the separation from his wife these habitual texts were his life-line to them. They did not always reply. It was Friday night and Finn, a good student and assiduously at his homework most weekday evenings, would be at a film with friends, therefore unlikely to respond quickly. Mikey, twenty months younger, was more trigger-happy with his new smartphone, and likely to whip back a message if he wasn't occupied with his recent Wii console.

He picked up from the desk one of his books about Trieste. First the Romans, then centuries of Hapsburg rule, now Italian, and surrounded on all sides by Slavs. A city at a crossroads, once a cultural melting pot, a hive of artistic and commercial activity. A model of religious tolerance. Now, an ageing population, ethnic tensions, a declining birth rate. Regeneration projects. Headquarters of the international coffee brand Illy.

He took a bottle of beer from the mini-bar and went onto the balcony, restless in his desire for company. The sound of traffic had abated. His eyes adjusted to shades of darkness. The sky had cleared and was star-lit, the air soft with spray. Large tankers opaque in the darkness flickered light onto the petrol-blue night; shimmering beacons climbed the sky to the east ... a block of flats, a row of villas, the famous lighthouse. A rectangle of small yellow dots slipped sideways out of frame ... must be a cruise ship moving down the channel into the Ionian and then onto that jewel of all seas, the Mediterranean. Just as it had been in his great-grandfather's time. Theodor Motz, father to his grandfather, Stephen Mott. Both long dead. One vanished into the past of this city. The other cremated, ashes scattered on a loved rose bush in a suburban garden in Surrey.

Above the orange wash of the city and above the elegant stone balcony from where he gazed out, the North Star peered down, a timeless landmark on the vast horizon. He stood for a long while unable to move. Finally, the throb of arthritis in his left hip caused him to return inside where he lay on the wide smooth bed until sleep finally came.

At breakfast he walked straight up to Jane. She was sitting on her own, reading glasses tipped on the end of her nose, head bowed over a phone. She smiled when she saw him and he was reassured.

There was a slight ache in his temple, which he rubbed with his palm. He was tired. Sleeping less and more fitfully. Through the night his unconscious had wrestled with dreaming images of water tanks and ghostly mansions; he had woken, still dressed and exhausted, to the thunder of early morning lorries.

They exchanged a few pleasantries. He asked her to join him for a drink later, but it came out awkwardly. Not quite the smooth talker he had once been. She contemplated him, taking her time to respond. Momentarily he felt dissected; it was not an unpleasant feeling – rather like being a familiar specimen under friendly routine inspection.

'Ok, yes why not.' Her lively expression lifted his spirits. She got up from the table. 'If you want, stop by the conference room later. A Joyce expert, the librarian from the Joyce museum, is giving a talk today at two. It'd be good to have you there and you never know, you might find some of it useful.'

He spent the morning wandering the city centre. Tomorrow he would begin the task of taking formal notes; today he walked and looked, unfolding his senses to what surrounded him. The local aroma of pastries in the *pasticceria* and a hint of – what was it called? *kren?* – from the doorway of a buffet (he checked his guidebook: *kren*, the local horseradish). He strolled the main shopping street and along the intersecting avenues.

The geometry was arresting: large bold squares and avenues arranged in a grid; then crooked narrow lines and crescents on the horizon. Trieste had taken shape in a bowl, flanked on three sides by steep green hills leading up to the Karst Plateau, and on the fourth, facing west, straight onto the Adriatic. Just as his grandfather had described. The vast canvas of a city: sometimes it might be a Braque with its verticality, other times there were Kandinsky's marks or Matisse's sensuous warmth. Trieste was difficult for him to grasp: a medley of histories distinctly expressed yet somehow at odds in the natural setting. It was at once familiar and equally strange.

As a boy he had heard many stories about the city. They would come to him during family visits on a Sunday when he would sit on Grandad's lap after lunch and pour over the large picture books taken from a high shelf. Inevitably his grandmother's eyes would roll. 'That place again!' she'd scoff, exasperation and a hint of jealousy in her voice as if her husband was rolling out an embalmed mistress. In later years, as he became a teenager, and visited less frequently but often on his own, he realised that she had never seemed to quite adjust to her husband's foreignness; to accommodate the inflection of German in the old man's speech to their distinctly English milieu. He had on several occasions over the years pushed his mother to talk, a little, about them, only to be met with reticence. Grandad was Jewish, there were lost relatives in the Second World War. It was a familiar tale in its generalities. He had not succeeded in getting any details from her and now it was too late.

Jacob's work had taken him to many places around the world. He was fifty-five and it was only now, now that there were more years behind him than in front, now that – what might he call it? – this gap in his life had appeared that the stories told to him by his grandfather returned with unsettling clarity. Grandad. Stefan to his own mother and father. Then later Stephen. Never Steve. There was the voice and there were the stories and there was the mystery of old Theodor's disappearance in Trieste. A good enough place to start.

He slowed his pace at the top of a long dark narrow street which opened onto a piazza, and blinked. It was approaching midday. New beginnings. Another chapter. These phrases looped disconcertingly in his mind. Overcome by fatigue, he found a table in a nearby cafe.

The city echoed its name: Trieste, 'triste', sad. Quite different to the colourful place of his grandfather's recollections. Even with the sudden appearance at lunchtime of city workers filling up cafes and browsing shops, a felted atmosphere pervaded. He sensed this surface masked something. His curiosity was aroused; there was something to be discovered here. He was reminded of how in one city or another throughout his working life a sudden heaviness would descend on him, inexplicable and unbidden; and how quickly a tantalising – could he call it intuition? – an intuition would restore him to the world and carry him on to the next engagement.

This city had secrets to be uncovered and he would find them. He remembered why he was here. With renewed energy he returned to the streets.

———

The librarian had begun his talk by the time Jacob slipped into the small executive meeting room. Jane and her colleagues were sitting around a table, boardroom style. Jane interrupted the proceedings and pointed him to a place on the corner. 'Apologies all – this is my friend Jacob, the one I mentioned earlier, the journalist doing a piece on Trieste.' He nodded a general greeting and sat on the hard chair a little apart. The speaker, a youngish Italian, resumed with a nod in the direction of Jacob. A large pile of books was stacked on the table. Jacob could just about make out the name 'James Joyce' on most of them. He wondered if he should arrange a private meeting with the librarian. Might be useful for his feature.

The talk was interesting: Joyce's madcap drinking and the excitement of a city at the crossroads of Europe; the mélange of languages which Joyce assimilated with the ease of a child-genius.

Then there was the wife Nora, the dark Irish beauty; and also the grinding poverty, the language teaching. A time of great activity, creative fertility. This, the librarian proudly announced, is when his genius was first noticed, this is where he completed *Dubliners*, and this is where he worked on *Ulysses*. He finished on a flourish of excited hand gestures, sat and was applauded.

Then the discussion started up among the women like the revving of an engine. Jacob was startled at the alacrity and energy with which they leapt at their subject, at ease in the sound of each other's voices.

They were alive with speech: relishing the colliding and overlapping of opinion, their cheerful shared worldview on this thing called the unconscious. Yes, they all agreed, Lucia's first consciousness was formed by a strong sense of Italian, that this language was the one with which she would communicate with her father throughout his life, this was, possibly, interesting ... Was her later breakdown, however, rooted in this pre-Oedipal phase? The bog Irish mother and her distaste for Daddy's girl, surely important to her later rebellion ... No, no, it was pure biology, problems with her brain chemistry. Hardwiring ...

Jane, what did Jane think? Jane addressed them all: little is known of those first few months Lucia spent with Nora and brother Giorgio – was the love there, did she bond with the mother? Or was there early infant trauma? The older brother, Mother's favourite, Lucia shunted sideways ... Difficult ...

Jacob noticed comments were most often directed at Jane. She was the leader, her intelligence direct and indefatigable. She would pick up an idea, begin to play with it, then another would join in, and they would be off again, overlapping and laughing, half-sentences and ripostes. At one point, Jane quietened the group – he noted that she didn't do this crudely, it simply happened that when she spoke the natural authority of her tone acted like a judge's gavel – and asked the librarian what he thought about Lucia and her creative relationship to her father. He, poor man, tried to look interested, though the turn of the discussion clearly alarmed him, a reaction with which Jacob felt a certain sympathy.

He did not trust this kind of talk about psycho-this and that; so much nonsense. But Jane captivated him: her queenly presence radiated warmth and protection. Even the librarian visibly relaxed when her attention came to rest on him.

'Jacob!' Jane called as if reading his thoughts. 'You know a lot about Joyce's writing. What do you think?'

He offered a few words about the playful linguistic nature of Joyce's work. Whether this was something that could be linked directly to his daughter, again, like the librarian, to whom he gave a friendly nod, he was not in any position to comment. 'I knew nothing about Lucia until Jane told me yesterday she was born in Trieste and later sectioned.' Then he said, 'My grandfather told me he met Joyce; it must have been sometime just before the First World War. He gave my great-grandfather English lessons.' He warmed to his subject: 'My grandfather used to come here with his father, a Jewish businessman in Vienna. He had an office here. He'd come a lot and bring my grandfather who was of course only a boy at the time.'

The librarian perked up: 'Yes, at a time when Joyce works on *Ulysses*. The city on top of its powers also.'

Eagerly Jacob continued: 'I remember my grandfather talking about a speaker who made his father very angry, who told all these good bourgeois patriots to burn libraries. Later I discovered he must have been talking about the futurist Marinetti's visit.'

'It is so,' agreed the librarian. 'Joyce went to the famous lecture in the Teatro Rosso where the Futurist manifesto was made a spectacle.'

'Do you think Lucia saw any of this?' Jane expertly brought the conversation back to its subject.

Jacob did not have an answer because it was, to his mind, unanswerable. He made his excuses and left. His imagination was filling with the possibilities of his grandfather's encounters with the intellectuals and revolutionaries of the era. He wanted to jot down some thoughts while they were fresh.

Back in his room he wrote up his impressions of the day. He included the talk downstairs with some ideas about what kind of man Theodor Motz might have been, this Viennese Jewish businessman who took his son to radical talks and had English lessons with James Joyce. It all went onto his laptop in the form of a journal. Later, back in London, he would begin the task of shaping it up.

He was in the bar at the agreed time. Jane arrived five minutes later. She was dressed more lavishly in a wine-red tunic with simple gold jewellery around her neck. She did not wear a wedding ring, though he knew this was hardly unusual for professional women of their generation. He had bought a bottle of the local wine. He hoped she didn't mind? When in Rome … He congratulated her on the afternoon session.

She chuckled: 'I think we irritated our speaker. The subject of women and their madness can make men uncomfortable, even when they think they should be interested.'

If this was a challenge, she mounted it with casual ease; he side-stepped with equal ease. He had spent years ducking much trickier opposition from his estranged wife. He was more concerned with progressing to the next stage of the evening. They had not agreed on having dinner together but he had indulged his hopes and located a restaurant nearby.

She sipped wine, sat back in her chair and considered him.

Again he felt as if he was an object of study. Again it was not unpleasant. After a moment she asked: 'What do you make of

Trieste?' He suppressed an urge to reply, 'What do you make of *me*?'

He told her he sensed he was in a city where most of what was interesting seemed to have happened in the past, that something undefined lurked in the atmosphere. Yet he sensed it was all coming alive again. How curious it felt. He mentioned his grandfather's love for the city, for its animation and colour; the old man's scattered memories; about visiting his grandparents when he was young: 'They lived in Surrey. I don't think they liked each other much. My grandmother was very home counties. Grandad had a slight accent and I realise now was probably quite remote.'

'Yes,' Jane laughed, 'I can imagine. Something similar was going on between my parents.' She continued, 'Have you heard of an Italian psychoanalyst called Ettore Jogan?' He said he hadn't. 'This is what he said about Trieste,' and she quoted: 'If by "neurotic" we mean someone who lives in the uneasiness of a past which conditions his present, then Trieste is neurotic.'

Her intelligent green eyes brightened as if this statement contained a wider truth that might include him. He felt drawn to the possibility, curious about how it might throw light on his relationship to Grandad and the family legacy. Later, much later, he would come to understand, quite precisely, the layers of meaning contained in her quote. How stories passed from one person to the next, across generations and countries, between sexes and nationalities, could spark war and loss, love and adventure. Death.

That evening he did not want to talk about his past and whether his present was conditioned by it. He ignored the quotation and praised her necklace instead: 'Looks like an Iceni torc, the kind worn by the likes of Boudicca.'

'That's me, a warrior queen!' She tossed her dark hair. 'Inspired, in fact, from drawings of the great Hindu goddess Kali.' He detected a glimmer of irony in her tone.

So what about this book idea, she asked, this ancestor? He

told her the bare bones. His great-grandfather Theodor had lived in Vienna from where he ran his business, Motz und Sohn. He kept an office in Trieste and would bring his son during the holidays. This was in the early 1900s. The Sohn, Jacob's grandfather Stefan, was then sent to England as a young man after the First World War when hyperinflation turned the company's fortunes to small change. Stefan stayed in Britain and married the daughter of an English stockbroker. His mother, born in 1934, was their only child. No one knew what had happened to Theodor when Austria became infected with Nazism. The trail disappeared with an address in Trieste from 1938. A postcard had been found among Stefan's few belongings on his death. Its cover photograph was of the large main square; written on the reverse side, a simple message in German: *My dear, 38 Via di Scorcola*. According to his mother, Stefan had never heard again from Theodor, nor from his own mother, Johanna, after her flight from Vienna to Prague in 1940. In a final burst of what Jacob now understood as grief, Grandad had consulted Bad Arolsen, the large archive of missing victims of the Nazis, and discovered his mother had died in 1942 at the concentration camp Theresienstadt.

'Both of us then!' Jane's comment carried surprise and delight.

'Both of us what?' He was confused.

Before she could answer, her mobile rang.

'Charlotte!' The greeting expressed an eagerness that provoked in him an unexpected twinge of jealousy. 'Great.' Her smile broadened. 'See you in about ten minutes … Yes, Margot and Rachel'll join us … Not sure … Somewhere near the hotel? … Good. Oh and' – as an afterthought with a quick flash at him she added – 'and Jacob … yeah, him, that one … he might join us too.' She turned to him. 'Will you? Join us for dinner?'

'Love to!' He tried not to sound opportunistic. He would have preferred Jane on her own, but a dinner with her friends constituted company, and this was something of which he felt himself in baffling need most days.

She returned the phone to her bag. He guessed she didn't have children; otherwise she would've checked for messages. He always did. Earlier he had spoken to both sons, and WhatsApped them images of Trieste with the message, *Your ancestors once lived here!* Finn had replied, *Cool!* Mikey sent a series of exclamation marks whose meaning was not quite intelligible to him.

'Charlotte owns a small flat in the green part of the city, up by the university. She knows the city well. There's a place near here she says is great.'

'She lives here?'

'Not really, but she comes here a lot, it's her only home. She's in Bosnia working for a children's charity. I don't get to see her much.'

'She's British?'

'Oh yes.'

They sat quietly. It suddenly occurred to him that Jane and Charlotte might be former lovers. He looked at Jane with more intent, rolling around in his mind this possibility.

'So, tell me,' he asked casually, 'are you and she very old friends?'

'In a way. I've known her for – goodness, what would it be now? – almost twenty years. Not what you'd call a typical friendship. We met in pretty raw circumstances and I haven't seen her for several years. We've been losing touch. One of the main reasons for organising this trip with my book group was to get a chance to meet up. She'd told me she was going to be here and the timing was right.'

This did not tell him much about the nature of Jane's interest in Charlotte. He admitted he had found Charlotte a little – spooky. She made an impression, certainly. 'Yes,' Jane agreed, 'she always has. She has a way … and then there's the – oh, whatever.' Jane shrugged, suddenly preoccupied. 'Shall we go?'

They walked out together and were joined by Margot and Rachel.

The trattoria was housed in the old city, the *città vecchia*, a warren of alleys glowing yellow from an ochre finish and subtle street lighting. Along the way he observed a pile of old stones encased in glass with a plaque attributing their date to 1 BCE. Remains of Roman Trieste. After the Romans thirteen Italian noble families commanded these streets. By the arrival of the twentieth century and James Joyce it was a place of brothels and seedy bars, *osterie* where Jim would spend hours of the night drinking. A den. Now bijou boutiques and cafes. A designer hotel. He fingered the notebook in his pocket.

The restaurant was oblong with a vaulted ceiling. The walls carried rustic artefacts and a pair of large black and white photographs of the city.

Charlotte was waiting at a small rectangular table, head held high. He was seized by an impulse to exclaim rapturously at the picture she created in the flickering candlelight as if the head of a Botticelli painting had been transplanted. Their eyes met. He sensed she was aware of her effect.

Jane embraced her: 'You're here already!' Then in quick order she introduced Margot and Rachel, and pulled back a chair for Jacob, saying, 'You two have already met.' She looked from him to Charlotte. He tilted his head in acknowledgement first at Jane, then, in taking his time, at Charlotte. She smiled in return. He noticed she had hollowed cheeks and soft bruising under her eyes; then faint lines criss-crossing luminescent skin. Her ash-blond hair fell glancingly about her shoulders. Shifting glints of distance and curiosity in the eyes. A perfect mouth. The phrase 'a rare beauty' came back to him.

The talk was of things common to Jane and her colleagues. Margot was a forensic psychologist employed by the prison service. Her interest in Trieste was focused on shopping and where Lucia Joyce had lived as a child. She was younger than Jane and Rachel by a good many years and aware of their seniority. He had not noticed her during the discussion of the afternoon for the reason, he now realised, that she had not spoken a word. He felt for her youth and awkwardness, and warmed to the energy of her personality. Rachel, possibly in her sixties, was a consultant psychiatrist with a slightly eccentric air. To his mind they formed an odd trio: brought together by geographical proximity, an interest in reading and linked professions, yet culturally and temperamentally seemingly very different.

He turned to Charlotte: 'Do you like living here?'

She sipped her wine and gazed beyond him, her eyes settling safely on a photograph of the central city square. 'It's a good city. Low-key. It suits me.' She spoke softly.

'What's your charity?' He could not imagine this delicate beauty at work.

'In Sarajevo. It's called Hope, for children who have suffered landmine injuries.'

This was picked up by Jane: 'Remarkable organisation. Putting children back together.'

There ensued a discussion between the professionals about whether such a thing was possible in the psychological sense. Margot was of the opinion that once broken, never mended. She had seen enough of those who went to prison to know that rehabilitation was practically a pipe dream. Rachel turned with disdain on her much younger colleague to remark that the complexity of trauma was such that no one really knew what worked. All you could do, she argued, was to bring a scientific precision to what could be diagnosed and to treat accordingly.

'With medication alone?' interjected Jane in a tone edged with disagreement. To Jacob she said: 'With my psychotherapeutic training I want to work with the unconscious. I also don't think healing happens without serious work on what happened in childhood. Rachel disagrees.'

He followed the debate as best he could. They were in a territory of professional discourse whose complexities and dimensions eluded him, much as it had during the afternoon's discussion.

Charlotte had fallen silent during this exchange, like him, and was bowed over a plate of pasta. He noticed Jane seemed to turn most often to Charlotte. A certain disquiet that he could not quite pinpoint had descended on their little group.

His attention wandered. A consistent thrum of Italian filled the air, suggesting to him that most of the customers were local. He had written about many such places in his years of travel: prosperous small restaurants that had a nose for market trends, an ability to provide the traditional with its inherent offer of quality and continuity alongside consumer demands for style and fashion. The ubiquitous cuisine of pasta, pizza and regional dishes. This particular place had a clean uncluttered look and soft theatrical lighting. The overall effect was one of intimacy. He patted his notebook again, an automatic reflex developed over years.

Rumbles from the refugee crisis and the tearing of social cohesion seemed to belong to elsewhere. He would visit the industrial zone if he had time; a snapshot view of what conditions of living might be outside the preserved and prettified central area. He liked to include details of the local politics in his travel pieces; it somehow appeased his guilty conscience, a constant feature of his daily life. Often they were cut. He had given up long ago fighting with editors about this.

To a stray diner he would be the lone man, middle-aged, among a group of women of all ages. The discerning might see that one of the women was not of the set, that her manner and dress had something different about them. It is possible the word 'aura' might be used. One of the younger diners might guess wrongly she was a model, or maybe a celebrity. Those with little conversation between them and a distracting curiosity in others would pick up the shift in tone that occurred abruptly halfway through the main course.

It happened because Charlotte sat bolt upright as if remembering a forgotten event and said in a voice that was oddly inflected: 'You have to talk. Even when it's the worst thing in the world.' Rachel and Margot stared impolitely. He detected anxiety in the way Jane communicated encouragement to her friend: 'Say more?' He shrunk back in his seat.

Margot jumped in: 'You should hear the talk I get every day. A lot of misery and fuck this and fuck that but you can tell when they're lying. You feel like really sorry for some of them, you know, domestic violence victims who end up doing stupid things, like push drugs, that kind of thing.' She shook her head in memory of these women and offered a tentative smile to Charlotte who said: 'Yes, I understand. Many of the mothers I meet through the charity have experienced the most awful things.'

'Enough,' boomed Rachel, throwing Charlotte a sympathetic bone. 'This is getting depressing for you I'm sure. And boring perhaps for our male guest.'

'Not at all,' was his polite reply. Charlotte nibbled on an index finger.

Jane stretched behind him and put her hand on Charlotte's shoulder. With a small shake the latter disengaged her friend's grip.

'The thing is,' continued Margot, not deterred by the injunction to change the conversation, 'the thing is, that you can talk as much as you want, in a therapeutic manner – I mean like –' she directed her words to Jane – 'I know it's what you do and it's like you really believe in it, but you can't treat criminals the same as patients. There'd be chaos.'

Jane noted her young colleague's assertions with a slight raise of her darkly arched eyebrows and flipped the conversation to him: 'Jacob, why don't you tell the others about your magazine commission?'

'It's really inspired by my grandfather, he used to come here as a boy and loved it. The Trieste of yesterday versus the Trieste of now. I'm also thinking about a book project, a personal story about a missing ancestor.' He placed his notebook on the table in affirmation of his credentials.

Charlotte: 'Did you know Italy's only death camp was in a suburb of Trieste?'

He said he had not yet read much about this aspect of the city's history but he looked forward to visiting the site and finding out more. Margot tittered and was ignored.

'It's haunting,' Charlotte continued. 'It was turned into a memorial in 1965. It was first a rice mill then a police prison. Perfect for when the SS took it over. It had a high chimney and an old oven. Communists and partisans in the main. And Jews of course although most of them were sent to Auschwitz. Did your relative die in Trieste?'

'I've no idea. He lived in Vienna and came here for business. He kept a flat on the Via San Nicolò. Had to give it all up after the First World War. Then I don't know what happened to him. All I have is an address from 1938. Over in the smart area to the west of the city.'

'I know the neighbourhood. My flat's not far from there. You've got your work cut out for you.'

It was not an invitation to pursue this line of conversation and he did not know why Jane had asked him to join them. He had nothing to contribute to the discussion about prisons and he was of no interest whatsoever to Charlotte – whose odd presence was asserting an irritating hold over him. He looked around the trattoria again and made a mental note of the architectural detail. He would include it in his feature on Trieste linking the neighbourhood with Joyce. He patted his notebook and nodded at the surrounds. 'Different to what it was in Joyce's day.'

He reclaimed the table with a short talk on Joyce's drinking haunts. His open grin invited the others to join in. Charlotte's renewed silence was a challenge. He was not used to being treated dismissively by a beautiful woman. *Amour propre* roused him to eloquence and he spoke roundly about the history of Trieste.

Jane was enthusiastic: 'Just imagine the different sounds, all those languages – what's the local dialect? Triestine? And then Slovene, is it? German, Italian. English. Greek. Turkish …' She counted them off her fingers. 'Must have been intense. Difficult for Lucia. A real babel.'

Margot piped up: 'But also a fascinating place. Her childhood must've been so lively. Trieste was like a hub back then, wasn't it, Jacob?'

Yes, it had been. A fascinating medley of people had passed through the city: the famous British author and explorer, Richard Burton, the French writer Stendhal, and then there were the exiled royals. And so on.

To his own puzzlement something strange was happening: he found himself able to focus only half-heartedly on what he was saying. Charlotte in her uncaring presence was distracting him. Out of the corner of his eye he saw she had begun to twist her fingers as if knitting.

Margot was talking again: 'I think Lucia was lucky. Must've been a great place to be when she was a kid. Really multicultural. I think she went off the rails later because it's who she was. And

like the toxic stuff of her dad and her not being able to dance.'
She shrugged in support of her opinion, a youthful gesture of
'whatever'. He checked his irritation at the draw Lucia seemed
to hold over these women – all of them, that is, with the exception
of Charlotte whose hand now twitched on the table. It occurred to
him that it was rather like sitting next to a puppet whose mistress
was invisible.

The professionals talked on.

Rachel was saying something about Lucia setting fire to a house
where she'd lived. Margot said it showed that her mother and
brother had been right to have her sectioned. Jane disagreed, at first
calmly and as the discussion heated up, with increasing passion.
Rachel's position was that if Lucia had had access early on to the
drugs they used nowadays she would have been able to have a
pretty normal life. No, argued Jane, the normal would not be
normal, it would just be facade. Margot said brain science could
now show there were people who were born with serious problems
in their biochemistry.

'There really are irredeemably bad people in the world,' asserted
Margot. Jane challenged: 'Do you really think people with mental
health problems like Lucia fit that category? Should all be locked
up? That's daft.'

'If medication doesn't work, then certainly,' affirmed Rachel.
'The priority for the judiciary must be to protect society. It was
right and proper that Lucia was put in an institution, she had shown
herself to be a danger to herself and to those around her.'

'Can you blame her? Her rage? The mother humiliated her –'
and Jane was off.

'Oh leave her mother out of it,' Rachel cut in. 'They're always
used as easy scapegoats, and by men at that.' Jane knew that, didn't
she, the awful influence of patriarchy on women's mental health –
'Yes,' interrupted Jane, 'but my point is –'

So steady and charming during the discussions of the afternoon, Jane had become shrill and hectoring. No longer the unofficial arbiter, she argued at some fundamental level as if her sense of self was being attacked. They all did. He was excluded from this discussion. So was Charlotte. Yet he had the impression that everything Jane said was for Charlotte's benefit. He sat between the two of them exasperated and a little scared by the force of emotion zinging about the table. Confrontation of any kind made him apprehensive. Abruptly Jane appealed to him: 'What do you think, Jacob? You seem kind. Surely you don't think leaving the mentally ill to rot in an institution is humane?'

'You're twisting things,' said Rachel. 'That's not my position.'

'Nor mine,' asserted Margot.

He said tentatively that he thought it was a very complex issue and that really he had no opinion. What he wanted was for this argument to end.

As he spoke he felt a strong shaking as if a slight earthquake was under way. Charlotte. Tremors were running through her. Alarmed, he put his arm around her shoulders. Then just as suddenly the trembling stopped and she composed herself.

'No, no, it's OK. I'm OK,' she whispered. He looked at her sharply. There was shame on her face, then determination.

Then she spoke, bringing their argument to a halt.

'I was in a mental hospital, seventeen years ago. Jane came to my rescue. She helped me. It does help, I can tell you. It helps a lot to have people who really listen, who don't think you're the worst person ever. I had lots of treatment, medication, group therapy, they helped. Without them, without Jane, I'd still be there, in a kind of prison.'

An embarrassed pause followed. He glanced around the restaurant. Two tables of two, one of three, one of four. All now concentrated on each other. And the pleasure of eating. Had they heard? He scraped the remains into his mouth of a delicately flavoured white fish.

'Anyway, I thought I should say something. That's probably enough now. I think I should go.' She got up. So did he, polite. Jane stood too.

'I'll come with you.' She spoke across him to Charlotte.

'No, thanks, I'm fine, just tired. I'll see you tomorrow, OK? Goodnight everyone.' The finality in Charlotte's voice was clear. She wanted to be gone, she wanted to be alone.

He watched her leave: as she walked through the glass door, she cast a quick, almost imperceptible glance back at him – Jane noticed too. It surprised him; he was reminded of Robert Doisneau's famous photograph, *Parisienne:* the dazzle of a young woman's face half-turned, caught in a moment of seductive communication with the cameraman; the way in which the image captures a complicity between the photographer and the woman.

Jane said to the table: 'She must be tired.' As if in explanation, or apology, she added: 'We go back a long way, she's had a really rough time.'

A tolerable civility re-entered the conversation. Chat replaced rancorous talk. No one mentioned Charlotte. They paid the bill and returned to the hotel.

Margot and Rachel said goodnight and disappeared into the lift. Jane dawdled. He had no desire to return to the loneliness of his bedroom on the second floor. Was Jane on the same landing? He remembered her room number: 28. Yes. Perhaps they might have a drink together on his balcony. The temperature was clement, the sky clear. It would be good to breathe the night's air. Steadying. Charlotte's behaviour had provoked in him a small dread and a little leap of excitement. Jane seemed to be in a similar state: she was twiddling her room key and shifting her weight from one foot to another as if unable to shake something.

Presently he asked: 'Would you like a drink?' She nodded distractedly. Fixing his features into what he hoped was a pleasing expression, he suggested they go to his room where in his mini-bar he knew there was a bottle of the fine local Friulia and a lovely view from the balcony. The dimly lit lobby offered cover. It was difficult to read her reaction.

'Yes, I'd think I'd like that,' she finally said. 'I feel a little shaken . . . you know . . . Charlotte, what happened this evening. It's emotional for me, seeing her again. I hadn't expected to feel so churned up.'

He murmured words of sympathy.

Once in his room they stepped outside. There was little traffic down below. A stillness had settled on the night. He offered his jacket and arranged the chairs side by side so that they both faced the now black sea and brightened stars; then he fetched the bottle of wine and two glasses.

There they sat in companionable silence for perhaps a couple of minutes until he took the tentative step of holding out his hand to her. Was it a pass? He wasn't sure. Should he? And would she? Too many nerves. It had been a while. She squeezed and let go. Not quite knowing what to do next he put his hand on his lap. The contact might be a moment of touching communication, it could equally be rejection.

'You've been kind, Jacob. Listening to us, witnessing that stuff with Charlotte.' He waited. It was unclear to him what might happen. 'Violence,' she continued, 'sometimes I feel it permeates everything.' She peered into the darkness, and then up and around the elaborate masonry of the balcony half lit from the bedroom lamp glowing through the window. Her eyes were dark and inscrutable.

She went on: 'History. There's your great-grandfather. That legacy is powerful. The bankruptcy, the Jewishness. It was very immediate in my case. My father had left behind a family in India. It was during Partition. His father had been English and had got him to London for university. Most of his Indian family were killed. They were Hindu. When you grow up with that shadow, even in the comfort of a staid ordinary suburban home like ours, with its petty bickering and settled compromises, even so, you can't escape. It seeps into you.'

He understood a little more now. She too had a line of loss in the family history. There are so many hidden in the tucks of time. He asked if her father was still alive.

'No,' she said, 'he died a while ago.'

'I'm sorry to hear that. So did mine.' A cul-de-sac.

He could see she was thinking and that her thoughts were leapfrogging from one thing to another. All at once agitation took hold: 'There's also what happened to Charlotte.'

Charlotte. More about Charlotte. The disturbed mood that had prevailed over the night's gathering was in her again. She had something to get out, a cleansing to perform. He got himself a warm jumper and from the bed a throw, which he draped over her knees.

Let her talk. He inhaled deeply the salt air. Perhaps then …

He settled into his chair, wider awake.

'Charlotte never comes back to Britain,' she went on. 'She experienced awful trauma. Then she went to work for the charity and she's been doing it for about fifteen years. It's funny what brings people together, isn't it? Invisible threads.'

He saw the three of them bound by a piece of string on the edge of this fat sturdy balcony performing a circle dance. It made him chuckle. Jane wanted to know what was amusing. 'No, nothing,' he murmured, 'just – no doesn't matter. You were saying?'

The night was stretching ahead. He must make a list of tomorrow's activities. A visit to the Revoltella, a museum of modern art.

He thought it was named after its founder, a merchant baron of the nineteenth century. His exuberance for this kind of research was unbounded. Bit by bit, like a jigsaw, the culture of a city would acquire shape and a story would begin to emerge. Notebooks would fill as an ever-increasing pile-up of fact and conjecture were collected. It made him feel like a credible human being, a citizen of the world. A bridge between cultures. A communicator.

Tomorrow beckoned. So much to do. Time to say goodnight.

But he didn't move. He did not want to leave Jane's side. He wanted to know more about her. He felt drawn to her by something he did not understand.

The sea air was now making him feel pleasantly sluggish, the momentary alertness gone. He suppressed a yawn. Jane sipped her wine and sighed at the vast space in front of them. The openness brought her even more into herself.

He had time, all the time in the world.

———

'You see, Charlotte can really get to me. I'd almost forgotten that about her. You must've found tonight's – what can I call it – outburst a bit much. We've been through a lot, the two of us. Oh it was many years ago and we've both moved on but … I don't know, you see she's special to me.

'We didn't meet like most old friends do, at school or university or through mutual acquaintances. I was in my first job. It was about twenty years ago or thereabouts. About this time of year. I was a clinical psychologist back then. I'd just finished my training and was working with the family mental health services in Gloucester. I was idealistic and rather inexperienced.

'Don't look surprised! Most of us coming out of college together were like that. It's normal I think. But in my case, well, let's just say there were unexpected consequences. If I'd only been a bit savvier you see. I don't think it was just my youth, I think I was just one of those types that sees herself as a rescuer and then, well, not to be too boastful, but I'd got really top marks for my PhD. It's a long story. A sad one. But I remember it all as if it were recent. Odd sometimes what we remember most. I've gone over it so many times in my head I sometimes wonder at where the line is between what really happened and what I've made up. That can happen, can't it?

'It started when I was asked to make an informal evaluation of Charlotte and her baby Sylvie. Yes, it was surprising. But you see questions had been raised by the consultant paediatrician after her GP had confided in him. That was pretty unusual. I've thought a lot about that since, about how it came about. It was outside the usual protocols. I think the GP felt undermined by Charlotte. He felt his authority was being challenged. He and the paediatrician were old friends. They were part of a sort of boys' network and I think they both had it in for Charlotte right from the start.

'No one in my department took the business with Charlotte seriously. I knew this because the task of interviewing her and meeting Sylvie had been fobbed off on me. That's not self-deprecation. As I said I was young and new to the department and though I thought I was pretty good I knew that if it'd been serious someone a lot more senior than me would've handled it. The other odd aspect of it was that I was told to go to her house. Social workers visit homes all the time but not psychologists and counsellors. Thinking about it, as I've done so often, it was because of her privileged position and her husband's influence. He didn't want her to come into the clinic. We had no choice.

'The idea was that I do a visit, ask some questions, fill in the form. Then file the paperwork and everyone's happy. Job done. Yes, it's very different now. Procedures for this kind of thing have been really tightened. Form, protocols, checks. But then. Well. It was a different world. Before the common use of the web and smartphones and email, Twitter, and the rest. In some ways it seems to me like a better time. There was room for improvisation. Downsides to that too, of course. I'm well aware that I can sound like a grumpy old woman to my younger colleagues.

'Charlotte lived in one of those old Cotswold manor houses. Warm golden stone. Down a drive in what felt like an enchanted valley. I remember it so clearly. I didn't know anyone who lived in a place like that. As I say I was pretty unworldly. I suppose I was self-assured but I wasn't very savvy in a kind of common sense, knowing-about-the-world way. My upbringing had been ordinary. Those things I told you about my father didn't come out until I'd left home and I was at university. Growing up I thought our family was pretty much like most others. My dad worked as a kind of data analyst for GCHQ. I knew there was a story about colonial administration and Anglo-Indian relations in the past but it was too distant to be of much interest to a hard-working swat like me. Mum was a housewife at first then got a part-time job. So you can see why going to Charlotte's was like visiting an exotic country that you'd only ever read about in glossy magazines. Then there was Charlotte's beauty. Well, you know. You've met her. Men became quite silly around her. Women too. That much was obvious. There was a time when that would've really annoyed me. Women as objects, eye candy. Not so much anymore. But at the time it seemed pretty clear to me the suspicions raised about her were sexist. I thought the paediatrician had made a pass at her and been rejected. That was only surmise of course, my imagination running away with me, but I still think my instincts were probably quite close to the truth. Charlotte and I have never talked about those early days.

'Anyway. This was the sum of my briefing: Charlotte had insisted on treating Sylvie's ailments with alternative medicine.

32

Homeopathy. Very fashionable now. Less so then. Heresy to doctors of a certain generation. Sylvie had a high temperature and respiratory problems. Charlotte brought her into the surgery. Apparently, she was calm and quite in control of the situation. Later I found out she'd studied medicine as an undergraduate and then given it up before marrying. She told the GP she was only there on the insistence of her homeopath. She'd had a private birth and wasn't registered for health visits. The GP referred her immediately to the hospital. She didn't go. He followed up with a phone call and she told him Sylvie's temperature had subsided after a dose of something called . . . something, I don't remember the name for it now. A treatment of sorts. This happened again, several times in fact. The GP felt she was rubbing his nose in her obstinacy and neglecting her child. This is what he communicated to the paediatrician.

'I'd met the consultant paediatrician on a couple of occasions, the one who informed social services. He was full of the research he was conducting on children who died sudden deaths. You'll know it by its lay term, cot death, when infants die suddenly in their sleep and no one really knows why. This paediatrician had become involved in several cases where he believed the mother was causing the problem. I thought he was way off the mark. I still do as a matter of fact, but that's another matter.

'Then there was the business of his arrogance. In his view, psychologists were even further down the chain of being than social workers. That many of us in both professions were women added to his condescension. The whole situation struck me as ridiculous. Part of me couldn't believe social services had taken it seriously, but Mr Shottley, the paediatrician, carried a lot influence in our small community. And I must admit another part of me was excited. I'd been given this particular responsibility, a case in unusual circumstances with a kind of glamour. I felt chosen. It does seem quite bonkers now and it probably was. I was just too young to know. And I'd been told to go there by my supervisor. I didn't feel I could refuse. They've really tightened up procedures since then. But I'd never know Charlotte if it was all done by the book.

'I got lost down a country lane and was late for the appointment. Charlotte was gracious and I was very nervous. You can imagine, can't you? The other thing to say is that this was the first interview of its kind I'd conducted on my own. And my god, with what a mother. It was rare if not unheard of for someone like me to find myself interviewing someone like her. Parents can be very defensive in such a situation. They know they're under the worst kind of scrutiny. But she was – so kind to me. We sat at her kitchen table and drank tea. There's a fairly standard list of questions you ask, about her feelings at being a mother, about her marriage, how she finds the pressures of looking after an infant, what support she has. There was an absurdity to our conversation. Most cases occur in homes where there is substantial deprivation, obvious signs of addiction or personality disorder – chaos. I don't know what the statistics are on care orders being issued to wealthy people, but I would imagine so negligible as to be practically non-existent. I don't mean abuse doesn't happen in those kinds of families, of course it does, it's simply easier to camouflage when you have money.

'The only moment in the interview which gave me pause for thought was when we got onto the subject of her marriage: it was a tiny flicker of hesitation on her part.

'She told me she and Alex, that was her husband, they'd married quickly after meeting at a party a couple of years earlier. *Coup de foudre* was the expression she used.

'She had that long hair, it covered her face when she looked down in such a way that I found myself trying to duck and peek sideways as if I were talking to a child. It was a strange game of hide-and-seek.

'Then I noticed a photograph on the kitchen counter: it was a casual snapshot of her and Alex on holiday somewhere. They were tanned and laughing. She told me it was taken when they were on their honeymoon. And here's where the hesitation came – I noticed her lips tighten. That was interesting to me because often, you know how it is, people, when they look at someone they love, or when they mention them, will show some sign of affection. It could be a softening of the expression, a slight smile, a certain tone in the voice, but she didn't, she tightened her lips. I continued.

'"Do you feel he's a supportive father?" She replied by telling me how hard he worked and how he provided for everything. She also added, as if an afterthought, that he adored his daughter.

'Her home was immaculate. Not a penny had been spared on the decor. The kitchen where we sat was bigger than my whole flat and was very designer. You know what I mean? Expensive tiles, huge range cooker. There were few signs of Sylvie – a wooden high-chair arranged neatly at the table and a rinsed bottle in the drying rack. I wondered if she breastfed. Sylvie was only two months or so. I asked whether she had a nanny, it all looked so, I don't know, just so ordered. And that's when she yelled at me, "No! Never!"

'I was so taken aback I just sat for several seconds my mouth wide open like an idiot. Then I quickly looked at my notebook to gain some time. When I looked up again she had regained her composure and was gazing somewhere off into the distance. Calm again. Then she said to me in a friendly voice: "I don't think nannies are a good idea, do you?"

'Apparently, Alex had wanted her to have one but she'd refused. She was determined to look after Sylvie herself.

'Her look challenged me to disagree with her. "So you feel you're coping?" I soldiered on.

'Going back over all that now, even now, with all the years that have gone by and with all that I've experienced and learned, I make my own toes curl! I was trying to be light and conversational. To put her at her ease. That's what I'd been taught to do. Keep the questions simple, straightforward. Make a connection. If there's a problem they'll betray themselves. You see, the narcissistic extension between mother and child is quite normal, especially when the child is still an infant but there are ways in which you can detect whether the symbiosis is veering towards the pathological which is what I was meant to be doing. Sorry, that's a little technical but what I mean is that there are signs that trained people are taught for detecting mental instability. I could've pressed her on whether she was coping, but I felt it was too early. Also, truth is, I really was way out of my depth.

'Predictably, she put me down. She didn't exactly scoff, but she came close, and I felt silly for having asked. Coping? Of course she was coping!

'She then looked at the kitchen clock and suggested we wake Sylvie. I followed her through the house. The all-consuming luxury acted as balm on my frayed nerves. I kept thinking, wrongly as it turns out, that everything was going very well.

'There was an impressive staircase and a stone floor. I also noticed a couple of large oil paintings on walls and thought they might be of ancestors. The thing was that, in spite of the formality, the house was a welcoming place. You felt instantly protected from the world as if those severe long-faced people on the wall were somehow guardian angels. It was really strange. I don't think I've had that experience again.

'Charlotte noticed my looking around and offered a kind of explanation. She told me about her feng shui expert. Now I know all about feng shui but then I hadn't a clue. She told me she'd wanted the house to have a positive energy for her child. The word she used was qi.

'Her tone was urgent and sweet. I nodded politely and looked vaguely at a portrait of an old man with a long face. Was he *positive energy*? The introduction of New Age terms – or what I thought then was New Age – raised the unspoken question again. Were there any signs of disturbance in the mind of this woman? Things like feng shui and alternative treatments are mainstream now, but not so back then.

'The word "normal" is problematic, even with so much more understanding about mental health issues. In my profession the more quickly you dispense with judgements about what's normal, the more chance you'll have at getting to the root of behaviour. Yet there I was in this amazing house with this striking woman and I couldn't stop myself from thinking there was nothing normal about any of it. Either in relation to her privilege or to her own singular presence. Certainly I was reacting to the material circumstances but there was more to it.

'Over the years I've often thought about that first meeting and what I keep coming back to is the overwhelming impression of perfection everywhere. It unsettled me more than anything else. The other thing I remember was how defensive I felt on her behalf. I felt she was vulnerable and under attack though I wasn't entirely sure from whom or what. I wanted to fight her corner. I still feel that way.

'Then there was Sylvie. She was very sweet. Tiny little creature. When we got to the top of the stairs I could hear her crying. I wondered where Charlotte's baby monitor was. I hadn't noticed one in the kitchen. We walked quickly down the corridor and into a room at the end. Charlotte gathered her daughter into her arms and murmured little endearments. Then she handed Sylvie to me. I cradled her in my arms. It was an awkward moment. Back then I'd hardly ever held a baby. A family psychologist who'd hardly ever held a baby! But you see much of the training involved talking and interpreting but you never took care of children. That was for social services and others. Sylvie stared at me with her mother's large blue eyes and I felt an inexplicable lump in my throat. She strained to be out of my arms, she wanted her mum. She wasn't fooled by me and my attempts to be maternal.

'I watched mother and child interact for about fifteen minutes. Everything seemed to be perfectly normal. Staged, of course. That's in the nature of observations of this kind. But we have to do them.

'Then I left. Out the kitchen door the way I'd come in. Charlotte saw me to my car, Sylvie in her arms. She invited me to stop by again if I was passing her way. I could have been a neighbour on a casual visit. She showed no anxiety at what I might have thought or what I might report back. On my side I was delighted by them.

'In the car on the way back to the office I felt a small upsurge of emotion against the whole system that had brought me there. I decided that some obscure vendetta was being carried out by the paediatrician against Charlotte. And the GP. Old fart men. Oh, you know the type I mean!

'I wrote a short report for my superiors. I said I'd found nothing untoward. The matter was taken no further and my report was filed away with all such reports.

'I thought that was the end of my relations with Charlotte. Occasionally I'd find myself on a road out where she lived and I'd feel a small pang of – I don't know what it was – a kind of longing I think, for something, some kind of magical life that she seemed to embody, for her friendship maybe. I worked so hard back then I barely had time for anyone, not even my lover. Soon I was to discover how wrong I was about her life, but it's odd, a trace of that feeling has always stayed with me, that feeling of there being something magical about her. I don't know whether you felt it too? Men often do with her.

'Then one day she called me. It was about a month after our meeting. She'd tracked me down at work and wanted to see me.

She didn't sound upset exactly, but there was none of the original friendliness. Her tone was neutral, almost commanding. She asked to meet in a cafe in Cheltenham. I immediately agreed. I shouldn't have. It was unprofessional of me. I should've asked her to come to the clinic. But, I reasoned, she wasn't under our supervision or care, and perhaps she wanted some off-the-record advice. There was even a small voice in my head that whispered perhaps she wanted to be friends. I knew I was fooling myself but I didn't consider it important enough to insist she come to my office.

'We met in a cafe on one of the big shopping streets. She was there before me. Sylvie wasn't with her. I was surprised. She'd seemed so protective, as if she didn't trust anyone with her baby. I hoped nothing bad had happened. I held out my hand to her but she just nodded and pointed to the chair opposite. Like it was some kind of interview.

'"Is everything OK?" I asked. She didn't answer. It was a stilted beginning and I felt wrong-footed. I took my time getting out of my coat and looked around the cafe. There weren't many people, just a few women taking a break from shopping. I focused on Charlotte. She looked exquisite. I remember thinking that was weird. Most mothers I came across barely found time to shower. She also looked as if she'd lost an awful lot of weight.

'Her mood shifted as if aware that she'd not been very welcoming and she smiled warmly. We chatted for a bit about this and that. She wanted to know more about my work. She thought I seemed good at what I did. I was flattered. I was trying to be both informal and detached, achieving neither I suspect.

'Then something peculiar happened; her eyes started flitting madly about the room. It was a tic of sorts, like the one she has now, did you notice? How she picks at her fingers when she's nervous? Then it was flitting eyes as if she thought all the world was watching her. I sensed an undercurrent of something troubling. I asked her about Sylvie, whether there was a problem. The direct approach is often best in these situations.

'"She's so demanding!" Her eruption caused those at nearby tables to frown at us. She quickly corrected herself and went on to talk about how stressful it was looking after Sylvie. I acknowledged the truth of this and waited for her to say more. Her eyes continued to flit this way and that. I wondered whether she was after reassurance. She hadn't struck me as the type of woman who would express any kind of need; and even now, with everything she's gone through, and with what we've gone through together, she keeps a distance. It's as if the remote behaviour is a barrier against harm.

'Apparently Sylvie was with her babysitter. Watching her talk, I was reminded that, in spite of her edginess, she was imposing. She had a natural authority and an intelligence which asserted itself in each figure of speech. It was easy to feel inadequate around her.

'She described how much Sylvie cried and how wearing it was. She told me about the homeopath, interjecting, in the one acknowledgement of what had first brought us together, that she assumed I knew all this. Then she spat out how much she hated the medical profession. I was surprised. After all she'd trained before marrying. It was her parents, they were both medics, he'd been a surgeon, and her mother a psychiatrist.

'Charlotte told me she hated them, daring me, it seemed, to disagree.

'It was a dark winter day. I remember it clearly. Dank and grey. Lights were on up and down the busy shopping street. There were Christmas decorations even though it was only early November. It was a time of year that often made me feel heavy. Memories of harsh family rows tended to crowd my thoughts. For a while when I was younger I'd got into Diwali. I loved the lights, the celebration of goodness and wealth. It seemed to me then so much more appealing than the suffering of Christianity. It was, of course, also a way of claiming the Indian side of my father's past. But then other things took over my life and I reverted to the usual Christmas festivities, mainly for an easier life with my mother. My brother celebrates Diwali and likes to identify now as Anglo-Indian. But, for me, well, work always came first. I redoubled my efforts and spent as little time as possible socialising at Christmas. Sorry, that's a digression. Charlotte – she noticed my sudden change in mood that day and in a quick show of sympathy told me how she too disliked Christmas. Her mother had died, committed suicide, she told me, close to Christmas. When she was newly pregnant with Sylvie.

'That shocked me. She'd dispensed this information with as much nonchalance as my casual observation about the Christmas lights. I knew I had to tread carefully. It occurred to me she was exhibiting symptoms of post-natal depression. I suggested she might like to speak to a professional, like a psychiatrist. My suggestion was met with contempt. "They think they know everything, fucking doctors," she asserted. I let it go.

'Over the next half-hour I tried several times to find out why she'd rung me. I wanted to believe it was out of friendship, and, in a way, it was. In spite of the differences between us, not just back then in terms of class or wealth, but also clearly in temperament, I believe we simply liked each other from the start. Something in her trusted me and I, I don't know, I was just drawn to her.

'She continued to exhibit signs of anxiety and possible post-natal depression but I failed to get her to open up. To ask for help. Finally I left her with my card, suggesting that she call me again anytime she wanted to chat. I returned to my office in a pensive state. It's all I could do. There was no official reason for an intervention and otherwise it was up to her to ask for help. I hoped she would. I thought she was making an overture to friendship. My impression was of a woman isolated and distressed. I resolved to call her myself in a couple of weeks if I hadn't heard from her.

41

'Of course, she didn't call, and my own life took over and I didn't get back in touch. The next thing I heard was from my senior manager. He came into my office several weeks after my coffee with her and said: "Remember that mother, posh one, you interviewed a couple of months back? Her daughter's died. Cot death. They'll have to be an inquest and coroner's report. They'll probably want to talk to you."

'The news really knocked me. You see I believed I was in part responsible. Had I followed up I might have persuaded her to get Sylvie to the hospital. We know more about cot death now than we did back then, but even so, the post-mortem showed respiratory problems, something which is always connected to cot death and could've been helped by a hospital intervention. I couldn't help feeling some of what had happened was my fault.

'I resolved to speak to Charlotte and called the house. I was treading a fine line again between professionalism and impulsive compassion. It was likely I'd be called up as a witness, it was the usual procedure for cot death, but my need to see her far outweighed my worries about breaking rules.

'Alex picked up the phone. He wanted nothing to do with me, and warned me to stay away. People express grief differently, but this man sounded nasty. My first instinct about him was corroborated by the way he behaved later, but it took a while for that to come out.

'His threat made me all the more determined to see her. She had trusted me and I had failed her. I should've called her after our coffee. She so clearly needed help. So I got in the car and drove out to the house. It was a foolhardy thing to do but at the time I didn't question the impulse and I'm very glad I went.

'I recall my journey on that day as if it were yesterday: the clarity of the light, unusual for deep winter, a stillness in the air, hoar frost. It was beautiful. It filled me with an intense sadness, in the way that great art often can; it's the awareness of transience, mortality, you know?

'A Christmas wreath hung on their front door. It was a large evergreen and holly fabrication that looked hand-made. Alex opened the front door. He cut quite a figure: he was slim, very tall. A lot of grey hair. Actually, he looked dreadful. Haggard. I felt a moment of deep sympathy for this bereaved man. After a short clipped conversation he let me in.

'I found myself in the same central hall through which I'd passed on my first visit. There was the polished wooden staircase that led to the upper floor. And at the top looking over the banister stood Charlotte.

'Her hair was pulled back in a ponytail, it had turned to ash-grey. She'd lost even more weight. She stared at me in a curious detached manner. I called up to her. She came down the stairs slowly. Movement was difficult for her.

'I gave her a hug. Her body felt like a bundle of twigs. She stood stiffly. Then muttered the word "tea" and I followed her to the kitchen. Alex left us to it. She moved delicately, touching the wall as she walked, as if she might fall without this continual recourse to solid matter. The highchair was still in place. I stroked it. I felt utterly powerless.

'Charlotte opened a cupboard to reach for tea and mugs. It was difficult for her. I went to help and she gave a little yelp. You see, the police had taken away all Sylvie's treatments. In cracked tones, she told me about the persistent respiratory problems. "Didn't stop Sylvie being early to turn over," she said. She bent down to show me how spotless the floor was and nearly fell over, steadied herself, rubbed her hand over a stretch of kitchen floor and put it in her mouth.

'I helped her up and guided her to a chair at the kitchen table. Then I got our cups of tea and we sat, just as we had done at my first visit.

'Over the next few minutes, and then hours, and days, as I continued to visit, she told me in small bursts what had happened. The baby's breathing had become worse over a period of a couple of days and she'd visited May, her homeopath, who'd given her an inhalation for Sylvie. Alex'd just got back from a business trip in the evening and was really tired. And then in the early morning she had found Sylvie in her cot, no longer breathing. Alex called the ambulance. But it was too late.

'During my visits, Alex was a hovering presence, not exactly welcoming, but polite enough, as if I might help him in some way. He was no doubt also rehearsing the divorce deposition that he would later present to her. He never showed any affection towards Charlotte. They gave each other a wide berth. She was heavily sedated and on a whole cocktail of medication, as I later found out.

'Not long after the coroner's verdict and a brief trial, she had a complete breakdown. It was two years before I saw her again.

'After the trial, I continued at family services doing the demanding and often messy work of evaluating families, depressed mothers, damaged kids. But – Charlotte. She never left me. She was always there at the back of my mind. What happened to her? Where was she? I'd called the house several times. The recorded message told me Mr and Mrs Symmond were away and gave the number of an answering service. I left a message. I did this several times. I never heard anything back. Eventually I drove out there. A "for sale" sign stood at the top of the drive. I knocked at front and back doors. Most of the windows on the ground floor were shuttered. I peeked through some of the smaller windows but it was dark inside. The place was deserted.

'Where was she? That nagging persistent question. I felt I needed to know. She'd been in a way my first case. And it's rather like a surgeon losing their first patient on the operating table. You don't forget. I had failed her. I hadn't protected her.

'You see I was driven to do what I do by a strong desire to scratch away at the crumbly porous surface of human behaviour. I've never been religious – I mean my participation in Diwali all those years ago was about culture, not belief – so all the consolations and answers that I might have found in a god or gods weren't available to me. I was way too sceptical but I was also idealistic. I thought once you really had everything in your grasp, you could fix what was broken. I hated silence and secrets. I'm pretty sure this was in part a legacy of being the child of a father who'd survived Partition and drawn a cloak of secrecy over his whole past. The truth is I didn't even find out about my father's first family until after his death. My mother knew; when he died she gave me some photos – this pile of curling sepia-toned small squares. The figures were barely visible – a portrait of a young couple, formally dressed, he was in an elegant linen suit, she in a sari. She also handed me a pile of yellowed letters.

'I spent hours on them, trying to make sense of the barely legible script. They were from his first wife. Tara, she was called. Who was she? And who was this father of mine who had lived an entire life before becoming my dad? In another country on another continent. The letters were simple expressions of young love. Shy. Conventional stuff. I pressed my mother for information. She was tight-lipped and resentful. She just didn't want to know. I don't think she ever forgave my father his past. She felt ashamed, as if there was something dirty, some unwashed linen that might be discovered by her very respectable bridge circle. She said she hadn't known about his first life until after they were married. She'd felt betrayed. She only found out when he broke down one night and told her the real story, that Tara, the very young bride, had existed and was dead. Killed in Calcutta during a particularly violent night of fighting. His mother dead too. He was already in England. It seems so incredibly naive to me now. How on earth could she not have known he was hiding something so devastating? But you only see what you want to, don't you?

'She believed he was simply a nice young man from a respectable colonial family with an Oxford education and a gift for mathematics. Little by little the haunted survivor emerged.

'I found Charlotte in a psychiatric hospital by chance one day. It was out of my normal catchment area, a private institution that worked with the NHS, a few hours away. I was there for ... well, I won't go into that, not important. Anyway, she was there and I wrote to ask if I could visit, and she replied saying that'd be nice. So I did, and continued to over a period of six months or so until she was ready to leave for good. Alex had pretty much vanished. They communicated through lawyers. And there was no one else. I helped her move into a flat in Cheltenham. She appointed me her legal next of kin and gave me powers of attorney over her health. I was the only one, there was no one else.

'Her transition to living alone in the flat was difficult for her. Financially she seemed to be OK, she had group therapy and weekly meetings with her psychiatrist. I too had meetings with her psychiatrist as her official next-of-kin person. We thought she was doing OK. There was part-time volunteer work she did too, but, well, let's just say, it was really tough for her. Isolating. I'd see her as often as I could, but I was so busy with little time beyond work. I was retraining during that period in forensic psychotherapy. My timetable was punishing. Then one day, must have been about six or eight months or so after leaving the hospital, she was offered the job in Bosnia. She felt she could be useful to them.

'And that was that. Off she went. Her psychiatrist wasn't sure it was good for her going to a trauma zone, but she was determined. I visited her not long after she arrived to make sure she was settling in; and then a couple more times over the years. She's never been back to Britain. And now here we are. It's strange, familiar on

46

the one hand, but still, as if we're just getting to know each other again. I think I'm finding it really difficult. And now there's you! Jacob. Jacob Bedford. Mr nice guy journalist. God, how long have I been talking? You must be tired, fed up listening to me and all this awful stuff from the past.'

The sky greyed in the east.

Jane was shivering; she drew the jacket tightly around her chest. Up until then she had barely noticed the drop in temperature. He had. A slow seeping of cold into bones. He had moved only to fetch a half-finished bottle of grappa from the bedside. This had provoked a momentary pause in her narrative but had not brought her back to him.

She ran fingers through thick heavy hair, a habit she had, he noticed, when talking intensely or feeling nervous. Her pause stretched into silence. He glanced at his watch. It was nearing four.

The alcohol had dimmed his wits.

'I don't know what to say.' A bottleneck of thoughts prevented him forming the appropriate responses. Lend an ear. Get an earful.

'I talk too much when I drink.' She laughed. He thought she might be embarrassed. She rubbed her knees under the rug and then her arms, shivered again and rocked herself, glancing sideways at him. 'You're a good listener.' She looked at him more intently.

He nodded vaguely. He was befuddled. So much echoing and swirling in his head. Dead. A dead child. A breakdown. He had never known anyone intimately who had either lost a child or spent time in a mental institution. He knew people to whom one or the other of these things had occurred but they had not been within his social circle and the talk about them had taken the form of gossip. He could hardly say he had thought Charlotte ordinary; yet, this, this awful story. It was no wonder she conveyed such a troubling presence.

Clichés flooded his mind: 'I can't imagine' . . . 'Impossible to think about' ... 'I don't know how I'd cope' . . . 'I'd never get over it' . . . When she had begun to speak he had responded with the usual conventions, little interventions that took the form of polite prompts. For the first twenty minutes or so, he thought she might be giving him a few details about the unusual circumstances of meeting Charlotte as a way of buying time while she worked out whether she might have sex with him. But as her story progressed it became clear her focus was only on the telling, not on him; and in so doing she was reliving what had long since passed. Her present dissolved. As he listened his amazement grew. From time to time, to ease the numbness growing in his limbs he'd shift position. Now, suddenly he needed something that felt real, of the moment.

'Let's go inside. You're cold. So am I.' He took her by the elbow and drew her across the threshold back into the room and steered her to sit on the bed.

'I didn't mean to tell you all that.' She peered at him alarmed, then jerked around to the mirrored glass of the tall windows outside which the new day was asserting itself. 'It's just that, being here . . . well, you know.' He nodded, he did know. It sometimes happened that way, in unfamiliar places things spill out. 'It's seeing her again,' she said.

He laid her head on his lap. He could feel the warm exhalation of her breath through his trousers. He stroked her hair, then she slipped away and walked to the books piled on the desk where the old photograph of Grandad was propped. She picked it up.

'Were you very close?' It was a polite question and he felt no compunction to reply. She replaced the photo and walked back to him, her chest level with his face. He kept still. She took his hands and pulled him up. The excitement her closeness aroused in him was dampened by fatigue and too much alcohol. She was surfing along a stretch of strong emotion whose particular elements were unclear. Where were they going now? His earlier curiosity to see her naked had a *déjà vu* quality. He had been in this situation many times before. The anonymous room, the anticipation, the detachment. He took her head in his hands and pulled it to his. She responded with an urgency that surprised him. Her kiss was long and deep. Gracefully their two bodies fell to the bed. Entwined, they rubbed and kissed. He moved his hand to her breast and felt her pelvis grind to his.

A strong memory of lust was reawakened and desire took hold. He rolled on top of her and felt under her tunic. Quite suddenly she pulled away and sat up.

Shaking her head as if in argument she said: 'No, sorry.' He sat up too. She leaned over and slapped his arm like an old sporting pal. 'I'm all over the place tonight. You see –' she paused indecisively – 'I'm married. And, well …'

He got up from the bed with studied poise. So that's it, a husband somewhere in the world.

'But,' she continued, 'that was … rather lovely all the same.'

He nodded. She had made her decision and all at once his need for sleep overwhelmed.

They parted chastely at his bedroom door; he turned back into the large cool room. He was feeling dreadful. Wine … like the water of oblivion. Not for her though, for her it loosened the tongue. The story about Charlotte was awful. He texted his younger son Mikey who would be fast asleep but he needed the connection. A message came back quickly: *Hey, Dad, go 2 bed. I'm sleeping! Luv U.* It made him smile; Mikey had never been a good sleeper and was most likely now playing games on his phone in bed. He climbed under the soft duvet and pulled it tight around his chin. The boundaries of his corporeal existence felt shaky and for a second night in this city on the edge of nowhere he slept fully clothed.

———

Jane was not at breakfast. At a table by the window he noticed Rachel; he tipped his aching head at her.

It was Sunday. The museums were open. He could pay a visit to the Joyce Museum. Take a walk up to the medieval castle. He placed a map of the city on the table. The lines and letters blurred. He felt out of sorts and popped an aspirin. His blood pressure went up and down erratically. The aspirin was more talismanic than medicinal.

His phone bleep indicated a message had come through.

Sorry for last night. Didn't mean for things to get so crazy. Hope you're not too groggy. Jane

He texted back:

A little! Work to do.

Join me and Charlotte at Caffe San Marco later? Buy you a coffee to make up for it! Historic cafe etc Charlotte can help with Trieste.

He located the cafe on his map. He would gather up his things and take his time. He might join them. After all Charlotte might be able to help him, she knew the city well. And Jane. A bottom-drawer encounter.

There was in him a perpetual loneliness, of a being dispossessed. It subsided when he was with his sons but otherwise lay somewhere under the topsoil of his daily perceptions; his single state now a visible and shameful manifestation of his condition.

Had Jane sniffed this? Or was it really the husband? He liked her. He wanted to be around her. And Charlotte. He texted back *yes, will see you later.*

————

It was about quarter past eleven when he walked through the doors of the San Marco. They were sitting at the other end of the room under a large rectangular window. White net curtains reaching halfway. Dim light. Stray rays of sun. Mild. There were few customers.

He noted: entrance circa early twentieth century, yellow moulded ceiling. Museum feel. A hang-out of writers. Another note: shiny plaque on wall to commemorate Joyce, Saba, Svevo; tall contemporary book-filled case, panelled wooden counter, gleaming copper coffeemaker (real or reproduction?) . . . the bracing bora wind coming off the Karst, the huddle of men engaged in lively conversation, threadbare suit hanging off James, Svevo in his elegant businessman's attire . . . high on the air of intellect . . . outside the hurly-burly shouts of sailors and merchants, all manner of port worker, tradesman, banker, grafter, washerwoman, all gabbing, gesticulating and selling.

He kissed both women. They had a relaxed look. It seemed to him the mood had shifted between them, knots had loosened.

Jane winked, a swift flicker of one eye. Merriment. An irritating blush spread across his tired skin. He was in no mood for games.

Jacob, did he want a coffee? Come, sit! She held out her hand to him.

'Lovely, espresso,' he replied. The long night pervaded his limbs. His head throbbed. He was often plagued by headaches, brought on by an excess of alcohol and mild night terrors.

The entrance door swung open and shut, admitting to their sanctum small groups of Triestines, some old, most middle-aged; a few younger professionals in casual dress.

Life was in gentle play around them. They drank coffee, they chatted. He began to feel better.

'Il conto, per favore!' demanded Charlotte from the waiter who answered with a characteristic flirt. 'Carlotta bella, per voi, tutta'. She turned to her companions: 'I asked for the bill. Shall we walk?' He was undecided.

'Go on. It'll be fun. I think it'll be interesting for your piece.' She was coaxing. Oh, all right. Follow the yellow brick road.

She took them on a tour of the old Roman part of the city, San Giusto, named after the impressive Romanesque cathedral which stood at the top of a hill in the heart of Trieste.

They moved casually in and out of their triangle. Charlotte led the way, providing a broken stream of information about the sites around them. Her manner was different: gone was the austerity and weirdness of the night before, in its place a girlish ease. Her smile unintentionally dazzled as she skipped up the hill, kicking stray stones along the way, her stripy Breton jersey billowing in the salt breeze. The ghoulish fragmented images that had penetrated his dreams over the past several hours melted away; alongside him skipped a vital graceful woman. He was beginning to understand how Jane had become so – what might the word be? – so *intent* on Charlotte.

He admired the mosaics in the cathedral (and made a note: thirteenth century, Byzantine); stared out across the vast sea from the belvedere at the top of the castle; had a sandwich at a makeshift table by a coffee van, and talked about ordinary things. He learned that Jane's husband Sheldon was an American academic, an art historian. They had been together eight years. This surprised him. Last night's intricate dance had led him to believe her marriage was on its second decade, and like his, had moved into a zone of question marks and repetitions. He searched her face for traces of last night's encounter. There, yes, a little red on the cheeks. Pert. He felt momentarily pleased.

'You should meet him,' Charlotte was saying. 'He's rather marvellous. A big teddy bear and not in the least bit scared of Jane.' On further conversation, Jacob learned that Sheldon had visited Bosnia with Jane several years ago, not long after they had got together.

He wondered if Jane had confided in her friend any detail of last night's events in his hotel room? He could pick up no hint of shared information.

The conversation turned to Charlotte's charity and how it had just received a huge injection of cash from a rich donor that would allow them to establish a centre for prosthetics.

'I helped find them some rich people,' Charlotte laughed. 'After all I knew a few in my time.' Jane's description of Charlotte's early life came back to him: privilege, a rich husband. She wore it lightly, she wore it well.

He spoke more about his book project, and his boys. The older one, Finn, he was seventeen, he was doing his A levels, the younger one, Mikey, fifteen, his GCSEs. They were good sons, easy. Finn could be secretive, he sometimes worried about him.

'And your ex-wife,' asked Jane. 'What does she do, what's her name?' He could suddenly feel both women were intensely curious about this aspect of his life.

'We're separated. Not yet divorced. Her name's Kathleen, Kath. She's a creative consultant. She helps arts companies develop their brand image.'

He shrugged. So far away from all of this.

'When were you separated?' Charlotte asked.

He hesitated.

'Almost a year ago.'

It had been a vituperative high-octane affair from which he had emerged much relieved. Kath now had a boyfriend. They would decide after the boys' exams about whether to divorce. He did not want to go over any of it now. Thankfully they let the subject drop.

Occasionally he caught Jane staring at him with a gaze that suggested encouragement and a touch of confusion. Yes, last night's encounter had left its mark. Not so easily erased then. This reassured him. He had often been a fly-by-night fuck. His one-off companions had wanted him to be a version of a man that played into their fantasies for one night, sometimes even for one hour. He would be out the door as quickly as he had come through it. Jane was different. She liked him and he liked her. They might be friends. The prospect excited him. He had many female friends, but most were part of a couple, and those couples had been part of his and Kath's social life. A friendship with Jane would be something new.

And the other? Not so easy. He agreed with Jane: Charlotte exercised a magnetic pull. At times she looked at him with open curiosity. There was nothing coy in her gaze. He was amused. It was as if she was a young girl seeking out her first man. He could detect no sign in today's clear light of the horrors Jane had recounted. He wondered how much of what she had recalled had been accurate, how trustworthy her memory might be. But what had happened, whatever had happened, had happened a long time ago. And he found himself not caring one bit about its truth. He was, if only briefly, happy: he felt at the centre of the world.

Later, at the hotel, Charlotte gave him her mobile number. 'Call me tomorrow? I can show you more of the city if you like.' Jane was returning to England in the morning; Monday a new week, a new start. She and Charlotte were having a final supper together. Would they talk about him? The question idled somewhere in his mind. 'I'll be here until Thursday,' Charlotte continued, 'I look forward to seeing you again.' She kissed him robustly on both cheeks and disappeared into the night.

Jane turned to him; it was time to part. She held his eyes all the while getting ready to say something. The pause grew longer and he became impatient. He did not like goodbyes. . . .

54

'Jacob.' She started and stopped. He waited. 'It's difficult, saying what I feel. I've offloaded so much onto you. Things I haven't much thought about for a long time. Last night I started talking and couldn't stop. And then, well – you know, when we almost … I'm sorry, I was unfair and selfish. You seemed so – willing. You see, it's occurred to me that seeing her again, the wine, all that talking, in this strange city – what I've done is to reanimate the whole story. Do you know what I mean?'

Yes, he did. His unease was growing.

'She's hardly been in touch these past several years. I feel her slipping away. I've been so worried. And I do still have a legal responsibility to her. It really means something to me, that. I let her down before and I won't again. I feel better now. And you are here and I think the two of you will get on.'

'I'd like to see her again.' A momentary image of Charlotte's enticing beauty flashed across his mind's eye.

'She's in need of love. Connection. You see I believe most of us have a strong desire for happiness. Charlotte's no different, in spite of what she's been through. It's equally in our nature to damage, to inflict harm. The most difficult is the work of repair. It requires a kind of grit, both a distancing from self and a ruthless self-knowledge. This is the work I do with patients. It's not successful a lot of the time. Our psyche can only handle so much. We construct lovely fantasies about ourselves. But it's possible. Charlotte is my talisman, she helps me hold onto the notion of good. I want her to be happy. I think you both might help each other.'

It struck him that she was suddenly lighter, as if free from worry, and this signalled to him another important aspect of her character that he had not quite recognised: her optimism. For Jane there was always a way in which a story might end well.

'You never quite know,' she repeated. 'Anyway. Time to go. You're a good man, Jacob. Perhaps we'll meet again. I hope so. You have my contacts don't you? If you're ever in Gloucester . . . I come to London a lot. Well . . . Thank you for everything.'

They embraced and he surrendered to her wonderful warmth. He shrunk into the contours of her plump breasts, her rounded stomach and pleasing thighs. He held on for dear life, longing for an eternity in this strong hospitable body.

Finally, she pried herself from him, wiped a tear from her eye and with an efficient determination turned to the next stage of her evening.

He had breakfast on the balcony, relishing the balmy air coming in from the port. A strong sun. The famous azure blue of the sea. A delightful parade of ships criss-crossed the bay. He felt an exhilarating sense of freedom. He had slept soundly and was refreshed, impatient to get on with work. The story of Jane and Charlotte felt like liquid trickling downstream from him. These women had caught him in a whirlpool of charm and emotional turmoil so distracting he had got behind in his research.

Then something unexpected happened: when he looked at his notes a renewed excitement came over him, something on the borders of titillation and fear, an alluring and utterly unfamiliar mix of feelings. There in the pages of his notebook written in his large untidy scrawl was the story of Jane and the enigmatic Charlotte. Dashed marks he had made in the odd half-hour over the past two days.

He felt gripped again by something inexplicable. He wanted to find out more. He wanted to have sex. He had been celibate since his separation. Abstinence would open the way to gravitas. Then there was the moment with Jane when the possibility of sex became real again. For years he had slipped in and out of beds with an amnesiac's conscience but his recent resolve to remain chaste had brought him nothing more than a dull emptiness.

Charlotte. Her appeal was visceral. The kind of beauty that makes fools of loyal men. There had been a husband, a long time ago, but no mention of a current partner.

He put thoughts of her to one side. He must press on; time was running out and his deadline was looming. There would be time later for Charlotte.

Work always had the most efficient remedial effect on his moods. It allowed him to slip away from present disturbances into the realm of his thinking brain. It brought him rewards, it gave him an anchored self.

He emailed some thoughts to his editor. Potted history, the hotel, the cafe, the restaurant, a museum or two, monuments. Theodor and Grandad. A whiplash from her would spur him on.

He wrote up some impressions of his walks around the city then organised a meeting with the curator of the Revoltella Museum. If he spent the next couple of days in concentrated activity he would make up for precious lost hours – and have time for Charlotte. Today he would examine the Porto Vecchio, the old port, now a series of derelict buildings, once the pride of the city burghers. A biennale had been mounted there last year, murmurings of a new art scene. Perhaps the city was making a comeback. He had read about plans for a maritime development project. Money was flowing in from the tankers bringing oil to Germany from the Middle East. Cranes were visible on the horizon. Drab grey buildings were being transformed into pink and yellow confections, lovely restorations everywhere the eye scanned.

He set off along the waterfront that swept round the littoral curling into the old port. The place was deserted: numerous blocks of nineteenth-century stone warehouses, some two storeys, others rising high at four. Rusted cranes tipping off the edge of roofs. Broken windows and peeling frames. Tufts of grass straining through cracks in joints. The gleaming lines of disused railway tracks cut through the yards, linking one site of haulage to another place of storage. Jacob heard male voices echoing in a nearby building. Their invisible presence hung sharply in the air.

A breeze rippled through his light jacket and the brilliant sun lit up the desolate port. There were rows of parked cars yet not a single human in sight.

To one side sat a low building, with a veranda, growing a tangle of branches, a child's bicycle chained to the fence. It might have been a customs house, he speculated, and over there was an official Hapsburg building where the hub of imperial commerce was oiled. All this, this impressive array of function and form had once been the pride of the city officials, the baron princes, the Emperor himself. Stevedores and ship captains too.

Jacob looked back across the harbour to the urban waterfront, squinting in the bright light, matching his map with what he saw until he fixed on the top of the Via San Nicolò, where Herr Motz had kept a flat. There, that corner building from where with a small turn of the body Herr Motz could survey his domain. A man of his times, standing tall at the tall window of the neoclassical building. Herr Motz turns left to hear the clink of his money being traded at the stock exchange two streets over, and turns right to watch his goods chugging into the Adriatic on their long route east; then he gives a quick nod in the direction of his clerks in the small office as they assemble lading lists.

Jacob took from his pocket the old postcard of Trieste written by Theodor to his son Stefan in 1938. A nondescript black and white drawing of what had been the Piazza Unita. In spidery script was written, *Liebe, 38 Via di Scorcola*. No addressee. No signature. He checked the direction against his map. Over there, above the railway station is where Theodor was last known to have existed. Solid bourgeois blocks.

He looked at another postcard bought at a newsagent the day

before: it was a group portrait of early twentieth-century Triestine merchants, black-haired and moustached, in dark woollen suits, positioned at a proud angle to the lens. A rotund short man with an oval face and waves of hair appeared to be the most senior. He looked Slav, but equally he might have been Jewish, Italian, Turkish, Armenian, of mixed race. A 'mischling'. This was the term used by Viennese officialdom for someone who was not pure Aryan. It was on his great-grandmother's identity card found in a disorganised pile of documents at his mother's death, given to her, he assumed, by Grandad. She had left behind a sparse paper trail. There were certificates of birth, marriage and death. A few weathered news-paper clippings in German from a Triestine newspaper in the early twentieth century in which the name Motz und Sohn is men-tioned. A genealogist had done initial research, the trail disappearing with the postcard from Theodor.

So here in Trieste, the city decreed by Empress Maria Theresa as a free port, open to Jews as much as to anyone else, Herr Motz had prospered.

Stefan, Stephen, Grandad, dead when he was seventeen. He remembered the big ears and the kindly smile; the long jacket. He remembered the small brick house in a modern close on the edge of Surbiton. Disinfectant and tobacco. The shelves were lined with books, some in German. There were two or three large photo-graphs in polished silver frames of family members. Only the English ones. No Theodor, no Johanna.

He felt a sudden deep sense of loss; a tangy vivid grief. Stephen, formerly Stefan, the lonely son of this once proud Herr Motz and his wife Johanna. Standing on the jagged stone among these nine-teenth-century warehouses, orange and black with rust and dirt, the swirl and smoke of that era assailed his senses. A primitive urge to claim ownership of this place possessed him. Why had he not asked his mother for more information? Some time ago during a particularly becalmed period in his marriage, Kathleen had pressed him: what are you scared of? Exposure, he'd replied, being exposed. She had not understood.

He was back at the hotel early evening and began to assemble some thoughts on his laptop, the photo of Grandad next to him. Talk to me, he asked silently, tell me where to go. He opened a new file and began to fashion a story of princes, trade, merchants and art. He worked intensely for several hours, ordering room service for supper. A series of texts brought his concentration to an end. Cheerful messages from both sons to which he responded lovingly, the verbal equivalent of hugs. And one from Charlotte:

> *Do you want to visit Castle Miramare tomorrow? Trieste's greatest site?*
> *I can show you around. Also know a great small restaurant nearby.*

His heart leapt in a silly schoolboy fashion. He was being passed like a baton from Jane to Charlotte. He did not mind; more than that, to his surprise, he welcomed it.

———

She picked him up in a taxi. The glorious weather continued. The castle was about a half-hour up the coast. They sped along the *rive* in silence. She sat in sunlight on the bench looking out to sea, self-sufficient in her thoughts. Once, she turned to look out the window on his side and allowed her gaze to slide over him; this provoked in her a sigh and a crinkle of the brow. Seconds later she inched towards him.

The drive was short and captivating. The green-blue sea lapped against large boulders where ghosts of summer tourists shimmered in the sun; cargo boats and outsized tankers lined the sky; modern holiday flats fixed with metallic grills leaned into steep green hills; Triestines sipped coffee and shared news on the sun-drenched terraces of empty hotels, family-sized and welcoming. The coast had not suffered the worst building splurges of many other Mediterranean countries. It felt old-fashioned, delayed in time. Ahead the romantic castle jutted out on a promontory, seaward, fronting the stormy moods of its watery location; just as the heartbroken widowed Princess Carlotta had kept a vigil for her husband the Hapsburg Prince Maximilian, killed in 1867 by his rebellious subjects in Mexico (he noted: *famous Manet painting of execution, in fragments, at the National Gallery*). Theirs was a true love match, so the story goes. The construction of their marital nest came to an end at his death; it remains a monument to all great loves, lived and lost down the years.

They were the only visitors. The guide was exuberant. She and Charlotte talked in Italian while he picked up what he could. Charlotte navigated their way around the edifice with the same beguiling poise with which she had taken them up San Giusto the day before. She was shy when she was not explaining a detail of its history. He scrambled to help her up and down the sweeping white marble steps, he bowed and scraped in and out of stately rooms. He played the courtier, the gentleman. At times, their hands brushed and this made her jump. He was conscious of her vulnerability. Of a skittish energy that was sexual.

They lunched in a small tavern on the edge of the water. The tables were laid with stained green cloths. The menu was a mixture of grilled fish and potatoes. They agreed it was surprisingly good.

They talked about trivial things: the sparkling sea, the haunting appeal of Miramare. The best place in Trieste to buy the local polenta, original to the region.

'I'll take you there!' She offered with an enthusiasm that led her to blush.

'That'd be nice,' he responded cautiously. She seemed to be engaged in a struggle with herself. He was not sure what it entailed.

It was as if he was the first man with whom she had been alone for a long time, yet he knew the charity work she did was demanding and required long hours, many spent no doubt in the company of male doctors, administrators and functionaries.

'I'm distracting you from your research,' she apologised in a half-playful tone. 'You need to find out more about your ancestor, don't you?'

'There's time for that.' He did not want this heavenly lunch to come to an end. The light was a strong autumnal shade of copper, a gentle breeze ruffled the water, a lone fishing boat knocked against the mooring. They could have been the only people in the world, forgotten on this small quay in a restaurant from yesteryear. The portly owner, a craggy middle-aged Italian, sat at his table in the corner, punching heavily on a calculator.

He told her about his wander through the old port the day before, how easy it had been to imagine the life of the docks a hundred years ago and how eerie it was now with its tall derelict nineteenth-century warehouses, broken windows and rusting joints.

'What did your great-grandfather export?' She seemed on surer ground when the conversation was directed away from herself.

'Fezzes to the East!' The absurdity of this enterprise struck them both and they laughed.

'They made hats in Vienna,' he explained. 'Vienna had the confidence of its imperial power in those days. I think their business was prosperous.'

The conversation tailed off during coffee. They stared out to sea and sipped espressos. Once she turned to look at him with sustained concentration. He felt like a model for an artist, as if she was mapping the topography of his features with studied sangfroid.

She invited him back to her flat. It occupied one of the upper storeys of an elegant block with balconies and views across the bowl of the city and the harbour. Simple. Little sign of anything personal.

He drank some grappa, she some fizzy water.

The sunset cast a red tint across the sitting room. The city below was fiery and pictorial, illuminated like a medieval manuscript.

She went to the tall window. He watched. She released her hair from its elastic and shook it free. The long blond mane fell around her shoulders and face. She wiped strands from her eyes and looked around at him.

What happened next happened quickly.

They made love on her bed; it was over in several minutes.

Her jeans and knickers hung off one foot. Her T-shirt was rucked around her breasts. His boxers dangled at his ankles.

He was dazed, separate again. Separated. She tugged her long T-shirt back over her bottom, hiding her hands in the loose extended sleeves. He pulled her into his arms, a matter of habit.

She pushed away from him, sat up against the headboard and in one swift movement kicked off the trouser leg. She then looked at him, curious, it seemed, about what it was that had just taken place. He sat up too, caressed her hand and tucked hair behind her ear. She let him perform these acts of tenderness. He was in need of them.

'I –' she began. Then drew up her knees and rested her chin.

The violent red of the setting sun had diminished. A gentle pinkish hue was inching across the door. They sat in the sharp twilight. Her white skin gleamed, translucent against the soft pale texture of the bed linen. He tried again: he stroked her bare thigh. She watched this movement, detached as if it was happening to someone else.

He took his hand away and peered into the room. Like the sitting room, the style was plain. Other than the bed, there was a modern wardrobe, an antique chest of drawers, a mirror above it and an upright wooden chair in the corner. The two large windows gave onto the back of the building, terraced against the green hillside. The only clue to its owner was a photograph of a baby, staring away from the camera, as if distracted by the laughs of a bystander. Sylvie.

Recognition provoked a sour memory of Charlotte's unhappy past and he swung his legs round to the side of the bed, ready to move on.

Her hand ran down his spine, arresting his movement.

'I'm sorry,' she murmured. 'That can't have been a lot of fun for you. You see, it's the first time since – I haven't done that in a long time.' She hesitated and continued: 'I – thank you.'

She withdrew, retreating from him again.

'It was all so sudden. I was too quick. I'm the one who's sorry. Come here.' He reached out and took her into his arms. No ambivalence. She let him. They half-lay on the bed in an awkward embrace. Her body was taut, the naked sinews of legs a cold bone china. Her soft fur on his bristly leg. Damp. He did not want to let go. He wanted some sign that this women propped the length of his body was happy to be there.

Gradually the room descended into fuller darkness and with it Charlotte relaxed. He could feel her muscles loosen into his own. Her breathing became deep and regular. Sleeping.

He shifted his leg in order to settle more comfortably but the slight pressure woke her and with a start she cried out: 'No!' She turned on the bedside lamp. Her eyes were unfocused, fearful. He absorbed her disquiet into his own.

'Oh. Oh dear. It's OK now. It's you. Here we are. Shit.' She leaned back against the headboard. 'I wish I smoked.' A small laugh. 'Shall we have a drink? I can make us a quick supper too, if you like. I have some fresh pasta in the fridge. It's late, isn't it? You must be hungry. I'll get on with it.' She leapt off the bed and slipped into her jeans, grabbed a hair scrunch from the top of the chest and came face to face with the photo of Sylvie. 'Did Jane tell you?' The question was asked in a low voice.

'Yes.' There was no need for him to elaborate.

'She can talk, can't she?'

He nodded.

'She says you're a good listener. She says you're kind.'

He made a modest acknowledgement of these compliments.

'She thought it would be good for me if we – well, had sex.'

This took him by surprise. Like many men he was aware of the intimate nature of female chat, but he had never quite adjusted to how much women divulged of their emotional lives and the amount of time spent discussing its components. Had Jane told her about their skirmish in his hotel bedroom? Had he passed some test?

'Was it?' He asked timorously.

She inclined her head in a thoughtful manner. 'Yes.'

The recent memory of her sexual hunger came back to him; overwhelmed by an unexpected feeling of longing he let a groan escape his lips. She sat.

'I don't know how to begin to explain. There's so much.' She shook her head as if trying to elude the unwanted flood of events that had shaped her life.

'No need,' he murmured.

'Jane wouldn't agree. She wants me to let it all hang out. That's her job, isn't it? Talk. It's all so messy. Do you know how we met?'

He was unsure as to where this conversation was going.

'She was very eager, so awfully confident. You can imagine, can't you? She's never given up on me. I could so easily have not made it.'

She reached into the drawer of the side-table and withdrew a silver locket. He helped her do up the clasp.

'I took it off yesterday. I felt it might free me to – you know ...'

A chilly draught filled the room. The shadowy twilight had distilled into clear night. Dark clumps of foliage outside the windows protruded like spies in the sodium glow of a nearby streetlight. No voices, no traffic. The creak of a branch.

'The terrace door is still open. I'll start supper.' It was a brusque end to their first encounter.

Some wine, fresh pasta. Interrupted conversation about buying the flat. A good view. Was it lonely, ever? He treaded with care. She inclined her head. 'I have some friends at the university. I do training there. Different courses on trauma injuries. It's OK.'

They were back in bed an hour later.

'Please don't go,' she asked quietly. 'Please stay.'

And so it was he spent the night with Charlotte.

During those long charged hours, in between the awkward and delicate business of their lovemaking, she talked in fragments about a first boyfriend ('we didn't know what we were doing, it was all play-acting'), her mother ('she was an insecure brute'), her charity work ('it saves me'), Jane ('She's dear, but really so formidable, I was scared of her for ages'), and once, Sylvie.

'It's so difficult to keep remembering. I have to work at it, to keep her beautiful face strong and alive to me. It's a kind of meditation. The important thing is to be very precise. She is always absent but if I can continue to see her, then she still exists.'

She allowed him to lift up her long T-shirt. He gazed at her breasts, a little heavy with middle age and faintly scarred. Her slim thighs opened onto a surprising round bottom, and in between the perfect slit of her pussy. He committed to memory the intense sudden arrival of her orgasm, the openness of her fucking and the need in her physicality. He had slept with many women, most completely unknown to him, but he had never felt pleasure like this.

In the morning, in the early fresh rays of the sun, he left.

———

He spent another three days in Trieste, alone. He wrote Charlotte a series of grateful wondrous text messages. He visited San Sabba, the rice mill that had been turned into a death camp by the Nazis, and looked through the Jewish registry. No sign of Theodor Motz. He left her a long message, too long. He rambled about his grandfather and great-grandfather, about the distance that separated them. The voicemail cut him off mid-sentence. He visited the Via di Scorcola, scouring number 38 for clues of Theodor. Indifferent to his quest, the building offered up no signs of a former life. From there, he took the tram to Opacina up on the Karst where once weary travellers had stopped to gaze at the glittering city below and marvel. Perhaps Theodor had made his way up here and hid somewhere on the vast plain. He took a photo on his phone and sent it to her with a caption: *miramare!* The memory of their lovemaking lived on in every one of his senses. He sat in the dark stillness of the Greek church so beloved of Joyce, and wrote her texts. He visited the Joyce museum and the public gardens where busts of the city's most famous writers stood. He saw the Maritime Museum and talked to an administrator about the shipping companies. He ate pork and sauerkraut at the famous Buffet da Pepi and texted her.

Her replies when they came were brief and courteous.

They talked once before his departure.

'Can we stay in touch?' he asked, unable and unwilling to conceal the needling sadness in his voice.

'Jacob, that's not a good idea. I had an amazing night with you. You've given me more than you'll ever know. But – you have your own life in London, your wife, your boys . . . after all.'

After all.

PART TWO

'I should like to formulate what we have learned
so far as follows: our hysterical patients suffer
from reminiscences.'

Sigmund Freud, *Five Lectures on Psycho-Analysis*

THE CALL CAME ONE MORNING MIDWEEK IN EARLY December. 'It's Charlotte.' She sounded hesitant. 'Can we see each other?'

He met her on a corner of a street in Kensington. The cold day was dark and featureless. Clouds hung low, heavy with snow.

She was waiting for him, wrapped in a black coat, fidgeting with the silver chain through folds of a patterned scarf. Hair swept up. Radiant.

He hurried to her; a gentle sweat had broken out over his body. He still dreamed about her in twilight hours between waking and sleep; her face would appear to him with the sharpness of an engraving, only to vanish on opening his eyes.

The reality of her sudden appearance thrilled him. Her embrace was warm, her pleasure in seeing him felt miraculous. He smiled like a fool.

'I'm staying with Jane in Gloucester,' she explained. 'I had to come up to London to do some things . . . it's good to see you, Jacob.'

He had no questions, no urgent pleading or bullying pressure to persuade her of what had become the most perplexing experience of his middle age: infatuation. He was content to be once again in her company, something which he had never thought might occur. His life was simply his life, a long determined condition.

'Are you well?' Her question was perfunctory, but in it he

detected a hint of worry, and was reminded of the way in which she switched quickly from open emotion to formal conversation. Yes, he nodded, yes, he was well, after a fashion, so much better now, in this moment, standing here with you.

'Why are you in London?'

'Just some personal things to sort out . . . Jane – she sends you her love.'

'Please do send her mine back.' Jane. The maestra, the minx. Their friendly exchange of emails had given him no indication Charlotte would be visiting. Occasionally he had dared a *heard from Charlotte?* And received a few vague snippets of news: *Seems fine, always busy, so good to see her.* Why had Jane not informed him of Charlotte's visit? As if hearing his silent question Charlotte explained: 'I made a last minute decision to come. Sort of took Jane by surprise. I don't think Sheldon's too pleased.'

She was becoming more fidgety, pulling on her silver chain.

'Jane thinks maybe we could all get together, a kind of reunion.'

'Great!' A snap of warmth went through him.

'There's a pub just up there. Shall we have a drink?' He pointed down the road. She paused for moment, her eyes seeming to scan the rows of buildings, registering both scrutiny and alarm. Slowly she nodded.

It was still early and the pub was empty. He got himself a pint of ale, she chose elderflower cordial. They sat at a round wooden table near the front door. The lights were on and a fire burned in the grate. It was the kind of local that had changed with the fashion, offering now a menu of organic food and real ales. Discreet colours, smart decor. She chatted nervously about the grim weather, the gleam of London, the new houses all over Gloucestershire . . . how different it was to what she remembered from all those years back when she lived there. She continued to twirl the silver chain around her fingers. Soft powder-blue jumper. He noticed that the cuticles around her fingers were ragged. He noticed the perfect mould of her breasts.

'How was your feature? Did it go down well?'

It took him a moment to understand what she was referring to. A feature. Then it came to him: the piece on Trieste. The one that had brought him to her. He said it had, that it would appear in the Italian edition of the magazine next year. Silently he calculated, another several hundred pounds of income. Such mental arithmetic had become a tic.

'It was cut a lot. I was hoping they'd keep in the story about my grandfather and his father, Theodor. You know the one that disappeared. But apart from a few brief sentences they cut most of my personal reminiscences. It was just a simple travel piece.' He smiled. Who cares.

'Will you come again to Trieste?' He explained he would if he could make enough headway on a proposal to persuade his agent that he had a viable book.

Silence fell and he resisted filling it. Instinctively he knew there was a reason she had wanted to meet but he did not have the courage to ask what it might be. He hardly dared believe she might have suffered a change of heart –

– and in that instant arrived a nugget of hope, a niggling persistent entity that lifted his perceptions and planted in him the expectation of love.

In an abrupt movement she got up to look out the window. The pub terrace was empty, its trees bare, its tables wet and encrusted with ash from old butts. He watched her slender back, the slight tensing of her shoulders and the stretch of her trousers across her shapely thighs. Beyond the terrace, brown trunks jutted from the pavement, a promise of lush green in sunnier months. Comfortable manicured houses presented themselves: some two-storey cottages with pretty front doors, others made of brick, four storeys high, stretching to meet the low sky. It was a colourful neighbourhood with shiny brass door knockers and dainty front gardens. The blinking red eyes of security systems up and down the street reminded him the wealthy lived here.

She returned to the table, resolve and anxiety in equal measure written on her face.

'God. I don't know why I thought I should see it again. I promised myself I would. God knows why. Over there, that's my childhood home. Jane wondered about me seeing it. I don't know. But all this stuff … it doesn't go away.'

A gift, her bright sapphire eyes.

'Jacob.' There was flirtation in her voice. 'You're a kind man, you're so awfully attractive, that lovely smile. I suppose most women don't resist you, do they?'

It was a question to which he had no appropriate answer.

'No,' she conceded. 'I didn't think so. That's good, that's OK. The important thing is you listen. You're neutral. You're the stranger at the table. That's what Jane calls you.'

He wanted to protest with the full force of emptiness echoing through the years and was quiet.

'Over there, d'you see? That house on the corner. That's where I grew up. I haven't seen it in years.'

Following her gaze he saw a flat-fronted bright-white Georgian townhouse. It had an impressive double door crowned with a crescent fanlight. A small front garden and stone path recalled a country vicarage. The house shone brightly in the dismal mid-day. The lighted fat Christmas tree, an array of gold, silver and red, dominated the sash window on the ground floor. The picture evoked in him a longed-for childhood where days were sweet with adventure and nights spent safe in dreams. His own youth was spent in a 1930s semi-detached on the boundaries of North London with a stormy frustrated mother, an insecure absent father and a bullying older sister. Holidays in Lyme Regis and presents from Woolworths.

'It's a beautiful house.' He sounded like an advertisement.

'We never had Christmas trees,' Charlotte said. 'Did Jane tell you about my mother?'

He acknowledged he knew her mother had died when she was pregnant with Sylvie. He hedged his tone, unsure about where this conversation was going.

'She committed suicide. They said she took an overdose. They said it was accidental. I didn't believe them. She was a wrecker. She couldn't bear that I was no longer hers. Out of her orbit, I'd thought, finally I've made it, I'm safe. You see those first months with Alex and then being pregnant with Sylvie ... I thought I'd freed myself from her.'

She interrupted herself again and gripped the side of the table. He stroked her hand, a personal appeal. She pulled back.

'It's so great to see you,' he said gently.

She looked at him quizzically, then sat and continued:

'That house. So lovely, isn't it? See the top floor? That was my bedroom. It had everything a girl could've wanted. Flowery wallpaper and matching bed, desk and wardrobe. Stuffed toys, doll's house, bookcases.'

He stretched to better see this gracious home where the woman at his side, who he barely knew, who had chosen him for some obscure purpose to reawaken her body and receive her memories, this place where she had been a girl, and a girl again now, or so it felt to him, encased in her woman's body, travelling back through the years. He could only wonder at what nasty fairy tale had gripped the house.

'Boxes within boxes. That's what it was like.' She pointed again at its pleasing facade. 'See there, beneath those black railings, the kitchen, a large gloomy underground world.' She shuddered. 'There was also the utility room and the pantry, dark secret places where I used to hide. At the back a small sitting room opened onto a courtyard, there were steps leading to the garden. It was a dull room with cracked walls and a tatty deep armchair where Mrs Bowler our housekeeper sat most of the day, often drunk.'

A few beads of perspiration broke over her face.

'I don't think she liked me. I'd buzz around her like a friendly fly, only to be swatted softly from time to time: "Go play, dear, there's a good girl," she'd say.'

'I bet you were a good girl,' he said affectionately, 'a dear good girl.'

Charlotte furrowed her brow. She drank without glancing at him and resumed her tale.

'Perhaps. I don't think any of them thought so. Not that I knew anything about them. For all my mother's radical pursuits, she was very much of her class – those that worked for her were servants, their lives were of no account outside their service to her. I never knew whether there was a Mr Bowler, or little Bowlers. A cleaner came most days, a nice middle-aged woman with a thick Scottish accent. I rarely saw her actually clean. It was the sort of house that looked marvellous until you examined it closely. It was only when I became a teenager and hyper-alert to the smallest comparisons between myself and others that I began to detect signs of neglect.'

She started on this word in sudden fright. 'Go on,' he whispered, relaxing all his features into as tender an invitation to trust as he could consciously manage.

'Neglect.' She repeated it slowly. 'Neglect. Years later they told me I'd suffered neglect during my childhood, they told me it's why I became ill. I didn't notice. I still have difficulty grasping what it means.

'They loved me, both of them, I think, in as much as they were capable. At least that's what I tell myself. Over and over again. You see if I forgive her, then I forgive myself. With him it's different. He disappeared such a long time ago.'

He nodded obediently. It occurred to him to cut her off, to shut down these sad stories. The next question slipped out in pursuit of its own logic: 'What was your mother like?'

'She was a tiny girlish woman, she had layers of feathered pale hair and bright blue eyes which seemed to flash lightning. Loads of jangling jewellery. She was beguiling. Men found her very attractive. My father and I hovered as close to her flame as we dared get.'

His mother had died ten years ago, roaring at life even as it was leaving her. Beguiling was not an adjective that he could associate with a maternal figure. His father had suffered a long decline from alcohol and nervousness culminating in a fatal stroke soon after his own marriage to Kath. He had never felt neglect. They were like most parents of their day, he reckoned, like most parents today, 'doing their best'.

Charlotte was staring again at the house across the street.

'Did you like living there?' Polite.

'The house had a lot of closets where I hid. The one under the stairs was crammed full of moth-eaten coats that no one wore. My father's old greatcoat hung in there for years after his death. If I tried hard, I believed it was him, roaming around the inside of the large man-shape. I could fit myself into it, all snug, and sing his songs.'

Pause. He stemmed an impulse to hum.

'The pantry was lined with shelves carrying rusty jars of honey and pickle and mustard. The mop and bucket stood in a swampy cavity in the corridor off the kitchen, being in there was like being in the jungle. Sometimes I pretended to be a captured explorer waiting to be eaten in a big fat cauldron of boiling vegetables.'

He interrupted in an excited rush to recognition: 'I used to do that too, in our back garden, with mates, we'd built a kind of den and there was a big old drum.'

She half-heard, ignored and continued: 'These places were all safe, they couldn't be locked. There were no keys to determine who could get in or out. At the top of the house next to the bathroom was the linen cupboard. This could be locked. She hid her fancy jewellery among the piles of sheets and towels. The key was kept in her desk.'

She looked down at her long narrow hands, the skin still childlike, marred only by small nicks. She laced her fingers and put them on the table, a new raw expression on her face. She was deep in the years of her younger self yet a wised-up look in her eye suggested to him a presence of mind that knew exactly where it was. How could he explain that he felt like an elected being? That the sound of her clear voice held him captive. That the sad tale of her childhood, so brutal and lonely, filled him with an ineffable pleasure. That her striking beauty blew through like a fresh spring breeze. That for these few moments, she was his.

'Go on,' he urged, '… the linen closet. She kept the key in her desk.'

'The desk was long, it had lots of drawers. It was a very important object. I knew that because of how much time she sat at it. It lived in her study, there on the ground floor, you see, that big square window where the Christmas tree is. It had high ceilings and on the walls she'd hung lots of art from other cultures. African masks. She'd never been to Africa but they were, "So real, so true, darling!" Books lined the room too. Up and down two full walls. I had a recurring nightmare about them for years: I would be playing and they would start jiggling, and then in a big avalanche crash down on top of me. All the big names, Freud, Jung, Winnicott, Klein, Joseph Campbell. Aldous Huxley. Her god was Laing. Ironic, don't you think? The man who put the family at the heart of it all and my mother, the divided self, incapable of creating anything resembling a family life. We were all just odd little pebbles rolling around from one box to another. She helped other people, I really believe she did, she was magnificent and bold and maverick. She was a monster to me.'

He pretended to know what she was referring to. The names were familiar, how could they not be? What they meant was another matter. Unlike many of his peers, he had studiously avoided being bogged down in the currents of therapy-think. But to Charlotte they were important. And her mother was a monster. Like the adjective beguiling, the noun for a destructive beast seemed incompatible with a description of a mother. Images from Hieronymus Bosch crowded his brain, the pink slithery nude figures, the monsters cavorting in the sky, a carnival of the grotesque.

'Monster?'

'Yes. The first time I remember her really losing it I was about four I think. It's so difficult to have all this clear. Even after all the years of treatment.'

He smiled encouragement, faltering. Dark clouds stumbling over the horizon. A storm approaching.

'What I think I remember is this: one afternoon I came into her study on all fours, intent on a solitary game of hide-and-seek. I used to play that a lot. I crawled behind the high straight-backed chair that stood closest to the door and peeked around its leg. My mother wasn't at her desk. Suddenly her bangles jingled loudly and she was above me staring down with this terrible expression. I remember so well the sound of those bangles, even now when I hear wind chimes or the clanking of any chain my heart skips a beat. I looked up at her and at the huge bookcase and I thought "It's going to fall."

'"Mummy!" I shouted. Her hair was all tangled and her lipstick smudged across her lips. I jumped up. She backed away in horror, all the way across the room, away from me, and bumped into the desk. There were papers all over it, falling off the side and strewn across the floor. They crackled under her feet and she jumped from one foot to the other like she was stepping on hot coals.'

Pause.

'Then?'

Her words sprinted in short bursts.

'I ran to her and put my arms around her thighs. She pried me loose and I lunged again at her. She was strong and had me bundled under her arm, up the stairs and into the linen closet in seconds.

Click. Door locked. I buried myself in the linens and gradually my fear went. Ages later, I don't know how much time passed, she let me out, as if nothing had happened.

It became so that I'd go in there on my own. I didn't hate it, I liked being there. It was a nest of soft towels and smooth sheets, smelling of all things clean and safe. I'd sing songs to myself. My favourite was one my father sang a lot.'

She lilted across the table:

> We'll drink a drink a drink
> To Lily the pink the pink the pink
> The saviour of our human race
> For she invented medicinal compound
> Most efficacious in every case.

He hummed the last few lines in harmony as if they were sharing a memory. At the next table a suited middle-aged man stared. She didn't notice.

'They say you should never take LSD on your own. She did. She also wrote herself prescriptions of new psychotropic drugs. These made her collapse in a daze for hours; sometimes she'd hallucinate, and I'd hear shrieks and laughter coming from her study. Once I dared go in. She was huddled in a corner. My appearance gave her a fright, then she went for me. "Get out!" She screamed at me. "Little

Devil! They're growing, right here" – and she banged her index fingers on either side of her head. "What, Mummy, what's growing?" Panic rose right through me and I grasped my two pigtails.

'She ran at me. I wasn't quick enough, and before I knew it I was being chased up the stairs and into the linens, into the soft dark clean haven away from her lunatic ravings.

'Another time I stole the closet key from her desk drawer.

'"It's hiding!" I goaded her by waving it above my head. She tried to swipe it. I giggled and scurried down to the kitchen round Mrs Bowler, through the sitting room, up the stone stairs and into the garden. It was summer, a deep wilting hot summers' day. Trees protected us from neighbouring eyes. There were large white lilies and little daisies and red geraniums. The sweet scent was overpowering. I must have been about eight. The smell of lilies has made me feel ill ever since.

'"Bitch," she shouted, and went back inside.

'I found her at that big desk rocking in her swivel chair. Above her head hung a beautiful painting, a small oil from the Northern Renaissance. It was the only possession I kept when she died. The long blond girl above and the drooping one in the chair below. For many years I confused them in my head.

'I climbed onto her lap and put the key neatly back in its place in the top drawer. Then I put my arms around her neck and my face into her neck. "Sorry Mummy, sorry." She held me tightly, swinging us both one way, then another, on that chair for I don't know how long.'

Charlotte looked fixedly at a point on his forehead. Her breathing had shortened as if she had just finished a strenuous exercise regime; her face shimmered in a pellucid half-wild glow, defiant. A sudden shadow brought shame and looking sideways she bowed her head. This allowed him a polite moment to absorb her story. That kind of monster, a wicked abusive mother-monster. The revulsion in him thundered and sparked. He was speechless. How was it possible that a mother could treat her child in this way? An innocent, just a little girl. His machismo swelled up like an inflatable balloon and as if readying for battle he half-rose from his chair. Charlotte had never known love. He would show her love.

He grabbed the corner of the table to stop from losing his balance and reached out with the other to grab her shoulder in solidarity. The gesture made her gasp and draw away.

'I'm sorry!' Embarrassment came over him like a rash. 'I don't mean to alarm you. It's an appalling story, you're amazing. To get through that.'

She ignored his compliment. Lurking at the bottom of his thoughts, a very small voice wondered at her tale, at its florid touches and arresting flow, its show of drama and verve. A question mark came and went through his conscious mind with a ghostly flicker. Was she sane?

He sat again, caught between a clanging desire to talk about wholesome things, everyday topics shared between normal people – say, the ongoing weather, how his kids were doing, Jane and Sheldon, the price of fuel – and the captivating force of her ravaged childhood.

'No, I'm sorry,' she softened. Several long seconds ticked by and then: 'I don't think much about all that. I keep busy. Work takes it out of me. But I attend a group therapy session in Bosnia. It's for trauma victims of the war. It helps me keep things in perspective. I talk about these stories sometimes there, I write them down, all different versions, but this is the first time I've told anyone I –' she hesitated and slipped a bashful smile at him – 'anyone I've been intimate with. That house. It's all so immediate, so clear.' She trembled.

'How long did she – did this go on for?' He asked. She put hands under her thighs and bit her bottom lip.

'As I grew older I wised up to her antics and eventually she left me alone.'

'Your father, where was he?'

'I used to cry out for him in the closet. He never heard. He was at the hospital mainly. He spent most of his life there. He turned his back on his great love, his "darling one" as he called her. He closed his eyes to her addictions and shook himself free from the tyranny of her needs. I don't blame him. I discovered years later from a medical school acquaintance that he'd had a long affair with the head matron. Apparently everyone at the hospital knew. I'm glad. That he had someone. You see I never thought of myself as part of a family. I have trouble even now understanding what that word might mean. We were hardly together, the three of us, and then we were just two. He died when I was ten leaving me and her to rattle about that big house together.

'There were no large Christmas gatherings or festive family parties. I had an aunt, my father's sister. I remember her vaguely: a soft round woman with helmet grey hair and a flat voice. She lived in Birmingham and worked as a secretary. My mother didn't like her. "Not one of us," she'd confide. What was this "us"?

'Oh dear, I fear I'm rambling now. It's seeing the house over there. Almost unchanged. You see I've kept away from it. They say you must face everything. What is the point in returning?

'It was all so –'

She stopped herself with a light shake as if tossing off sand.

'Jacob, excuse me. This must be so boring for you.'

He answered with a prim laugh. The cold seeped through the draughts in the front door. The fire in the grate burned with an ethereal flame. The room had filled up with a local crowd looking for warmth and food.

He stroked her thigh. He remembered her nakedness, how her skin felt. He had an irresistible desire to smell her. He inched his head towards her taking in deep breaths through his nostrils. A slight, ever so slight, tang of – lavender, no, mustier, amber.

She hesitated and raised an eyebrow. He removed his hand and pulled back. She returned inward. Anger crossed her features, she shook her head.

'Everything. You want to know it all. Well, I can tell you, she wouldn't have liked you. Not top drawer. You're handsome all right, and clever, she'd have liked that. Bloody top drawer. That was one of her favourite phrases. "Darling!" she'd exclaim, "you must meet the Vesney son. He's awfully clever. Top drawer." You see my father wasn't but he was awfully successful. She liked that. Alex was tippy top. She hated him.'

Alex. The husband. He tried to remember what Jane had said about him. Wealthy. Abandoned her.

'"What do you talk about?" she'd ask.' Charlotte stared again at the window where her mother's study had been. 'Then she'd go on, in a really awful tone, "He doesn't seem to have much conversation." And I'd say, "You know, this and that. Nothing much really."

'I was telling the truth. We didn't know each other. How could we? He was so – all together. In charge from the beginning of his life. He had a number of sisters, they were rather nice and they didn't like me but they thought he was marvellous. So did his mother, a short haughty woman whose two loves in life were her garden and her son. Father, jovial, pompous, sexist. I'm sure you know the type. Alex never questioned himself. He went straight at his goals with no turning right or left. It was exhilarating. Sex was like that too: he made love like the most streamlined computer, all smooth and quick. He tolerated nonsense, my nonsense, because it never touched his sense of the world. His world was entirely under his command and entirely under his control. He could make anything happen.

84

'One thing he couldn't do was bring back the dead.'

Charlotte stopped again. Her eyes spangled in memory of her passionate younger self and she threw back her head in a throaty chortle, barely conscious of her current surroundings. His mood had changed from elation to envy. He did not like this story about Alex. He did not want to hear about his confidence, his credit card and his performance in bed. Me, he commanded, me, I am here.

Charlotte gave him a look that dared him to remonstrate. Intelligence and a strange gaiety danced in her eyes. Then she turned back to the window, to the discernible outline of her childhood home. The Christmas tree bulbs shone like stars. Inside the pub the fire burned on. Clients huddled together, rubbing hands, noses red. The cold slowed down time. Charlotte wiped her forehead and face with her palms as if in benediction.

Her presence commanded the gaze of those nearby. Not just the businessman next to them, others too: the eyes of both men and women slid over her and then returned quickly to stare. A jamboree of emotions collided in him: so utterly gorgeous she was! He wanted to help her, to protect her, to impress her. Yet. She was only interested in this past of hers, this superman husband. How rich was he? And she, how rich was she? She was snobby, precious, superior! No. Fragile, an ephemeral being made of broken glass. 'Leave,' ordered his inner voice. He sat.

Something difficult to recognise, a kind of repugnance, stirred in him. His miniscule presence in her life did not count. Her operatic tale of this whirlwind courtship with a rich powerful man outstripped any small offering he could make. 'I am ordinary,' he thought. 'My life, quite pedestrian. Go quietly now,' he repeated to himself, and again he ignored the instruction.

'Jacob, I have a favour to ask of you. Something I need you to do.' She hesitated. 'I don't know anyone in London anymore. A few professional acquaintances. But this, this is personal. I daren't trust it to just anyone.'

And he was hers again. Anything.

'That painting. The panel. Inherited from my mother. I want to sell it. It's been with Jane all these years. I need to have it evaluated and put into auction. Sotheby's showed an interest ages ago. It should be easy. If I organise to have it delivered to them, will you make sure it all goes smoothly? Act as my agent?'

He could barely imagine how much something like that was worth. A shameful thought cut across his turbulent feelings: would he get a commission? A quick calculation pointed to the possibility of his pocketing several thousand from the transaction. The child support, the exorbitant cost of his small rental in Kensal Rise. His diminishing work and rising bills. Most important, he reasoned, it would keep him in touch with her. She would have to pay attention.

He agreed.

'Good.' She became hurried. 'Now I must get a train back to Gloucester. Will you come this weekend then? Jane and Sheldon have plenty of room.'

It would have been his weekend for having the boys. Kath had rearranged the schedule, without asking, for a visit to their grand-parents. He had an aching, sometimes unbearable longing for them. But they did not like visits to his poky bland flat. It was not their home. Their home was several streets away in a large Victorian house with their mother, a conservatory, large garden, plasma screen television, their own bedrooms.

Yes, he could visit this Saturday. He would take a train.

They walked together up Kensington High Street, their breath mingled and dissolved in the cold dusk. It was half past four and the day had retreated. A mosaic of lights sparkled up and down the wide congested street. She walked quickly, eyes flitting, alert to dangers bearing down from the weight of her past, the bustling indifference of shoppers, the giggling pubescent schoolboys and girls on their way home, coats open wide to the winter air. She walked past the entrance to the tube, quickened her pace and stopped further on, looking all around her up and down the street.

In the near distance stood a huge modern hotel, a monolith from the 1960s in concrete and glass where mass consumer needs were handled with functionality and spas. A coach was parked in front. An eyesore. He had never been inside. What promise it now offered! An airy room in beige and grey with a king-sized bed, dimmer lights, wall-to-wall carpet. Room service would bring champagne. His thoughts tumbled one after the other. He would undress her, oil her pearly skin, carry her to the crisp tightly made bed, make love slowly over many hours. Or, quick, into the room, fumbling to pull off each other's clothes, urgent pawing at buttons and zips. Jumping at the touch of cold hands against warm skin.

She suddenly asked: 'Where is Barkers?' There was anguish in her voice.

He told her the department store had disappeared a while ago, along with most other independently owned stores. The art deco palace was now home to an expensive organic food emporium and various offices.

'I had a friend, Marie, her father was some kind of manager at Barkers. She was at Montessori with me. I – I didn't remember, till just now. I played with her. She lived in a modern council house, on the other side of the railway. I think he was a kind man. I ignored him.'

He felt impatient. Her insistence on recalling the past was a blockade. Over there, just across the street, a new life beckoned. The vast hotel offered anonymity and protection. Choose, he urged silently.

She did not hear his internal plea. She turned heel and together they walked back to the entrance of the tube where she kissed him on the cheek, confirmed their arrangement to meet on Saturday in Gloucestershire, and joined the crowd in the neon-lit passage.

She looked back as she put her ticket into the electronic barrier. Neither waved.

It was a nippy, invigorating afternoon when he arrived by train in Gloucester.

Jane met him at the station. Her greeting was effusive. She thanked him for the flowers and then drove in near silence to her home, a Regency townhouse overlooking a garden square in the middle of the city. He sensed not all was well.

The house was hushed, an organised and comforting array of rooms on four floors each wooden and book-lined. The colours were sage, soft blue and limpid yellow. Modern in tone, it was a gentle home, one where he felt you could retreat from the world. Only two of them lived here, Sheldon's study at the very top, next to the bedroom in which he was to sleep; Jane's at the very bottom, leading onto a cobbled courtyard.

In between they found Charlotte in the drawing room.

She stood by an ice-blue sofa. Above hung the painting, hypnotic in this casual domestic setting. It was much smaller than he had imagined: a neat rectangle of intense animation and colour. It seemed to be a medieval allegory at the centre of which was a young naked woman with long curly golden hair falling down her skinny child-like body. Tiny perfectly round breasts. She was standing in a wainscoted room amid the clutter of her daily life. A big window on one side looked onto brown fields and green hills. At the top end of the room, a dressed man was coming through the door. The question the painting seemed to ask was whether she was delighting in her own naked solitariness or anticipating the prospect of lovemaking. Or both. It was charming and surprisingly modern. It had the peculiar effect of blurring all notions of place and time.

'Exquisite,' he remarked. Charlotte bowed her head. He kissed her on both cheeks.

Tea was laid out on a low glass table.

'Welcome!' Charlotte gestured at the sofa. 'Thanks Jane,' she added over his shoulder. 'Tea?'

He sat in an armchair, took the delicate china cup and assumed an air of agreeable distance.

Jane raked hands through hair, and tossed out words about the city and its downtrodden atmosphere as unemployment rose; Sheldon's return later from a conference, the enduring cold. Charlotte sat next to her, serene.

Outside, the square was silent apart from the song of a bird that disturbed the crusty air at irregular intervals. The windows grew dark, casting their selves in pale reflection. He drifted.

Jane rose and drew the curtains with a quick tug. She offered another round of tea. He nibbled on a piece of carrot cake. It was as if they were meeting for the first time. There were no signs of the tangled weave that held them together in fragile communion. The long years of friendship between Jane and Charlotte, begun in torment and grief, were now being measured in cups of tea. And here he was, a stranger, aware that he might never penetrate their secrets; nor find the solace he craved.

———

Sheldon returned around seven and assumed his role as host. He was a big genial man with a crop of grey curls and a careless bonhomie. His arrival immediately relieved the tension in the air. Jacob warmed to him on first sight.

They ate in the large kitchen enclosed by white shutters at either end. A wood-burning stove belted heat and an inviting set of sofa and armchair completed the picture of comfort. Jacob began to relax.

'One helluva shame,' Sheldon asserted as an afterthought to Jacob's casual questions about universities in the States. Sheldon spent much of the year teaching well-funded undergraduates at a liberal arts college on the East Coast. He continued, 'Y'know, the whole damn system is corrupt. When our fine institutions, great places with some of the best minds in the world, when you can't even rely on them to know what a conflict of interest is, then –' And he wiped his hands in a theatrical gesture.

'People are scared,' argued Jane. 'They think it's all going to hell. Rats and sinking ships. Students are up in arms. No wonder they –'

'Nah. Bunch of cowards.' Sheldon stretched his long legs to the side in punctuation.

'*Sauve qui peut* mentality. They think they're in the shit; they're sensitive; idealistic; you know how it is with young people – it's all ideals and black and white. Especially tough being young now.' Jane countered with persuasive charm. Jacob found himself admiring yet again her confidence.

'Oh tosh,' continued Sheldon. 'You go on merit, that's it, those were the founding ideals, anyone can get there, you work hard, you get rewarded. It's simple. Look at me, it's how I did it. No leg up. Things have changed. You don't let students in and give them A's just because Dad might donate a painting to the museum.' His generous physique lent substance to such plain-speaking.

'Sheldon still believes in these things,' Charlotte said with a wink at Sheldon.

'Someone's got to,' he retorted chuckling. 'You Brits take it all with that laid-back irony.'

There was a twinkle to his conversation, as if aware that his role as American blunderbuss was all in an evening's performance.

'Oh stop now,' Jane delivered this rebuke with a grin. She turned to Jacob and carried on, 'He's just trying to provoke you. He believes English people think of Americans as idiots.'

Jacob threw hands up in mock surrender.

'Who could blame them,' commented Sheldon, suddenly serious. 'A country that elects bozos with barely a brain cell to lead them – OK so there was Obama, granted – but look at what's happening now. Damn shame. The country disrespects basic notions of civic responsibility, is full of religious nuts and privileges the rich over everyone else.'

'I like Americans,' Jacob offered. 'I had one of the best experiences of my life there in the early 1980s. I often think of my British cohort of colleagues, journalists, writers, and the like, as a small group of squabbling adolescents by comparison. And look what's happening in this country. Hijacked by throwback imperialists. Dreadful inequality. Looming chaos. Hardly any better. I encountered a refreshing openness in the US. It was impressive.'

He and Sheldon preened with benevolence, each trying to outdo the other. Jacob was aware they were engaged in a friendly masculine performance, like a piece of theatre. Jane intervened, mediated and moved them on. The affection between her and Sheldon was strong and encompassing.

Underlying Jane's social composure ran a troubling current. It had to do with Charlotte. It was as if she was earthed to her friend by a live wire. Every slight shift in Charlotte's behaviour was felt by Jane. It reminded Jacob of their dinner together in Trieste with Jane's colleagues. Sheldon practised an avuncular condescension to Charlotte which slipped from time to time into obsequiousness. Jacob suspected there had been rows between Sheldon and Jane about Charlotte.

She followed the discussion with the occasional offside comment thrown in. She was not interested in matters of political ethics. Her thoughts worked on something quite different. 'Me,' he wondered, 'are they on me?' He sat at a perpendicular, hoping their feet might touch.

'Charlotte,' Jane turned to her friend, 'in Bosnia, you've seen things over the years, the war, the intervention by NATO, the rebuilding of the country. Do you think it's all so hopeless?'

Charlotte looked down at her plate. Jacob leaned towards her; so did Jane and Sheldon.

'So many children were killed. Many continue to be wounded by landmines. The forests and hills are littered with them. Gashes appear in walls and streets ... scars everywhere. I don't really know. I tend to kids. I change their bandages. I make them tell me their stories. I try to learn things about their lives. There was Katya. She was eight. Arm gone. Her mother was a junkie. Her father, God knows where. She lived in a tower block that threatened to fall down any day ... Hearing the details of their lives, the very specific stories each has to tell, it keeps me sane. It keeps me away from myself. As for the rest – ' She brushed the air with her hand, her fingers tugging the end of a long sleeve.

'Yes,' Jane reached out to her friend, 'yes, I understand, and what about looking after yourself, finding your own pleasure and nourishment, these things are also important.'

Charlotte nodded very slightly in Jacob's direction. He beamed.

'There was an eminent American psycho-historian,' Jane changed tack, 'he said children were poison containers, used by adults through centuries as a repository for all our emotional muck. He thought wars came out of bad childhoods.'

Sheldon countered: 'Jane thinks more breastfeeding in the world would stop crazies from making a grab for power.'

Jane turned to Jacob: 'Did you know that studies into parenting practices in Prussia at the turn of the twentieth century revealed shocking practices of abuse inflicted on children, real abuse, in the name of building strong character? Tell me that didn't produce a number of brutal Nazi guards.'

Jacob found himself caught in the spotlight: there was an expectation of something, an opinion, a tug of acknowledgement, coming from Jane. He pulled himself up and said, 'Politicians and their rich friends want power and when they get it they want to keep it at all costs. They'll invade countries, brutalise civilians, grab land and resources. Make themselves rich and important. We're now all governed by a super-shadowy elite which has different rules to the rest of us. It's a plutocracy. And we all follow, too busy or embattled in our little lives to take much notice. Until a catastrophe happens and then we're shocked. I don't know what that has to do with nice childhoods.'

He had rehearsed this argument many times over the past years, not invested as he once had been in the importance of the assertions but attached all the same to their truth. He felt distant to himself, from the younger man who had erupted in pubs about the unfairness of society. At this moment he was preoccupied with the next half-hour and whether Charlotte would give him a sign that his presence meant something to her.

Sheldon sent him a commiserating smile. 'Ah Jacob, indeed, the erosion of democracy. The rule of Mammon.'

To his relief, Jane and Sheldon picked up the threads of the discussion. Jane said tyrants had suffered abusive childhoods. Sheldon said not all those who committed atrocities were tyrants. Jane said she meant tyrant in a looser sense. Sheldon said good people did bad things. Jane said we all had this capacity. Sheldon said then it didn't just depend on mother's breast, there was a matter of conscience, there was a question of collective ethics. Jane and Sheldon agreed. Jacob turned to Charlotte.

She announced: 'I'd just like to say Jacob is going to oversee the sale of my painting. I hope you don't mind. I think it's time for me to let it go.'

Sheldon gave a belching laugh. Jane exclaimed, 'You never said anything to me!' She reacted as if she had been attacked. Jacob immediately wanted to apologise.

Charlotte: 'I decided a couple of weeks ago. I've been in touch with Sotheby's. The auction should take place in the New Year. Jacob's in London, it's easy for him to manage it. I didn't want to bother you.' Jacob nodded in affirmation of this, shrinking back from the tensions that had suddenly bubbled up.

Jane: 'But Sheldon can do that for you! After all, art is his field. Bother ...'

She wiped her mouth, folded her napkin in a neat square and put it on the table, a full-stop. Jacob held his tongue.

Sheldon replenished their glasses. 'Hey, honey, it's her decision. I'm sure Jacob can handle it all just fine.'

'Jacob,' Jane leant over and squeezed his forearm. 'I'm sorry, I didn't mean to suggest you were somehow incompetent. But, this painting, it is, well, many things, isn't it, Charlotte? It's not just money we're talking about here, is it?'

'It is basically the money. I want the cash.' Charlotte smiled graciously at them.

'Your mother ...' Jane prompted, reminding her friend of something vital.

'I haven't seen this painting in years. When I saw it hanging there I thought, "Oh, all the stuff that went on ..." I'm afraid I bored Jacob with some of it this week – seeing the old house ...' Jacob nodded at her. At this she frowned. 'It's just a painting, and it's time to move on.'

Sheldon got up from the table and put a new log on the dying flames. Charlotte's slim fingers picked at each other.

Jane piled plates, knives and forks, crumpled napkins, and a white porcelain serving dish into a teetering stack.

'There's fruit if anyone wants it.'

Charlotte got up and stood by her chair, hands clasped together as if waiting for grace to be said.

Sheldon went to the sofa by the wood-burner and balanced a glass of wine on his stomach.

Jane at table, sat in front of the wonky pile, tapping her fingers on the wood.

'No thanks. Time for bed. I'm afraid I'm a little tired.' Charlotte kissed Jane on the head and brushed her lips on Jacob's cheek. Was it a sign? She did not linger but walked over to Sheldon and patted his curls. Jacob could see Sheldon was irritated. And why not? Charlotte had thrown a proverbial spanner in the works of their genial gathering.

She closed the door and they listened to her light step on the stairs.

Sheldon: 'Come over here, Jacob. By the fire. Get comfortable.' Relieved, he moved from the table to the armchair.

They sat looking into the flames. A sudden noise of chairs and crockery signalled Jane was clearing up. He stirred and Sheldon extended a restraining arm. 'Let her do it, it'll calm her.'

The log burned and Jane bustled and upstairs the faint sound of a door opened and closed. It was getting hotter by the fire. He removed his jumper. Her bedroom would be directly under his.

Jane sunk into the sofa and crossed her arms. 'So Jacob, what's going on?'

'Honey, just let it be, OK? Just let her get on with whatever it is she's doing. Right, Jacob?' Sheldon patted her leg.

'Let it be? Something's going on. She comes back to England for the first time in years. She borrows the car, she wants to visit the house she lived in with that brute Alex. She goes up to London, not telling me why, she sees Jacob, she invites him here without asking us. She tells us she's selling her painting. She's not talking to me but she's animated. I feel it. Something's going on. I sense it. Jacob?' She fixed on him a kindly determination.

'Honestly? I don't know. In London she showed me that house in Kensington where she grew up. Told me stories, awful things about her childhood. I don't know why. After Trieste I never thought I'd see her again. But now, she wants to sell this painting, I agreed to help.'

'Are you in love with her?' It was a direct hit. He nodded slowly, dubious. 'In love' was not a phrase he felt confident about claiming for himself. 'Powerfully attracted' seemed more accurate but coy and vague.

And there was so much more he felt he could say to Jane and Sheldon, these nice people who seemed to him in this moment to be interested in him. He might talk about his years of bed-hopping, a habit formed in his teen years in response to the reactions he inspired in girls; he might mention his sense of irrelevance; he might talk about his wife and their separation. His love of his boys. And more about what he felt was his essentially peripheral nature. But he held back; this was perhaps not the right time for confessionals.

'What does she feel about you?' Jane continued in a probing voice. Her manner encouraged honesty.

'Not much,' he admitted, hoping to be contradicted. Sheldon clicked his tongue.

'How do you know?' She pressed. He corrected his posture into the upright.

'I'm here because I was invited, because I want to spend every minute with her in the hope that she might notice me, because I like you very much and want you to help.'

'Jane'll fix it,' Sheldon said to no one in particular and poured more wine. 'You know how we met?' He smiled at Jane. 'At a conference about art and psychoanalysis. She came right up to me, bang, with that sassy goddamn gorgeous face of hers, all smart and laughing. I was a mess, my wife had just left me and I was separated from my kids. She knew it, just sort of got it. We talked and talked, and weeks later I rearranged my life, and here I am. Damn good thing too. But be careful Jacob, Charlotte – ah, now, she's a whole other bag of tricks.'

Jacob found himself pacified by the abundance of the wine and the heat of the fire, both of which seemed to perfectly embody the good intentions of his hosts. He thought he knew all about tricks. He wanted them to know Charlotte was different. Yet, there he was, the one usually so fluent reduced to emotional stuttering.

He tried again: 'You know her well, and I don't. She is so full of sadness. But she is full of life too, with such – '

'Intelligence,' asserted Jane.

'Class,' added Sheldon.

'Strength,' he concluded.

Jane wanted to continue with this conversation about Charlotte and his feelings for her. She had taken Sheldon's hand in an affectionate clasp and kept her eyes on him. He was reminded of an ancient priestess, glittering and wise. He envied Sheldon. He too wanted Jane to take his hand. For many years he had slept at one side of the matrimonial bed and his wife at the other, each one slipping in and out of their respective sides and crossing by chance on their way here and there as the routine of daily life imitated intimacy. He was grateful to Jane and Sheldon for taking seriously his feelings about Charlotte. It was up to him to explain . . . something, though he had no account of himself to offer.

'I take it your marriage is over?' Jane asked in a tone that was entirely neutral.

The simple answer was yes. He was not sure Kathleen agreed.

'It's complicated,' he answered.

She nodded, impatient, and waited for more. What answer could he give her? He had married Kath because she was beautiful, she was a bitch, she made him feel real. He had been impressed by her competence in the management of their life and in her ambition for their joint future. Then came their son, Finn, and twenty months later, Mikey. It had crept up on him over those first years when they came into being as if from air: he finally understood love, its delicate focused vulnerable nature. He realised what he felt for Kath was not love. It fell far short. He resumed old habits. The end was bound to come. None of this he felt he could sum up for Jane in a manner that escaped abject guilt.

He tried: 'Charlotte. She's the first woman since my separation I've – ' He hesitated. It seemed unsavoury to mention his night spent in lovemaking.

Jane's look again suggested impatience. She was ahead of him. She knew about complications, she knew about sex.

He announced: 'I've been celibate since my separation. I can't explain to you why I feel so much for Charlotte. All I can say is I've never felt like this before. I've known many women, sexually – this is not to my credit. But Charlotte. She's bewitching.'

'Yep,' intoned Sheldon. 'She sure is that. Always out of reach. Janie thinks I'm too hard on her. But I see Janie tie herself in knots for this woman. For what? She lost her baby. It was a long time ago. I'm sure it was awful. Dreadful ordeal for everyone. But it's over. She's got money, she's got a life, doing good things across there in Bosnia. Now she's finally had sex. Great! I'm very happy for her. And you, Jacob. You seem like a nice guy. I just think every time Janie gets caught up with Charlotte, everything else goes to the wall.'

Jane: 'That's just not fair. God, I hardly ever see her. You're still cross with me because I left you on your birthday to fly to Sarajevo to spend the anniversary of Sylvie's death with her. That was four years ago!' She tilted her head, raised an eyebrow and said, 'Do we need to talk more about that?'

Sheldon yawned, closed his eyes and shook his head. 'Anyway,' his words caught in another yawn and he opened his eyes again. 'It wasn't about me. You're this great woman, you have this amazing career, you teach, you lecture, you deal every week with the criminally insane with more courage than I can imagine, people love you – but, one little tremor from Charlotte and you lose all sense.'

Jane turned in on herself. Her thoughts quickened and flashed across her face. She stalked the room, tidying and touching loose objects along the way. She went round three times and came to rest once again in her chair with a resolute focus that she turned on him.

'It's the cash, isn't it? She wants it for something.'

'No doubt, but she certainly didn't tell me what for and I didn't ask. Seems to be her business.'

'Will you get a commission?' Jane's shrewdness was at its sharpest. He looked to Sheldon for support. The latter was now alert, sitting up, swishing the dregs of wine around his glass. He said: 'Time for bed, buddy. I'm whacked. Come on, honey, you too. We can resume this in the morning when her ladyship is with us.' Jacob was thankful for Sheldon's bluntness. He had no wish to discuss the embarrassment of his finances.

Jane and Sheldon's bedroom was next to Charlotte's. They whispered a goodnight to one another. There was no light visible under Charlotte's door. Up one flight in his garret room, he yanked off his boots and let them fall to the floor with two thuds. He stripped and slipped between the smooth linen. His body felt as cold as snow. He shivered; his teeth chattered. The silent night was broken briefly by the sound of a car. He turned off the light and was thrown into gloom. Streaks of silver shone like ice through gaps in the curtains. The moon that night was at its most intense. The house creaked, moving on its old joints, settling like its residents into hours more of chilled darkness. He concentrated on the silence. Was that a sigh? Another car, more groaning timber. A cough? Was she, like him, naked in frosty sheets? He curled up to warm himself and fell into a deep, dreamless sleep.

Jacob slept well, waking with the slow winter sunrise. He got himself a cup of tea and had a shower. By the time he came down for breakfast they were all up. Sheldon boiled some eggs; they ate in silence over the Sunday newspapers. The mood was lighter. Charlotte looked at him a lot, and when he caught her eye she cocked her head and sent him a gallant smile. The shift was small but pronounced. Slowly she was allowing him to enter her being. He wondered if he might stay an extra night. Time was an important element in their advancing relations and soon she would be back in Bosnia. A new optimism buoyed his spirits, and briefly that morning, in the comfort of the pleasant ordered home, the future seemed a friendly place.

When they'd finished their second cups of coffee, Sheldon suggested a walk to the cathedral and a pit stop in the cafe. Charlotte wasn't sure. Jane jollied them along. Sheldon asked Jacob if he'd ever visited the Cathedral. Jacob said he had, a few years ago, when doing a feature on locations used in the Harry Potter films.

They set out together along the connecting streets, some as ancient as the cathedral, others lined with concrete modern blocks curving through the city.

They walked through a small alley and came into the picturesque cathedral close. Charlotte stopped short and muttered, 'Oh my god.' Facing them was a soaring magnificent edifice stretching up and round, dwarfing everything in its vicinity. She said in a small voice: 'That's where I got married.' Jacob stared at her in surprise. He hadn't imagined her so unequivocally socialite.

'Must have been quite some do,' teased Sheldon.

Charlotte laughed: 'You could say that.'

She walked ahead of them impatient to reach the entrance. He followed. Sheldon and Jane strolled, arms linked. The sky had turned a crystal winter blue, a strong sun hung low, the threat of snow in abeyance.

An advent service was under way. The incantatory voice of the presiding cleric calling the congregation to prayer was answered with a collective murmur: '*A-a-a-me-e-enn.*' The words echoed in his head, the residue of his childhood when as a choirboy he would recite the Anglican liturgy weekly.

Charlotte walked through the porch. He turned back to Sheldon and Jane. They signalled towards the side of the cathedral and made a gesture of drink. He waved and shouted, 'We'll join you when we've finished.'

Charlotte circled the back sticking close to the wall. There were many people bent in prayer down the nave. Beyond, rising up from the stone, the glorious eastern stained glass window astonished in the bright light.

Charlotte's hands were shoved into the pockets of her padded coat, her head protected by a thick scarf. A deviant religious. He took her arm and together they advanced a few more steps to the top of the aisle. 'I walked all that way alone.' She talked in a loud whisper, blue eyes dilated. He stared down the middle of the nave, to the altar, the lectern, and beyond to the quire and heavenly window. I'm looking in the direction of God, he thought, she walked towards Him all on her own, strutting a sacramental runway.

An officer of the church went to the lectern and began a reading: 'Behold, a virgin shall conceive and bear a son . . .'

She led him to the northern ambulatory, a protected corridor where the tomb of Edward II lay. The words from Isaiah followed them and dimmed. There was just the two of them now in this quiet lay-by muffled by centuries of stone and bone. She continued in a low wavering voice, her eyes travelling from the effigy to curling masonry and across the smooth flagged floor to the outside. He sat on a bench, light-headed.

'What was it like, getting married here?'

'I don't remember much about my wedding. "I do!" Then whoosh, back down the aisle, into a car all the way to Alex's family estate. There was so much champagne and so many people, everyone kissing me. I can't remember a thing about the speeches and then we danced in a white marquee. And my mother, swaying in a corner, trailing lavender silk and getting drunk.' She was looking beyond him, her magnetic eyes caught in a gleam of sun.

The drone of another deep voice travelled from the lectern.

'At this time of year, as we await the joyful celebration of the birth of our Lord, we pause to think about …'

He and Kathleen had tied the knot at Westminster Town Hall with a few friends and some family. It was an informal cheery occasion, civic and legal. No obedience, no honour.

All her attention now rested on him. She was beseeching him to understand something. Something about this story of her wedding, about this marriage to the important and wealthy Alex.

'Do you see? Then suddenly there I was, Mrs Alex Symmond, purring through the country lanes in a sleek Jaguar, a husband behind the wheel, a gold band on my finger, en route to my new life.' She waggled her left hand, the ring finger extended towards the light, the imagined icy diamond flashing before him.

'I was living in a dream. A silly fantasy. But, oh, the summer's day – it was so beautiful! A golden sun, like an eternal glow. We drove along as if on wings to our new home.'

Her voice was tinged with rapture, and her bearing, caught in the mood of this portentous day, bore down on him with the force of an avenging angel.

'We turned into the drive. There were these amazing green oak trees, they went all the way down, like guards welcoming us. And there it was in front of me, still warm from the summer sun, my house! I had presided over every detail right down to the handle on the front door. Alex swept me over the threshold and finally it was just the two of us, standing in the big hall, staring into our future.'

She now gestured as if laying out a grand plan, her whole face lit up with the urgency of this remembered time.

The reading from Isaiah continued, filling the enclave as if from above while stray beams turned the stone a gilded organic hue. Amid the numinous signals of this great church and the ecstatic animation of Charlotte's flight, he was a tiny nothing.

'Let's go back outside.' His voice was dulled by tension. He needed to get out. He was parched from the dry air, from the bitterness that burned in his mouth, from the poetic beauty cascading from her dewy lips. She allowed him once again to take her by the forearm and together they crept along the south aisle to the front porch.

The choir was singing a *Te Deum Laudemus*, amplifying the vaults with sweet sound. He felt the welling up of tears.

'Shall we join Jane and Sheldon in the cafe?'

She noticed the light wetness around his eyes. She hesitated. 'I need you to know these things.' Shame swept across her face. 'It's OK, isn't it? It's such a beautiful day. So clear and bright. Let's sit for a while. Poor Jacob. But, you –' she took a breath – 'I – want you to know …'

Why, why poor? Why me? He was not a vessel into which she could pour her past like some reality television participant. He glared at her. 'Over there,' she pointed to a bench and he allowed himself to be led to it.

She turned to the low fierce ball of yellow absorbing its rays into her body as if for strength and huddled deeper into him with a child's tenacity. 'You see,' she murmured, her breath close to his ear, 'it's all so clear. Vivid pictures of what was once a life. The colours and the places and how I felt.' He wanted to know if it was like dreams, the eerie distortion of the familiar into the scary and lurid. He wanted to know if she was in love again with this dead life. 'OK.' His voice was crisp. 'Tell me.'

She paused and drew back from him, reflections of her white-blonde hair shimmering in the golden chill. A jagged halo. And once again he saw in her eyes that quick-shifting from cornflower to peacock, the deepness of a midnight sky, and in them a gathering of storms. Her glories, he thought, her hair, her eyes. She checked him with a mocking, half-concentrated look. He rebelled inwardly. You are not as mesmerising as you think, he scolded. He recalled in a blur the women with whom he had shared his body. Some had even said his intelligence, his charm. One day, he thought with a satisfying resentment, you will be not much at all, you will be like the rest of us, old and left-over.

She was talking now like a girl at a cocktail party performing a trick. Talking to air, he thought. He turned to her: it was evident she was barely aware of him.

She checked herself as if picking up the faintest crackle from his thoughts. He was surprised yet again at her hypersensitivity: it swung from the smallest flutter of emotion to the wide open universe. She rushed on, the words gaining pace.

'Alex didn't believe in feng shui, he didn't believe in any of it. It amused him and he paid the bills. He went to church and said he had faith and when I tried to say it was all a similar thing, he stroked my hair and said, you funny thing, to think you come from a medical family.' She swallowed a giggle.

He smiled in spite of himself. 'You funny thing.' He reached out and touched her hair. She was sitting upright now, away from him, her long neck showing white in the unforgiving light, crinkles of ageing skin delicate above the layers of wool. A sliver of silver circling her neck, the memento mori. She tugged at her gloved hands and closed her eyes as if in sudden sleep.

A hymn rose up from the body of the church: 'In the bleak mid-winter, frosty wind made moan, earth stood hard as iron, water like a stone.' Those familiar words recalled a time of believing now lost, and again he blinked back tears. Charlotte, startled from her memories, stared up, high up, at the towering spire. 'Snow had fallen, snow on snow, snow on snow, in the bleak midwinter, long ago.'

She slumped roundly like a defeated teenager. 'Such an odd time of year, isn't it?' Odd, he thought, odd all right. 'It's melancholy, a time for remembering. But we should be celebrating shouldn't we? Celebrating the birth of the baby Jesus, we should celebrate all babies shouldn't we? It's death too, it's all so sad because we know he died. Like Sylvie.' She went on: 'I bet Mary didn't feel strange about being pregnant, even if the circumstances of her conception were out of the ordinary.' She paused several long seconds. He watched his exhaled breath disappear like vapour.

'When I fell pregnant – my world – everything stopped. I was terrified.' She looked up. 'Like I'd fallen off the top of that spire, and was just left to hang in mid-air.' The words slipped out in a low embarrassed tone and he noticed a tiny fleck of spittle caught in the left corner of her mouth.

Her gaze led his to the long grey stone arrow stretching to the sky and he felt gripped by queasiness. The choral melody faint, a small sound floating on air: 'but his mother only, in her maiden bliss, worshipped the beloved with a kiss.' I will be your beloved, he thought, in time. I can wait. You will rest your head by mine at night, and we will love. He shuffled close. Her hair smelled of almond. He encircled her with his arm to catch her from this terrible fall from on high. She wriggled from him with a click of her tongue and announced, 'May saved me.' May, he thought, who the hell is she?

May, the homeopath. Warm, generous, loving woman. Remedies and the natural order of things. And so on. Alex again. Alex, and his perfect wife. On she went, more words. His resentment returned; he felt stirrings of hunger and wondered whether to text Jane. His train returned to London in several hours. He roughly pulled away and looked at his watch.

Abruptly she stopped talking and tears began to fall. He patted her back awkwardly. He had caught only a phrase here and there. She hid her head in the rough wool of his winter coat. We'll sit some more, he thought. He yawned widely. Not enough sleep last night after all. She nuzzled deeper into him. The gentle nutty smell again found its way to his nostrils, infusing the air directly around his head with fragrant promise.

People poured out of the cathedral. There were many of all ages. It must be the time of year. Last Christmas he had taken his boys to a carol concert at their local church and been interested in how much they had loved the singing, the stories, the drama of the nativity scene. He and Kath had not brought them up within any religion but they had been dragged to a number of churches during holidays across Europe from the remote timber-frames rising from Romney Marsh to the elaborate splendour of Gaudí in Barcelona. Examples of perfect Northern Gothic, fine Renaissance carving, etc. It had bored them, they had all squabbled. This year he would be alone on Christmas Day.

Out of the corner of his eye, he saw Jane and Sheldon approaching, arm in arm. As they drew near Jane quickened her pace.

Charlotte looked up: 'It's OK, I'm OK.' She stood, releasing herself into Jane's embrace. Jane shot an inquiring look at him. He shrugged. Sheldon looked on, irritated all over again.

They turned homeward and passed the crown court, a polygonal building in mustard limestone nestled amid the modern sixties block of the Shire Hall. He remarked on the distinctive style of architecture and suggested they take a look inside. Perhaps there was a history, even a brochure, which might give a more detailed account of why it had been built in this way. He was drawn to the shapes and the possible stories contained within; a small pleasure loomed.

Charlotte paused and threw him a strange glance before being moved on by Jane. He was momentarily confused. Sheldon shook his head and murmured testily, 'The trial. Charlotte's. Held in this place. Bad associations.'

He jogged his memory. Jane had not gone into any details in Trieste about any trial and Charlotte had never mentioned it. It struck him as a minor blip in the grand operatic tale of her childhood and marriage. Drama, more drama. He was annoyed. He wanted to inspect the building. He and Sheldon exchanged looks of solidarity. They were tired of being controlled by Charlotte's vulnerability. 'Shame,' he said. But they walked on dutiful behind the women. 'I'll show you around your next visit,' consoled Sheldon. 'It's worth looking at.'

———

The argument started up after lunch. Sheldon had excused himself and retired to his study. He, Jane and Charlotte remained at the kitchen table with their coffee. He was alert to the ongoing sense of unease which plagued their little group. He wondered, briefly, whether to catch an earlier train. The warmth he had felt from Charlotte in the morning had evaporated.

He had a strong desire to see his sons. The tall window to the front looked out onto the street, the square and a robust fat oak tree. Boys were kicking a football in the square with older men. On Sunday, he often went to the park with Finn and Mikey to do the same. There were tennis courts and sometimes they played a few games. These outings had been part of his Sundays from the time they could toddle.

'I'm going to see Alex,' Charlotte began. 'I've googled him. There's loads there on him. He still lives in Gloucestershire in a big house. You can go onto the satellite bit and look at it from above. There's a swimming pool and tennis court. I felt like a spy sweeping down on him. There's also a new family, of course. In this biography of him I found, it says his wife is called Elisabeth and they have four children. That's a lot isn't it?'

Jane challenged: 'Is that wise?' Her tone had a generic therapeutic timbre, but her eyes flickered anxiety. A small lump formed in his throat. Charlotte was still in love with Alex! Still in love with her lost life.

'I feel I need to, just once. I never did, you know – after –' A slow flush crept up her features.

'Exactly,' asserted Jane. 'He left you isolated in that awful house, alone with a new baby and suffering. OK he stuck by you through the trial, the least he could do really, and then just abandoned you. In your deepest hour of need while you were in the hospital. I don't understand why you want to go there.'

Charlotte appealed to him; he nodded at her, conscious of the determination in her decision.

'Jane,' he cajoled, 'perhaps this is something she just needs to get out of her system?' Maybe she would exorcise forever this man from her life. 'Surely,' he continued, 'you would advocate this kind of closure?' As if trumping her with her own profession might deter her opposition.

'Closure!' she scoffed. 'She was in a hospital for almost three years, she's carved a new life, a new career, in the most inhospitable place, doing courageous work, it's a lifetime's journey, I don't think closure is quite the right word.'

He was cut; he had not reckoned on the sharp side of Jane's nature.

'Stop,' commanded Charlotte. She had drawn herself upright. 'This is my life, my story. Stop talking about me as if I was this object. Just stop.' On this last word her voice cracked and her eyes flitted like the wings of a rare blue butterfly – and in her voice, tones of an immovable will.

'Sweetheart,' reprised Jane, gentler, 'of course it is. But I worry, I wonder if seeing him will really help you. I think it might open up wounds. I wonder if it's necessary.'

'Jane, I need to talk to him about Sylvie. It's something I have to do even if it hurts. I'm going to do it.'

Her resolve struck him with the full force of its import and he barked, 'If you need to, then just fucking get on with it.'

Charlotte and Jane registered surprise.

He held their gaze: 'I'm sorry, that was uncalled for.' He articulated this slowly, savouring the brief aroma of power that came from his impatience. The women waited on his next words.

His reply was measured: 'Charlotte, I've come to care for you in our short time together, I think you know that, and I don't think it's a good idea at all for you to visit Alex. I agree with Jane. But if that's what it takes, then just get on with it.'

'Thank you Jacob,' murmured Charlotte.

Jane dismissed him with a slighting glance and renewed her efforts with Charlotte. Back and forth the two women threw words. Seeing Alex would set her back. No, it would help move her forward. There were things she needed to say.

'Like what?' Jane's cool was heating up, her will thwarted. He was again excluded. Charlotte grew icy: 'Things that don't concern you, Jane.' She stood tall like an imperial princess.

Jane slammed the table. 'I know a lot, and it's my opinion you're making a mistake. You don't know what you're doing.'

Charlotte replied: 'I do. I know exactly what I'm doing. I'm pregnant.'

Shock rippled through his body. Jane's hands flew to her mouth.

'It's early days. I wasn't going to say anything yet, not until I was past the first trimester. But you just made me. You've always said mental health depends on our being able to see clearly, to tell our story as honestly as we can, to keep telling it to people who listen. That's what I'm doing. I want this baby so very badly. I have to face these demons.'

Alarming and random questions flooded his thoughts: 'Is it mine?' and 'Will she marry me?' and in an agonising rush, 'What will I tell my boys?' and finally, 'How *could* she?'

Finally he asked: 'When is the due date?' Mid-July.

'Is it mine?' He needed to say aloud the word 'mine' and to hear her confirmation.

'Yes.' She smiled.

Eventually Jane exhaled. Defeated.

Charlotte said mildly, 'I thought you must have known.'

Jane shook her head. Charlotte turned to him, softened: 'I'm sorry, I wasn't going to tell you until I was sure about it. It feels like a miracle. We had just the one night . . . There are so many things for me to sort.'

He was coming back into a kind of consciousness. Briefly he exchanged a look with Jane in which a reciprocal sympathy was communicated.

'So,' Jane picked up the information as if it were a fragile and dangerous object. 'So you're going to have this baby.'

'Please God,' and she knocked on the wooden table.

Slowly Jane was absorbing and mastering the news, drawing all her reactions and thoughts into coherence. Charlotte sat again and Jane began to clear away the remains of the lunch.

Daylight was fast diminishing. The clear winter sky was deepening into a nightly blue. A crescent moon was emerging. His train was in an hour. He felt as if he was dissolving with the daylight, a fluid and evanescent entity. Charlotte needed cash because she was going to have a baby. That is why she was selling the painting. Charlotte was in London to see him because she was going to have a baby. Charlotte was telling him about her past life because he was going to be father to her baby. But – and this thought came to him wrapped in indignation – did she want him to be a father to their baby?

Sheldon wandered into the room. 'Just getting a cup of coffee.'

Jane: 'Charlotte's pregnant.'

Sheldon smiled broadly. 'That's wonderful news, congratulations.' He gave Charlotte a squeeze on the shoulder, and whistling softly he set about making a fresh pot of coffee.

In a normal situation a response would include expressions of felicitation just as Sheldon had uttered. Jacob tried out these words on his inner self, allowing a moment for them to take root amid the shock and confusion. He turned to Jane for direction. Tell me where to go now, he silently demanded.

She became brisk. 'Sheldon's right, it's great news. Very wonderful for you. Let's hope you make it through the trimester. As you say, a miracle.' She too knocked on wood in a perfunctory manner and gave her friend a crooked smile.

'Thank you. I want you to be happy for me, that's so important to me. You are after all my closest friend, my only person in the world.' The warmth in her voice was sincere and catching, and Jane laughed.

'It's just a shock. I don't know why. You're right I should've known. I just never thought you'd be a mother again, I never saw you that way.' She dropped her head and with it her voice.

'I want this so much,' Charlotte implored. He was struggling with a fierce and urgent desire to howl. Did he want this? Did she think about whether he might want this?

Sheldon planted a kiss on Jane as he left the room. It was more than routine, it held in it a message. Jane rubbed her cheek against his arm in a primitive need for contact.

'Jacob,' he said, 'come say goodbye before you go.'

He was reminded of the practicalities of the day. He was to take a train to London where he would return to his flat and finish off a feature about a forthcoming museum exhibition for a magazine whose copy deadline was tomorrow. He would write his blog about the magazine piece. He would tweet about the exhibition. He would deal with the many emails that he had failed to answer on his phone. He would talk to his sons and hear about the weekend with their grandparents, make plans with them for supper later in the week at Pizza Express. If his estranged wife was in a good mood, she would not want to talk to him; if her weekend had thrown up frustrations, she would want to take them out on him with a series of instructions about the boys. These expectations and exchanges were his life, their reliability brought him stability.

Jane broke into his thoughts: 'This is a lot for you to handle, isn't it?' He nodded. 'Will it cause real problems?' He nodded again. Charlotte murmured something he failed to hear. Jane said, 'No I don't imagine you did, but now we had all better start doing some thinking ...' The sharpness of her tone was offset by a slight clearing of her throat.

Suddenly he was overcome with anxiety. 'Let's just wait, OK?' It was his turn to implore. 'Let's be in close touch and after your first term check-up, we'll talk again.'

In the next hour a powerful driving purpose emerged from Charlotte. She raised the different hospital options. Bosnia, excellent but stressful. Trieste, possible, very good maternity hospital and she knew some of them from her training. Bristol, maybe ... But, threw in Jane, would Charlotte get good pre-natal care in Sarajevo? Oh yes, they're amazing people working there. She rattled on, but maybe . . . if the baby held – more knocking on wood – maybe, she was thinking she might finally return to England for good. She'd be OK this time, she had the support of her trauma group in Sarajevo for the pregnancy. Then a group back in England. It would be OK. This baby was a sign, her second chance. Facing Alex was part of her plan to make it all right. You can't leave these things undone, you can't, it's cowardly!

Jane volleyed her reactions. Jacob interjected when he could. Charlotte appealed directly to him: 'Don't you think so Jacob, now you know, don't you think I should see him?'

He frowned: 'I really don't know.' Cowardly was an adjective that troubled him. It had been attached often to him in his marriage and its bust-up. It was a predictable attack, one that he did not oppose or duck. Yet he also felt an injustice against him was contained in Kath's easy accusation. He did not believe honesty was the sole route to virtue, in fact most often he had found it acted as an excuse for cruelty. The need to be both in the right and a victim had led Kath to enumerate with energetic consistency his many failings. And there were many. Yet the deeper questions about his boys and his love for them were never mentioned. In himself, this father-love was primal, an inexplicable defining instinct. Was he to be a father again? He turned again to Jane, silently beseeching.

Practical, Jane acted like a secretary-cum-advisor. There was a numbness in her too, apparent in the manner with which she busied herself around the kitchen, turning on lights, closing the shutters, putting dishes in the machine. She too was deeply affected by the news. At one point, she dropped the water pitcher which broke, scattering shards across the floor. On hands and knees, she cleaned up the mess, sucking her finger where glass had cut. He bent down to help, and in so doing he saw silent tears fall down her face. All the while Charlotte talked, insensible to the turmoil that had settled in him and Jane.

Excitement gave her expressions a magical cast. Minutes ticked by and with them a bountiful replenishing of his attraction to her. He did not know why; he felt overwhelmed; in a panic; excluded. Yet hope, ever resourceful, found new avenues and while Charlotte talked about the maternity hospital in Trieste, he began to create a picture of himself with her and their child, his sons, a seamless extension of one life to another.

In the end Sheldon drove him to the station and he was grateful for the tacit support.

'It'll work out somehow,' Sheldon said. 'I expect there are going to be some bumps on the way. Of course she may miscarry. In one way a blessing, not that I should say that. If you need anything from me ...'

He continued: 'Jane'll do everything of course to help. It's tough on her. She'd always wanted children, real bad – but it was too late. My two live in Boston, they're grown-up now. This is kind of close to home you might say. Damn Charlotte, she's always got to upstage everyone.'

It had never occurred to him that Jane's childlessness was a cause for regret. Her compelling authority had the quality of some principle of deterministic intelligence. It always knew where it was going, so very unlike his own fumbles through life. The ambivalence of her response to Charlotte's news heartened him. She might prove to be an important ally.

Charlotte found an email address for Alex and was surprised by his immediate response agreeing to meet. She borrowed Jane's car and drove to his home deep in the countryside. The house was bigger than the one he and Charlotte had shared. There were many acres. The property had a swimming pool, tennis court, kitchen garden; it had a workshop for Alex's carpentry, and a studio where his wife made luxury handbags. He had his own tractor and a soundproof study with lots of computers on which he managed their investments. He had given up his city job. The four children ranged in ages between eleven and six. His marriage had taken place soon after the divorce to Charlotte had come through.

All this was clear and factual, reported to Jacob by Jane over the phone.

Jane also told him that Charlotte appeared calm on her return, and when questioned about what had occurred Charlotte said they had put ghosts to rest.

This was hardly satisfying to Jane, and under further scrutiny, Charlotte revealed Alex kept a photograph of Sylvie in his study. He hadn't forgotten her, Charlotte said, and Jane wanted to know if he had apologised. Charlotte had seemed surprised by this question. Why did Jane think Alex should apologise when she had been the one out of her mind? Because, Jane explained first to Charlotte, then repeated to Jacob, Alex hadn't helped, quite the reverse, he had abandoned Charlotte three times over, in the marriage, in her depression and then in the hospital.

Jane's indignation was resurrected as if the misdemeanours were being committed anew.

There was more too. In another phone conversation with Jacob, between parking her car and going into the clinic, Jane said that Charlotte was visiting places from her past but not saying too much about any of them. And there was the further complication of Jane's schedule; she was busy, she didn't really have the time to talk properly to Charlotte. 'Am I a different person?' Charlotte had asked yesterday while Jane was gathering her notes for a forth-coming assessment. 'We absorb our past,' Jane said, 'we assimilate it into our present.' The assessment was of a young boy who had been caught shoplifting and vandalising. 'It's important,' insisted Charlotte with an urgency that compelled Jane to delay her business. 'Yes,' she said, 'you are very different.' She told Jacob that Charlotte's question had prompted her to reflect on those weeks during the year when she first met Charlotte and to wonder at her own younger self. 'We have both metamorphosed,' she said first to Charlotte, and in repetition on the phone to Jacob. 'Just like butterflies,' laughed Charlotte, flapping her arms. 'You bet,' Jane chuckled, grabbing her phone and folders, hoping the magistrate was the more benign one. 'I just didn't have the time to give her,' she explained to Jacob.

During the final two days of her visit, Charlotte changed behaviour and avoided even small exchanges. Jane confessed to Jacob she felt relieved. She was teaching, she had two assessments, several patient sessions, a clinical group meeting and a professional dinner to attend. She felt guilty. Sheldon had flown back to the States. Charlotte was roving on her own. She told Jacob Charlotte talked a lot about her trauma group in Bosnia, the maternity care in Trieste. During the day, Jane said, she wandered around the city, sometimes she borrowed the car. What was going on in her head, Jane wondered, during all these solitary encounters with her past? Jane understood better than most that there were different kinds of talking, different messages communicated. Charlotte was trying to tell her something and demanded her full attention but Jane had work to do, there was no getting out of her commitments.

What had she said to Jacob?

Little. Charlotte emailed him on her return to Sarajevo:

I'm holding on selling the painting. Will let you know. Everything is in this dreadful limbo. I'm just trying to keep calm. Work is good. My group helps. Thank you Jacob. Love Charlotte.

Jacob went to the British Library. There was so much he didn't know about Charlotte. She was to be the mother of his child. Charlotte. A society wedding in a cathedral. An ex-husband who she was in touch with again.

He requested back copies of the regional papers in Gloucestershire from the mid-1990s. He sped through pages of microfiche until a black and white photograph of Charlotte popped up, in a wedding dress, a bit blurred. Like a black and white movie star. Then, every several months, there were mentions of charity attendances, hunt balls. Lady Charlotte, he thought, Lady La-La. Flashes of her white skin, scarred, came back to him.

Then some months later there was a sudden shift, a concentration of copy, a cramped paragraph on the third page of the *Gloucester Herald* dated 18 December:

> A four-month-old baby, daughter of Alex Symmond and his wife, Charlotte, was declared dead on arrival at St Hilda's hospital in Gloucester at 6.45 am yesterday morning. The cause of death is unknown though sources close to the couple say it was entirely unexpected and comes as a great shock. Consultant paediatrician Mr Shottley says nothing can be determined without an autopsy and inquest. Experts think it's likely to be cot death.

There was more in the 2 February edition:

> Glamorous young county socialite charged with murder.

And on 6 April:

> The trial started today at Gloucester Crown Court of Mrs Symmond, wife of the Alex Symmond, partner in the highly successful commodities brokerage Mercury. Charged with murdering her four-month-old daughter, Mrs Symmond entered a plea of not guilty.

He paused. Took out his notebook, a pencil. Trial for murder. Jane had not mentioned this. She had said a trial, always one after a cot death. Is that what'd she said? Her words were dim in his memory. He wrote the date, the charge. He illustrated with fancy doodles across the page; a sketch of Charlotte's face emerged, scratched lines, and a tangle of question marks for hair. It calmed him.

He returned to the microfiche. Over the next two hours he collected information from the court reports and the local gossipy features triggered by the trial. Charlotte and Alex, the house they lived in, its value; their royal connections. Homeopathy was discussed at length with reference to an illustrious prince, also a resident of the county, known to be a supporter of this healing method.

Charlotte had existed for him in a cloister of intimacy; yet here was another Charlotte, a young woman watched by the world; first as an object of benign fascination, then of lurid speculation.

He discovered she'd had a housekeeper called Mrs Eagle who worked five days a week, and often over weekends when Charlotte and Alex entertained. Mrs Eagle was a witness for the defence. She was on Charlotte's side. So was her daughter, Louise, who had babysat Sylvie. Jacob warmed to them. The court reports said both women had testified that Charlotte had found being a new mother difficult; they both said Sylvie was frail, had trouble with breathing, cried a lot. They felt Charlotte didn't have a lot of support. No family, husband away a lot. No health visitor. May, the homeopath, was put on the stand, and she too spoke in support of Charlotte, of the difficulties of being a young mother, the baby's breathing problems. All perfectly normal. The prosecutor didn't seem to make much of a case.

In his cross-questioning of Mrs Eagle, the prosecutor asked whether her employer ever got angry with the child. Mrs Eagle reported that Mrs Symmond did occasionally, and when pressed on this point, Mrs Eagle replied that Mrs Symmond would shout at

118

the baby sometimes and take her upstairs to her room and return to sit in the conservatory, leaving the monitor with Mrs Eagle as she often did. The prosecutor asked if Sylvie was ever ill. Mrs Eagle confirmed the baby didn't seem to be well a lot of the time. She said she didn't think Charlotte was well either. Depressed, is how she seemed to Mrs Eagle. When asked to elaborate, Mrs Eagle didn't have much more to say other than Charlotte often seemed to her to be not quite there and spent a lot of time either lying down or sitting in the conservatory.

He alighted on Jane's name. She too had been a witness for Charlotte. She asserted that her assessment of Charlotte had shown her relations with the baby to be perfectly within the range of normal and that Sylvie had shown no signs of distress. He read over the short paragraph many times. He felt bewildered. The balcony in Trieste and a starry night, the sea spray and her lilting voice. She had talked for hours.

The papers talked up Charlotte's barrister. Photographs showed a suited, smiling woman arriving at the courthouse, leaning ahead as if driven by urgency and ambition. A London barrister, puffed the papers. She was young, in her thirties, a fact she used to her advantage in the trial in the way she was able to communicate that she was both like Charlotte, just another modern young woman juggling the demands of motherhood in a busy, stressful world; and still fresh to the injustices and prejudices perpetrated against her sex.

The defining testimonies were given by Charlotte and Mr Shottley, the paediatrician. According to the court reports, Mr Shottley urged the jury to understand that it was not his wish to cause any further distress to a grieving mother and father, but that his years of research and observation had led him to conclude that Mrs Symmond's behaviour conformed with the patterns evidenced in a woman deliberately harming her child. He related how concerned he'd been when the GP, his trusted friend, had recounted the pattern of Charlotte's behaviour, her visits with Sylvie, the respiratory problems, the advice to go to the hospital, the follow-up calls, the deceit. Charlotte's barrister's cross-examination pointed out that these claims were unsubstantiated, based on opinion, and should be stricken from the record. The judge commanded Mr Shottley to stick to the medical facts. And these were scanty. The ambulance had brought Sylvie to the hospital at about seven o'clock in the morning. Mr Shottley had been the consultant on the case. He had declared Sylvia dead on arrival. There were traces of blood in the lungs, but, countered the barrister, were these not also consistent with children who had died a sudden death? Mr Shottley conceded this was so.

Finally, Charlotte was put on the stand. All the papers carried detailed accounts of her testimony. Sketches in black ink portrayed an angular slim woman of classical beauty, head bowed, hair falling forward. She was heavily sedated, the papers said – describing her as if appearing neither to hear nor see.

She was asked by her barrister to tell the court what happened the day of Sylvie's death. Her testimony was simple: Sylvie had been unhappy, her breathing was shallow. No more than usual when she had these small attacks. Usually, they went away quickly after a dose of pulsatilla. She took her to May. May held her for a while. This calmed her. She responded well to May. May listened to her chest, rubbed it. Suggested a mild inhalation. Sylvie had an afternoon nap but kept waking. She wasn't happy. The inhalation seemed to help. Had her bath, a rub on the chest with a gentle eucalyptus ointment. She didn't want sleep, wheezed when she was put down. But she did finally go off after being given her bottle. Alex returned from a business trip and they both went to sleep about midnight. Charlotte woke, according to the court reports, at about half past five and went to check on Sylvie, and found her not breathing.

Her voice came back to him, a low whisper from her pillow in the dark sweaty room, Trieste asleep outside the walls, deaf to her murmurings.

And that, apparently, was the end of her testimony in court. She was unable to answer any further questions. The judge urged gentleness. Alex led Charlotte away from the stand, holding her up. There were closing statements. The judge advised the jury to concentrate on concrete evidence and reminded them of the need for proof beyond doubt; the court was adjourned.

The jury reached its verdict in less than an hour. Unanimous. Not guilty.

Jacob turned off the microfiche machine, returned the spools to the librarian, collected his notes and left the library. Crushed beside his fellow workers on the tube home, he absorbed the information about the trial. The carriage lurched, stopped and started. The air was fuggy and damp. He felt light-headed, carried along by the weight of passengers, his hand gripped the metal pole. The public spectacle of a deeply bereaved woman put in the stocks outraged him. Jerking along, pain cut across his stomach, a deep-bellied empathy for what Charlotte had been put through; and he marvelled at Jane, their friendship, the warmth of their affection. And now he was part of them, through virtue of a night when his sperm found its way to Charlotte's egg. A sudden surge of people pushed him along the carriage, threatening his balance. A young man got up from his seat, and pointed Jacob to sit. He accepted with gratitude.

Jane, I'd really l like to see you. Will you be in London anytime soon?
Jacob

I've a committee meeting in London in early January. Am also going to Boston with Sheldon for a few days, leaving tomorrow. Just until New Year. Is it urgent? J x

It can wait. Can we put a date in diary?

Great. 3pm Jan 9th ok? Let me know where. I'll be taking train back to Gloucester.

Ok. Will text about where on the day. Have a good Xmas. Send my regards to Sheldon. x

His days were led in parallel worlds. The ordinary stuff of his visible life took him through the hours with a list of tasks and demands. He wrote, he blogged, he tweeted, he talked, he went to meetings and Christmas parties. Twice he had supper with friends, those that remained neutral in the matter of his separation from his wife. He talked to his agent Nicky about more research for his book proposal. Nicky, a long-time friend, told him he had to find the USP – why his story? His ancestor? I don't have time, said Jacob. Hire an investigator, recommended Nicky, search online, that's easy, free. I don't have money, or that kind of time, he replied.

He saw his boys: Finn had retreated more into himself; Mikey was fizzy like a firecracker. They said, Mum's boyfriend has gone, Mum is really cross, she shouts a lot. Come home, Dad, please. They came straight at him, fierce in their desire. He could do nothing but tell them no. He put his hands up like a shield then opened them wide and took his sons into him. He was so sorry but he couldn't, he couldn't go back. In the days after Christmas, they leaned into him at night on the cheap sofa, limbs interwoven, ate slices of pizza and yelled at the television.

The other world was full of Charlotte. Her emails were short and often sounded like weather reports. *Quite a calm period, morning sickness tailing off. A good sign.* Once she asked him about his past. *I know nothing about you. Have you had a good life?* He sent back carefully edited sentences. When he wrote of his past he was not lyrical like her. He was calm, uninflected.

He also wrote a long incontinent letter which he dragged to the folder marked 'Personal' on his laptop. It carried rage and hurt, bewilderment, and lust. He wrote about his boys, describing each one's trajectory from birth to the present. Their height, their colouring, their vulnerabilities. His soaring pride in them. He sketched out plans for their future all together. He could work anywhere, he would write his book, they would buy a house in Bristol with a separate bedroom each for Finn and for Mikey. He knew there was great sadness in her, he knew she had suffered, he knew about the trial and the awful breakdown. He would cherish her, he would protect her and their child. He could do all this.

He did not write about Kathleen, the long years of deteriorating communication, the life shared. The looming divorce battle. The diminishing income. His failure. He did not display his old habit of promiscuity, the forgetful ease of saying 'yes' to the advances of women he met in passing around the world.

He wrote to give his current circumstances shape. He wrote in the early hours of morning, before bed or after rising, when the streets were deserted. He wrote to conjure her into proximity.

I live in a small flat in Kensal Rise. Do you know this area of London? I imagine not. It's typical of so many parts of London now, a mix of long-time residents come from many parts of the former colonies in search of things I don't think they ever found, and people like me, prosperous and stressed and paying absurd prices for badly converted flats and subsiding houses. My flat is on the second floor of a late Victorian terraced on a narrow street. I've done nothing to improve its sterile atmosphere. There is a small second bedroom where I've put up bunk beds for the boys. They don't like it here. How can I blame them? It's cramped and dull. The man who lives at the top of this building had a real go at me the other day. He is as lonely as me and older but I think he has been alone for many years and has no one other than a mongrel for company. I was tidying up the front walk and he thought I was interfering with his dustbin. 'Fucking posh twat', he shouted at me. 'Stay away from my things or I'll set my dog on you.' At night I can hear through the bedroom wall the rows of a young couple. I think they're often drunk. 'I hate living here,' she cried last night. 'I hate it. It's small and depressing.' 'We're poor,' he said. 'This is it, this is all we can afford. Deal with it.' 'It's not fair,' she yelled back. 'I want to go home, get out of this fucking city.' They make love a lot, sounds of despair and pleasure reach out to me across the shared wall. People's assumed privacy makes them unaware of those around them. I never paid attention to any of this when I lived in my big house with my family. We were too busy with our own squabbles, our meals, our mess, our conversation, our love. We were turned in. Now it is all different. I live within myself as never before but all my senses vibrate to the intimacies of those I barely know. What is your story, Charlotte? Where is your head? Where is your heart? I want a second chance at this thing called love.

———

He and Jane met at a cafe round the corner from Paddington station. He had carefully prepared his questions. She arrived late in what he had come to perceive as a habit. He could also see she was distracted, a little brusque in her greeting to him.

They exchanged pleasantries about each other's Christmas. Then Jane asked, 'Have you heard from Charlotte?' He told her they'd been emailing each other; that she sounded fine.

Jane expressed relief.

'So,' began Jacob, 'I've been doing some research. About Charlotte's trial.'

A shadow crossed Jane's face. He continued, 'I'd like you to tell me about it.'

She nodded. 'What do you want to know?'

'The charge? Why murder?'

'I don't fully remember. It wasn't infanticide – that's a legal term for a mother killing her child when the child is under one – the law recognises that women suffer from moments of mental illness due to hormonal imbalance and this can lead to harming their children. It's an interesting law, it's been around for a long time; there's been a fairly recent review of it to see if the one year rule stands. And they decided it should. But none of this applied to Charlotte because she didn't harm Sylvie.'

'Your testimony.'

She nodded again. 'I told them about my visit to her, how there was nothing at all out of the ordinary.'

'Did you mention your suspicions about her post-natal depression?'

She shook her head. 'I thought it would be misleading. And she was in such a state of grief I thought it would make things worse for her. As it turns out, she was so deeply depressed, she completely broke down. As I think I told you.'

'What caused the breakdown?'

The irony with which she greeted this question grated on him. 'You could say grief, maltreatment by her husband, the grinding wheels of the system that put her on trial.'

'Did you think she was to blame in any way for Sylvie's death?'

'No, I didn't. The consultant psychiatrist was a real shit. All the evidence pointed to a clear-cut case of cot death. And then Alex was there as well, remember. He left her alone, he didn't get her the appropriate help. He should've seen how difficult it was for her.'

'What was she like when you found her?'

Jane paused for a long while. He held the silence.

'I came across her about two years later. I think I told you this in Trieste. She was in a private mental hospital. The hospital also worked with the NHS. I was there on another case. It's just by chance that I found out she was also a patient. I wrote to ask if I might visit. She remembered me, and when I arrived she was pleased to see me. She was fragile but stable. Alex and she were in the middle of divorce proceedings. By that time she was there by choice.

'She'd been released earlier but there had been no one to look after her. A few social acquaintances, her old housekeeper. She relapsed. Our first visit went well so I started to see her regularly. I became the point of contact with her psychiatrist and her personal nurse. We all agreed that I would help her find a home and take care of her. Both my professional training and our growing friendship made me the best choice. I was happy to. I'd grown very fond of her. She granted me powers of attorney over everything, just in case. Then, well, you know the rest.'

'Why did she go to Bosnia?'

'She hated the loneliness of her new life. She did everything we recommended, the meditation, the group therapy, her psychiatric sessions, but she was going down again. She was on medication, of course. She found the charity in Bosnia through an ad.'

'Do you think she was running away?'

'Of course, fleeing ghosts, fleeing guilt, shame. She put herself into a trauma zone. She made herself useful. It was the only way she could survive at the time.'

'Guilt?'

'Jacob, let me put it to you: if one of your boys died, through some dreadful accident, how would you feel?'

'Christ, absolutely devastated.'

'And?'

He saw where she was going: any parent would feel guilty for not having been able to protect their child.

He nodded. 'I get it.' And pressed: 'The homeopathy, she should've taken Sylvie to the hospital.'

'There is of course an argument about that kind of treatment and whether it's neglect. But if Alex had been around, if there hadn't been a private birth, if she'd been in the system, if she'd had adequate psychiatric help, all these "ifs". So little was known about cot death. And you know as well as I do that the medical establishment is often wrong.'

She looked at her watch. 'I'm sorry Jacob. I need to be going. I have a committee meeting in half an hour.'

'What about the post-natal depression?'

'Many women suffer from it. In more normal circumstances Charlotte would've been treated. That's my guilt. You know, I think I told you in Trieste? I should've intervened, I didn't. I didn't pick it up.'

'I guess you also think that appalling childhood had something to do with it.'

'Yes. It inflicted deep wounds in her psyche. But as you saw when we were in Trieste, not everyone in the world of mental health agrees, or at least that story, the Freudian approach, is not one everyone thinks is helpful as either a diagnostic or a healing tool.'

'You really do?'

'I do.'

'How can you be so certain?'

'I'm not, but how can any of us be? You try. It helped get Charlotte back on the path to recovery. Along with medication and psychiatry. Of course. I'm not anti-drugs. But you need a holistic approach. It helps the patients I work with, the ones who are really at the extreme end of society.'

She patted his hand. 'It'll be all right. And of course she may miscarry.' The possibility of such an outcome hung between them.

'Would that be better?' He kept his voice even.

127

'Not for her.'

Then she stood and gathered up her things. They exchanged looks in which were mirrored a range of feelings about the idea of a miscarriage, not all clear or straightforward.

'We'll talk soon, yeah?'

He put his notebook away. 'Let me know if you hear anything.'

In mid-January, he received an email:

I just had my first three month scan and all is well! She is so tiny, so beautiful. Please dear gods and goddesses may all continue to be well. The doctor says everything is progressing really well. I think we'll need to talk soon. Love Charlotte.

Then days later another one in which she told him she would not sell her painting through an auction house. He needn't bother about it anymore. Alex was buying it.

———

He rented a car and drove first to Gloucester to pick up the painting, then next morning to Alex's where he delivered it. It was wrapped in bubble and brown paper, prepared for departure the night before in Jane and Sheldon's drawing room.

Sheldon had approached their task with the fine choreography of a dancer. His large body moved with focused grace as he unhooked the canvas from the wall and laid it out on the carpet, running his fingers expertly along the frame and the glass. Jane was nervy, tossing indiscriminate pieces of string and tape to Sheldon. Her animation bounced off them with remarks about why, really, Jacob felt it necessary to deliver the painting in person, and why Charlotte was selling to this man, and whether surrendering a piece of her mother to the useless father of her dead baby didn't signify a neurotic transaction. He was a willing and amiable helper acknowledging all the while Jane's barrage with short indefinite phrases, 'I'm not really sure,' 'Perhaps' and 'Quite mysterious I agree.' They each performed the necessary functions with recourse to some essential part of their nature, and when the task was done they collapsed into the sofa and shared a bottle of wine.

He was not at all certain about why he felt it necessary to bring the painting in person to Alex. It was more than curiosity about this man to whom she had once pledged herself and to whom she now travelled so eloquently in her reminiscences.

That he had a sense of wanting to establish himself concretely in her story. That he wanted to impress. That he was marking his territory. That he wanted to assess.

The manor house sat on a hill at the end of a sketchily paved road that led only there. Protected by voluminous trees tailing into heritage woodland and facing a limitless view of rolling wooded vales, it invited him in through an iron gate and up a swept pebble drive. His rented car scrunched on the pristine stones. He parked alongside a sleek Range Rover, careful to align his tyres in an orderly fashion. Even on this mist-cold winter's day the denuded brown of trunk and twig heralded abundance. The grass was dark green, the manor limestone honeyed. The clean panes of the leaded windows on both floors sparkled in the opal light. Tiles sat firm on three pointed roofs like a coronet. Majestic, the property invited devotion.

He carried the painting against his torso up a stone path like a clumsy courier.

The door was opened by a long man. Alex. Steel-grey eyes in a linear face. Bristle-grey hair. He loomed over Jacob like a tilting windmill. They appeared to be the only humans within miles.

'Come in.' Alex stepped aside. 'Bring it here.' He led them into a room off the hallway, shut the door, took the brown parcel and placed it against the wall in a careless movement. 'Tea? Coffee?'

They were in his study. Computer consoles stretched across a wide glass desk. A well-behaved fire flickered in the grate of an inglenook fireplace. A plump sofa faced it. Some books on a shelf. Family photographs on walls. Smooth overhead beams. He said coffee would be nice.

Alex opened the door again and shouted down the corridor, 'Sorry to disturb, Angie, but could you bring us some coffee? Thanks!' Door shut.

So not the only human. Still no sounds from anywhere. Maybe Angie was a robot.

He did not want to sink into the sofa alongside this ectomorph but he could not see another option other than that presented by the chair in front of the desk. He shoved a hand in his trouser pocket and glanced out the window. 'Dull day,' he commented.

'No trouble finding it, I hope?' asked Alex. 'Satnav doesn't reach here. Lands you in a field.'

'With the cows?' He joked.

'Please,' Alex gestured, 'sit.'

He took up one end of the sofa, Alex the other. He found himself mirroring Alex's sprawl, legs outstretched, arm draped over the back. Their feet almost met.

'Good of you to bring the painting. I could've had it picked up.' This was spoken in a tone that suggested Alex meant the opposite.

'It seemed the safest way, given how precious it is.' Defiant.

Alex glanced at the package near the door and folded his hands together, meditating for a moment on something. The pause was interrupted by the arrival of coffee, delivered by a smiling middle-aged woman in an apron, 'There you go, I've brought some biscuits too, freshly made, in case you're a bit peckish.' She departed quickly.

'I plan to sell it.' Alex leant forward for the coffee. 'Milk?' Yes, and one sugar. 'Biscuit?' No, really, he wasn't hungry. Alex continued, 'Not much interested in that kind of art, but there's always a demand for it. Do you know about art?'

Jacob acknowledged he knew a little. 'Quite superficial really, but as an arts correspondent you see a lot.'

'So that's what you do is it?'

He saw his career carried the same weight as a puff of smoke.

'You probably know that painting won't fetch much, anonymous, provenance unknown. But – ' and here suddenly Alex's smooth voice broke – 'when I divorced Charlotte she didn't want anything from me. So – I thought – it might be helpful to her for me to give her a good price direct.'

'That's awfully kind of you.' The words slithered out of his mouth. He wondered at Alex's assessment of the worth of the painting. What was 'not much' to a wealthy man?

'Good karma. Beth, my wife, she's been saying for years I had to do something about Charlotte. Doing all right is she?'

Jacob saw Alex knew nothing about them. He thought they were lovers. Jacob and Charlotte, Charlotte and Jacob. A they.

'She is doing amazingly well. Yes.' The authority with which he delivered his statement was marred by a rush of emotion. He coughed.

'She told me she might be coming back to England.' Pause. 'What is it, ten years? More …' Alex shook his head in disbelief. 'Down to you, I guess?' He clacked his coffee mug back on the tray.

'Yes.' It was not a lie. She was going to have a baby, he was the father, ergo.

Alex nodded. 'When her mother died, there was only the house. I sold it, not for a great deal, it was the mid-nineties and a recession was on, and there were death duties to pay. But there was a bit so I set up that investment fund. When I asked her about it, she said it had gone up and down, she didn't really pay attention, she said.'

'No.' He was bluffing.

'But – the baby –' Alex stuttered in uncertainty.

131

She had told him she was pregnant. She had confided in him. He glanced at the brown parcel in acknowledgement of Alex's offer to buy it. 'I'm sure that'll help Charlotte. Give her some leeway. Most generous.' Why had she told him?

'They told me it could happen again.' Alex looked straight at his chest, where the heart beats. A fierce energy was concentrated in the gaze. Jacob turned away. This man could crush him if he chose. He was no more than a miniature.

He stared at the thin pale daylight on the wall. Earlier on in his life, when he was in his mid-thirties and still a bachelor, he had spent a brief period paying for the services of a financial advisor. He was earning well and fancied himself on the way up. His advisor had advocated a pension fund which since had lost most of its worth. The suggestion was also made that he invest in another property, to supplement his solid one bedroom, perhaps some little country retreat, affordable mortgage. He had studied the advertisements of period country houses in the glossy magazines for which he wrote, and occasionally made a foray into the country where he would follow a punctilious agent from room to room in a home, already then way too dear, too grand, and imagine himself into what the magazine referred to as gracious living. He never inspected those that he might have afforded – the village cottage, the Edwardian semi, the small Victorian in need of work. During this period his sleeping and waking dreams converged into sentimental stories of country house sagas, only to be cut through by desolate scenes of emptiness and panic. Finally, he stopped looking, and when he married, he and Kath sold their respective flats and bought a family house on a tree-lined street in northwest London with potential for much renovation and expansion, close to a park and a good primary school.

This world apart, this assembly of class and wealth, of planned beauty and expensive design reduced him to a supplicant. Before him, Alex, the embodiment of the fanciful figure who inhabited the empty country houses of his imagined autobiography, loomed and growled, and from him broke: 'Could've done something. Told her that when I saw her. She just stood there, like some – angel, more beautiful than I remembered. Karma. Christ! Even Elisabeth doesn't know what I went through. Awful business.'

Alex sprang from the sofa and went over to the wall of photos. Is he angry? Does he feel him uncaring? He apologised.

'All long ago, Jacob. You want to forget but you don't.' Alex took a picture and held it facing out like an icon. A baby. So innocent. Charlotte's enormous blue eyes. He nodded in appreciation and turned blankly to the dimming fire. Alex repeated: 'Long time ago.' And: 'You move on.'

Quite so. Time now to leave. He rose and brushed his hands on his trousers, penitent in the craven impulse which pushed him to slip away.

'It was the family,' said Alex in a show of emphatic anger. 'Couldn't put them through more of it.' The violent changes between coolness and unrest gave a rubbery quality to his chiselled features. 'Knew something was wrong. Didn't know what to do.' The confident lower register deepened and cracked.

Jacob peered again at the unliving square, a symbol of all that was left. Alex returned it to the wall, and stared down, hands in trouser pockets, fingering change. A clock chimed in the hallway, bringing the men back to each other. Pain shadowed Alex's dark metal eyes, a shield to further conversation. Jacob felt a surprising wash of fellow-feeling. He put out his hand and shook Alex's with fraternal warmth.

'I was mad about her, you know.' Alex's final words as he balanced tall on the threshold of his demesne flew beyond them to enter the open blanched view. Frosted green and winter beige.

Thank you Jacob. That was kind of you. I imagine you wanted to see what he was like, didn't you? He's not a bad man. Please don't think so. We need to talk don't we? She is doing so well, growing every day. Will you come to Trieste again? I can get a break next month. Love Charlotte.

'He was a brute,' repeated Jane down the phone. They were getting into a routine of speaking every week or so. In each conversation Jacob waited for a trace of further information to fall from her lips.

'Alex is still suffering. I think he blames himself. He's not a monster.'

'She was suffering and he didn't even notice. She should've been on medication, seeing a therapist, a psychiatrist, especially given her mother's death, all those things I've already told you. But they had money to avoid the usual controls. And he was certainly controlling. Private birth, no health visitor. He even got rid of May, the one person who really helped her. Then when Sylvie died, and that paediatrician got up a case against her, well, he should've knocked it on the head. Absurd. And to divorce her when she's being treated in hospital for a severe depressive breakdown, now that really was low.'

He could only agree, yet this explanation of Alex's conduct sat uneasily in him. The powerful lean human machine with whom he had shared a morning coffee rattled with unresolved passion. He attuned his inner temperature to Alex's, and in so doing discovered a commonality that tempered his envy: Alex had been as besotted with Charlotte as he was. Now he no longer had her. She was elsewhere, not his, flown the coop. Set free. And Alex was not immune to pain. Their child, a memory, dust and earth. Jacob had the advantage: his baby was the future. Their future.

PART THREE

'Pardonne N'oublie Pas'
Mémorial des Martyrs de la Déportation, Paris

Did you bury Sylvie?

He saw in his dreams a white dancing baby and an acid green grave-yard where he walked in frustrated circles. As he got close to the baby, the face of his son Mikey peered from the naked blob and screamed at him; he woke in a clutch of terror.

Her email back was subdued:

Alex buried her in the graveyard of the church next to the family home. I wasn't there. I visited it with Jane when I was finally discharged from hospital. A pink cherry tree was in blossom, soft white petals decorated the new stone. I remember thinking, how lovely, she's covered in confetti. I went back there last December. He keeps the grave well-tended. He doesn't mention me on the headstone. Just dates and her name Sylvia Beatrice Symmond, beloved daughter. I have leave from work and will meet you next week. Still ok? x

He booked his flight to Trieste and in the days before his trip he set about the task of ordering his life. He visited his lawyer, he had a meeting with Nicky. The one he instructed to write to Kathleen asking for a divorce. She could sue him for adultery. There was no point in delaying the inevitable. She earned more than him, he would make no demand on her income, her pension, their house. He wanted equal access. He lived ten minutes from the family home, close to their school. It was manageable. Finn was almost an adult anyway. He would not negotiate on this point. 'Are you sure, Jacob?' asked his lawyer over the phone, 'It's going to be difficult. Courts almost always award full custody to mothers. It's the way.'

To the other he spoke about a book proposal, a possible advance. He needed money. Nicky, corpulent and several years older than he, managed expectation with the busy efficiency of a health visitor. They sat in Nicky's office on the sofa he reserved for intimate conversation, and he plied Jacob with questions. Did his relative die in a camp? How big was his business? Was there a love affair? Wealth? A question of exceptional human suffering? Or bravery? Trieste. Could he trace a link with the boisterous cultural scene of Joyce?

'The story needs to be personal,' Nicky said, 'but it needs to be universal too. But not run of the mill. Definitely not. People want to read about heroism. Redemption.'

Jacob sipped from his coffee and listened. 'What else?' On the table in front of them lay a pile of recent books written by some of Nicky's clients. A first novel, prize-winning. *Hilarious and moving account of a coming-of-age story set against a background of stark deprivation …* read the blurb. A large fat hardback, a memoir by a naturalist who had discovered a series of waterways in search of Britain's changed landmass. *An extraordinary account of lost worlds in the lucid original prose that we have come to expect of such a distinguished writer …* tickertape across the jacket. He wondered if Nicky had read them. Everyone, it seemed to him, was producing a masterpiece.

'Not too much suffering,' advised Nicky. 'Could you tie it to something current, the state of refugees? The rising hatred of immigrants? Populism?'

'I don't know. Not yet at least.' He wanted to write a personal account about what had happened to his mother's grandfather, a Viennese Jew, during World War Two. That seemed a straight-forward proposal. That he had an ancestor, a whole section of family who had lived in a country and spoke in a language that bore no resemblance to anything he had ever known, was this not interesting?

Years of clever dealing and good timing had made Nicky a wealthy man. His eyebrows raised, 'No, it's not. You need a story. Trieste, there's an interesting angle. The disappearance of Theodor. Old Europe. With the rise of populism, perhaps,' he mused, 'there's a renewed interest in what Europe had been before the European community. Older people read books like this. Retired, prosperous people. That's your market. People like to read about suffering from the comfort of their homes. With good endings.'

'Can't you find some money for me? I'm in a real bind. What about a long-length feature?' Jacob pressed.

'I'll try. Angle?'

'Disappearance of Theodor. A mystery story. Only a postcard, etc. I'll dig up what I can in Trieste and write it as personal detective story. A plot. I'll draw some parallels with the current political situation. I'll find a hook to something that is going on now, an anniversary or some such. Good enough?'

The world that had allowed Jacob to earn money and build a reputation was dissolving and morphing with the rapidity of the melting ice in the North Pole. Advertisement and sales revenue for printed newspapers had collapsed. As had reader numbers. Everything was now online, print only one element. He sat in meetings about transmedia platforms and TweetDeck while images of a medieval execution platform appeared to him. The hooded executioner, the axe, the hapless victim on knees. An enthusiastic crowd baying for blood. No one was much interested in the kind of art he had spent a lifetime writing about. Everything now was old before it was even new. Some magazines were holding up. He had two retainers that kept his life underwritten. There had been a TV series about fifteen years ago when the boys were very little. Kath had hoped this might launch him into a bigger arena. You have your appeal, she'd said in a scabrous tone, your charm. Go for it. He had not. He had retreated from the brief glare of spotlights. A book, black advancing marks on a page, a permanence in lieu of himself. This he could do. He had a finished novel in a filing cabinet, written in his youth. A bad book. Then a published one, a product, stories about a handful of powerful louche arts dealers post-war. It had sold well. Nicky had been pleased. Now he wanted this, his story, his absent family. His hole to fill.

'Mail something to me. I'll see what I can do.' Nicky scrolled down his phone, a sign that Jacob's time was up.

———

He booked into a small hotel in a narrow alley in the old city, a different setting to the previous grandeur of the Excelsior. This place was hidden, monastic. Much cheaper than the seafront palace. He was shouldering his own expenses, and though tax-deductible, they cut into his cash flow. Charlotte had not invited him to stay.

The sealed neat box room contained his excess: a single bed in one corner onto which he had unloaded his books; his jackets and shirts poked from a wardrobe suited to the needs of a young backpacker; the minibar, compact under a narrow ledge on which he had placed his bits and bobs; a bedside table too small for a lamp which hung above. The shuttered window on the other side of which was a narrow shaft whose unchanging grey light obscured time.

It was perfectly proportioned and arranged, squeaky clean, silent. Up against the wall on the bed, caddy corner, he roamed his feelings. He was here on a dual mission. More research for his book proposal, archives to be plundered. *I'll need to spend some time*

140

searching city archives. Talking to a few officials too. My Italian is very bad. My German ok. Perhaps you could help? Yes, she'd love to, if there was time. She had made an appointment for them at the maternity hospital and she needed to sort out a birth plan. She had four days off work.

The official trail to his ancestor stopped short in Vienna in 1937. The family company sold for a pittance to a Viennese citizen, a *Privat*, a man of private means, an Aryan. A death listing for his great-grandmother Johanna Motz. Theresienstadt 1942. The concentration camp was in the Czech fortress village of Terezin, lovingly named after Maria Theresa, the great mother empress of Trieste, purveyor of religious tolerance and free trade. Circles and ironies.

Of his great-grandfather, Theodor, he could find no death listing. The only clue came from the address on the postcard. There was no signature. As if there was no shared blood, no lived history. Dated December 1938.

A story flashed through the compartments of his brain in disconnected phrases. If he could wrestle these into a narrative elaboration with copious research, if he could excavate the wounds of his ancestors, bring close to the page their trials and delights, and the terror – was there resignation, denial, fortitude? – he would have a book. Match it, perhaps, with contemporary interviews, relatives perhaps – a 'then and now' structure. Everyone thinks that about their own family histories, said Nicky in his crispest business voice on the phone to Jacob from the departure lounge at the airport. But, he argued, I'll turn up something.

He knew the feature he had written for *Class Travel* magazine about his grandfather and Trieste would appear soon in the Italian edition. Like smoke signals in the sky, he hoped a pair of distant eyes might read the signs and come forward with information. Clutching at straws, opined Nicky. Anyway, he said, the Jewish question is overcooked. Out of fashion. Too much tension between Israel and Palestine, the Middle East problem. But what about, he had remonstrated, what about, and then listed three books which had been picked up for review by broadsheets and gone on to win awards. All about the holocaust and personal loss. Well, that's true, Nicky conceded. See what you unearth. OK. Get it down on paper.

———

He met Charlotte at the Caffè San Marco again. Now early March, the temperature was of a different order to the autumn softness of his October visit. A strong sun, out of the ordinary, warmed the harsh air.

'I have come for you,' he said simply.

He followed her along the streets of Trieste through the residents deep in their winter wear to her flat in the elegant stone block high on a hill among a crown of bare trees.

His lust made him alert, volatile, submissive, cranky. He went with her and watched the drama in her eyes. He lost her words. He wanted no more of her stories.

When the consummation came it released him into the complexity of her body. Written across her skin was a story of self-inspired mutilation from her time in the mental hospital. He traced the faint white slivers on her upper arms where she had drawn with a paperclip. He licked the bumpy white tissue on the inside of her left wrist. 'They found me before I had time to finish off the job,' she explained, apologetic. He caressed the marks on her stomach, feeling the remnants of her pregnancy with Sylvie revived in the growth of their baby. He put his head on the taut small mound of her tummy and inhaled the luxurious aroma of her skin.

'Careful,' she said, pushing away his head and putting her hands over her belly.

'Sorry,' he sat up, 'I just want to be close.' He removed her hands and looked at the skin. She wriggled to the side.

'I couldn't help it – I –'

He suddenly realised: they weren't stretch marks, they were more scars from self-inflicted wounds. The desire he felt for her was kindled by the horror her suffering provoked in him. Texture and history.

The sex was direct, uncomplicated, open. Her amused guileless patience towards his unreliable erections. Her full earthy orgasms. In the morning, lit by rays of luminescent sun, naked, relaxed over the protruding bump of her middle she was gleeful: 'You are now twice in me. You have baptised our baby with your sperm.'

It was not a beginning. Charlotte marked the passage of time in discrete events. Continuity and evolution were happening inside her. Outside, her personality was refracted through the demands of each encounter. He was encased in her variousness. As his lover, she was hungry and tender, indifferent to the wondering pained gaze he brought to her body. Indifferent to his interior life. Her centre was always elsewhere, away from him. She was using him to bring her back to life. He gave in to her with the belligerent generosity of an adolescent.

'What about us?' He held himself defiant, bare naked, in the middle of her sitting room, high in the sky. She was impatient with his demands, blasé in her dismissal of his needs. 'You are cruel,' he spat out.

'No,' she replied gently. 'You don't know things, that's all.'

'Tell me,' he challenged. All of a sudden she was giggling at his undressed state, his scratchy seriousness. 'It's Alex isn't it? And the trial. Sylvie's weird death.' There sparked in his brain the notion that Charlotte was guilty, an evil person; she had neglected her child. She had not taken her to hospital. Who was she to be a mother again? It was a scintilla of poison that shot through him.

His words frightened her; she curled up into a ball on the sofa, a careful young girl with a whimpering desire to hide. She tugged the cords of her robe around her and retreated.

He grew in his manliness, arms on hips, swagger. Another voice in him jeered, 'you are ridiculous Jacob, you are making yourself ridiculous,' and harmonised with the painful yearning lover that sought reassurance.

'Tell me,' he commanded.

'Please don't. I never loved Alex. Her death – you don't know how painful.'

He surrendered, crossed to the sofa and took her into his arms.

Throughout the days, in these moments when they were alone, their lust slaked, he pushed his advantage, prodding here and there with a devilish question. Her stonewalling was triumphant and reduced him to a whiny boy. Her curiosity was piqued only by information about his boys.

In the hotel room, sifting through the thin file of his mother's documents and the genealogist's report, he forgot about her. His thoughts gathered around the mystery of his lost family.

He walked to the well-kept bourgeois apartment block on the Via di Scorcola. The deep blue sky covered the city. He stared up and around and down. He was at the beginning of a hill from which arose the railway station where once had stood warehouses and army barracks; from where the gritty operations of law, order, war and trade were implemented. He could hear the old-fashioned wooden tram rattle in the near distance. Beginning operation in 1902, it carried workers from the thriving bowl of the city to the windy plain of the Karst. Up there Richard Burton had worked in a solitary inn while he translated *Arabian Nights*. Up there in a suburban villa the celebrated Triestine writer Italo Svevo – pseudonym for the Jewish Ettore Schmitz, thought to be one of the many models for Joyce's Leopold Bloom – wrote *Zeno's Conscience* in 1923. One of Freud's earliest pupils, Edoardo Weiss, Ettore Schmitz's nephew, introduced psychoanalysis to Italy in Trieste. Freud came here to study eels.

Below, next to the train station, the skeleton of the Porto Vecchio stretched north. During the war, Theodor would have heard sounds of manoeuvres and grindings from his open window, night and day, as the city entered the domain of bloodshed. In 1943 the Germans had taken over the city, putting in place the killing machine of the Nazi high command. Multiple trains went from Trieste to Auschwitz daily. At the Teatro Verdi Wagner's *Lohengrin* attracted great crowds. On the other side of the city, in the genteel neighbourhood of San Vito, the Palazzo Morpurgo, former home of Elio Morpurgo, the merchant prince and ennobled Jew, was the Fascist headquarters. Circles and ironies. He had not found any death listing for Theodor Motz in the archives of the Jewish Registry from Trieste. The request made to the tracing service of the massive archive in Bad Arolsen, an archive that preserved and assembled the fate of 17.5 million people persecuted and murdered by the Nazis, had revealed the death of his great-grandmother Johanna at Theresienstadt. He did not know how she got there. Theodor was nowhere. Not there, not here.

———

Charlotte came with him to the city archives. The clerk, smiling and helpful, spoke good English. Company ledgers dating back to the early twentieth century were extensive and orderly. Many of those pre-1918 were in German. He did not need her help and found her restlessness irritating. 'Go,' he said, 'I'll meet you later.' 'The appointment,' she said. 'I'm coming with you,' he forced a gentle reply. 'I'll meet you at the San Marco.' His several hours proved fruitful. In the register of citizens living on the Via di Scorcola in the

1930s at the address from which Theodor has sent the postcard lived a number of families, all with Italian names. The register indicated these families were moderately well-off. Owners of shops and small enterprises, managers in the big insurance agencies. The Trieste phone book indicated many carrying the same names lived in the city today. Needle in a haystack. He began photocopying. A couple of hours later his task accomplished he returned to the pallid mid-afternoon light.

Charlotte was waiting as agreed at the San Marco. 'It's our place,' he laughed, 'now we need a song!'

'Shall we walk?' She massaged her bump.

They skimmed news kiosks and rows of scooters, a grand manicured church in a square surrounded by trees, recycling bins and a secondary school. Signs for Illy coffee advertised in cafe windows. He sniffed in the direction of the sea. His nose tingled, his eyes teared up. Today the bora was hurling and gusting. On some corners in the city centre there remained iron railings installed a long time ago to help pedestrians stay upright during the worst of the wind's assaults. He took hold of Charlotte's arm, pressing into her.

Another Trieste was revealed: this was the city of everyday. Tall neat rectangular apartment buildings, some shuttered, holes in the plaster; others newly painted in rose, ochre or cream; cement blocks mingled with more ornate early twentieth-century buildings garlanded with white trims and pretty friezes; balconies bearing satellite dishes and lines of washing. Shopfronts offered haircuts, insurance, handbags, groceries.

At the end of a green hilly neighbourhood they found the maternity hospital. It had a reputation for being one of the best in Italy. The attached research institute was known worldwide. Here all babies in Trieste were born. Here is where Charlotte wanted their child to come into the world.

It was cosily familiar and completely disorientating. The assured white cement blocks of the hospital that stretched down the Via dell'Istria welcomed him into a world of conscientious work, solid capabilities, uniformed workers; it was a place that transformed lives. Here, in the ordered low corridors painted hospital green, nurses in blue uniform strolled, waving hands and chatting in a language he barely understood. Echoes from a similar place in London reverberated in him: 'Look!' he had inwardly shouted leaving St Mary's with Finn seventeen years ago, irrepressible joy spilling over, 'Everyone! Don't you all see! The world has changed, Finn has arrived!'

In the consulting room, Charlotte was composed and professional in manner. Italian tripped off her tongue in quick precise sentences. He picked up what he could. They sat with the obstetrician, an older reserved Triestine who smiled intermittently as if transmitting in code a message of male solidarity. Charlotte translated the occasional phrase. 'He says I mustn't fly much after seven months. I must leave Bosnia and come back to the city in plenty of time.' 'He says because of my age they want to do some tests.'

There came a moment in the conversation when she stumbled. It was a routine question put by Dr Lucchetta: 'Is this your first?' She shook her head and in this gesture he saw an absolute negation of her earlier composure. Her fingers began to scuttle, her head fell forward.

Jacob tried: 'No, bambino, e morte . . . multo anni . . .' He made a gesture with his hand to communicate this happened a long time ago.

Dr Lucchetta nodded and asked a question. Jacob did not understand.

'Es speshal eelniss?' Jacob repressed an inappropriate giggle. The air thickened around Charlotte.

'Cot death,' he explained. The doctor looked puzzled, shrugged his elegant Italian shoulders.

'Culla – morte,' murmured Charlotte.

'Ah, si.' The doctor nodded, his eyebrows reasserting themselves in a line of compassion. A matter of fact statement followed. Charlotte did not translate but he detected a phrase about not worrying 'non preoccuparsi'.

'Si,' continued Charlotte, and spoke very quickly in a tone that carried within the sadness a command. He picked up the word for psychiatrist.

Dr Lucchetta's next shrug was accompanied by a bowing of the head and an upward lift of his eyebrows. They conversed together in expressive sentences that were lost on him. Charlotte's eyes contained a plea that did not match the assurance of her speech. Something she said brought forth from the doctor much nodding and a phone call to a colleague.

'He's setting me up with one of their psychiatrists,' explained Charlotte. 'I told him I had a breakdown.' Her countenance sent warning signals that distress was fermenting.

Dr Lucchetta made a few notes, then looked to Charlotte and gestured in Jacob's direction, 'Marito?'

'Non, il padre del mio bambino.' If, if I were your husband … and Charlotte? Her conditionals were of a different fabric, woven with prayer, turned inwards. Another quick question to her from the doctor.

Charlotte's eyes rested on his shoulder: 'Will you be here for the birth?'

'Yes. Si.' Such a short word, containing a promise and an unknowable commitment. He repeated loudly as if not taken seriously the first time, 'Yes!' It would be a July birth. Finn would have finished his A levels, Mikey his GCSEs. Kathleen and the divorce. A new life. His child born here in a city he barely knew, from a woman whose feelings towards him were no stronger than a distant cousin with whom he shared traces of an affectionate and enigmatic family lore.

———

Later he climbed into bed beside Charlotte and cupped her stomach. Through the rough skin of his hand he channelled a bustle of movement, a very small outward punch, a tremor in her body, and there, a slight gurgle. She was lying with her back to him: it was not an intimate spoon, it was an invitation to leave. There was so little they had talked about. She was exhausted after their several days of lovemaking, the hovering questions and the trip to the maternity hospital. They had been careful and hungry in each other's company, attentive to the slightest touch, resistant to the larger argument. He had zoomed in on a detail of emotion, nothing more. Normally he was the first to talk his way out of difficulty, slipping and sliding until he was just plain gone. Charlotte's evasiveness was composed of silence and dead ends.

'Please, Charlotte. Tell me something about your plans.' She was leaving the next afternoon.

'I want this baby. That's all I know. I want her to be healthy.'

'So do I. What about me?'

'You are the father.'

'Do you want me in your life? Yours and hers?'

'I don't know, Jacob. That's too far away.'

He tried again the next day, sitting at a cafe in the open sunshine outside the Teatro Verdi at half eleven in the morning.

'Do you want us to be together?'

'I don't know, Jacob. I have to see what happens after the birth. I trust this city.'

'Bristol is a good city. Don't you think? I've always thought Bristol would be a fine place to live.' He was belligerent again in his need for recognition. He had only ever visited Bristol twice for art exhibitions.

'I hardly know it. Maybe I will come back to England. Sometimes I think I will.'

Abruptly he got up and threw some coins on the table. 'I have work to do. I'm leaving tomorrow. Go to hell.' He walked away, felt a rising sense of panic and turned back. 'I'm sorry. I didn't mean to be mean.'

Her hands were on her bump. She was looking at the change.

'I know you didn't. It's me.'

He hoped to wrench her open from a different angle.

'I want to help you, be with you, if you'll let me. If not, if not yet, then please let me help you with our baby.'

She sucked in her breath, exasperated at his persistence. The resistance in her was made of the toughest material, like an ancient wall that had been built to keep out the enemy across a long expanse of emptiness, and now remained, its purpose lost but durable all the same. His spirit was different to hers, light, untethered. Together, he thought, together we can create something.

'I'm glad you'll be here for the birth. I really am.' She was sincere.

'Meet me again. Come to London. Stay in the flat. It's small, not so comfortable. It's only temporary. You can meet my boys. They're wonderful. Really good kids.' He was racing ahead, unable to restrain himself, aware she wouldn't like it.

'Maybe, Jacob. Please don't expect anything. Not of me. Just the baby, we will make sure she is all right together. I know you are a good father.'

He and Jane texted each other several times. His messages were positive and vague. *She's fine, the baby is fine. We are getting to know each other.* Jane wanted to know if Charlotte seemed OK. *What are her plans? I emailed her, not heard back.* She didn't like the idea of the baby being born in Trieste. Jacob became contrarian: *Why not? Excellent hospital, one of best in Italy.* She riposted, *Too lonely, isolated. She'll need a lot of support. Mental health an issue. You need to understand this.*

He was tired of understanding.

On Saturday he flew home. He called Kathleen from the airport. 'I want to see the boys tonight. Can they stay with me?'

'It's your weekend anyway, and Finn's going to a party,' she retorted.

'I spoke to Mikey, he wasn't sure what the plans were, said you might be taking them somewhere.' He was defensive, restless with longing and guilt. These emotions were familiar to him, constant companions through his life; now their intensified presence was making him stubborn. 'Tell them to walk over later. I'll be at the flat from late afternoon on.'

She did not mention the lawyer's letter. He wondered if she had received it. He had approved the draft in Trieste. It should arrive any day.

Kathleen opened the front door. She flushed and drew breath; his literal appearance momentarily knocked her. This was the first time they had seen each other since before Christmas. He normally rejected her requests to meet fearing the acrimony that would follow but Finn had left behind his laptop and needed it for schoolwork.

He handed over the machine on the doorstep. He did not want to enter.

'I was a bit groggy after my trip. I forgot to remind him about it,' he said defensively.

'You're spending a lot of time in Trieste.' She fixed on him a look of alert suspicion.

'I'm working up a book proposal about Theodor and Granddad.'

It was Kath who had given him the services of a genealogist for his fifty-fifth birthday last year, persuaded of the commercial potential in a project about the ghosts of his ancestors. She had long been fascinated by that mysterious postcard from Theodor. She had also felt he needed something to sink his teeth into, something with meaning and headlines. 'You're barely fit for purpose anymore,' she'd jibed, 'what with the whole print media becoming obsolete. You need something new.'

They had met at a prize-giving ceremony for new artists. She was director of the foundation that sponsored the prize. She was assertive, biting, stylish and petite. At a glance he saw she would be a dynamic partner and committed mother. He was alone, he was lonely. His estimate was sound. She was all he had intuited she might be.

Their courtship had been conventional and quick. Finn came along soon after. Kath had been just as eager for a family as he. She was two years older and losing eggs quickly (she'd joked).

He had not meant to leave Kath. Leaving Kath would mean leaving Mikey and Finn, their shared life. The thought had been too painful for him to follow through to its various outcomes. When the end came it was accidental, a casual conversation began one night after a dinner party that led to an admission of adultery from him. He remembered her face, whitened by the shock, and the crumpling of her body as each one of his words, forced from him at first then willingly spilled, landed on her. By one in the morning he was in a single room in a business hotel nearby.

The speed of the breakdown revealed the wholly unstable infrastructure of the marriage, almost as much of a surprise to him as his revelation was to her. With a tenacity of will that he had so admired in the management of her career, she had at first clung to the idea that in separation he would be brought to his senses, serve penitence for his misdemeanour and beg for her forgiveness.

His single most salient sense told him this was another example of her inability to know him.

Now he saw she was ageing well. Spurred by his betrayal, she had lost weight and changed her hairstyle. There had been a love affair with a younger man. He had accounts of all this from the boys. He thought she might have had work done on her face. Men had been in equal measure drawn to her by a flirtatious manner and a pixie look – and put off by a forceful will and keen ambition. He was not interested in her girlishness, he had wanted her steel. He had not known himself any better than he had known her or she had known him.

'I got your lawyer's letter,' she was saying, 'and you'll be hearing from mine soon. We need to talk.'

She saw his relief and flinched; then stood aside, an invitation into the house. He took a few unwilling steps across the threshold. The hallway was lit by a dim spot partly shrouded by the rack of coats and family paraphernalia which dominated the narrow space. There were Mikey's new Nike trainers and Finn's beloved military-style jacket. An old coat of his, a tweed left over from the nineties still hung in the far corner. Details came back to him with dizzying effect. That pile of old gloves in a basket on the floor, the smell of disinfectant from the loo wafting along the corridor. He absorbed it all through the eyes of a former owner, a cocktail of nostalgia and sharp familiarity accompanied the knowledge that it all belonged to the past.

She closed the front door. Braced, she dropped her eyes to the tatty rug. 'I don't want a divorce,' she said in a voice trembling with hurt and anger. She now looked up straight at him, and in this moment of high risk, her eyes rounded like a child.

'We could try again.' It was a plea, not a declaration of love.

He hoped his expression was answer enough yet there she stood in front of him willing the answer he could not give. Finally he said, 'Please, Kath, no. I don't want to come back.' He held out his arms in a motion of inadvertent helplessness.

'You fucking coward!' she yelled, all senses blazing.

He would not, not now or ever, be able to persuade her that staying in this marriage would be a surrender to weakness. She did not understand what had taken him such a long time to face: the simple truth that there was little love between them.

―――

The text was an instruction:

> *We need to meet. Urgent. Can you come here? I'm free tonight or tomorrow night. Jane x*

> *Can't make it till next week. What's going on?*

> *Can't say. Too difficult will tell when you come Jx*

> *Ok sorry too much to do at moment, will let you know when I have time.*

It was a lie. He could easily make time for an overnight visit to Gloucester but he did not want to. His obstinacy resisted the snowballing of commands hurtling his way and his sharpened instincts pointed to the unlikelihood of Jane's news being of any help or comfort to him. She could call him, she could email him, but instead she wanted his physical presence. This indicated to him that whatever it was she felt impelled to say to him was both too delicate for the brute communications of distance and also not nearly as urgent as her text suggested. Let her wait.

Two weeks rolled by before he boarded a train. His sense of *déjà vu* created an unsettling echo. He retraced the steps of his first visit: flowers bought at Paddington Station, a fetid crowded carriage, the zip through rolling green countryside; his own image visible in the window. The journey to deliver the painting from Gloucester to Alex had been made in a rental car in the flat grey of late January. That was almost three months ago, forty-three days after he had learnt about Charlotte's pregnancy, six months to the day he and Charlotte had spent one night together. Their baby was due in one hundred and two days. They could be exact, there was only the one night. He and Kath had not been able to pinpoint the date of Finn's conception, they were fucking so much in those early days. With Mikey it was easier, sex between them had become infrequent. A holiday in Rome with Finn asleep quietly in the travel cot at their side.

Jane was not at the station to greet him. She was engaged in a conference call; Sheldon at work in his study. He was to take a taxi. The harsh drizzle blew horizontal across the crowded evening streets. The clocks had gone forward. Light was coming. He drew into his raincoat. He was looking forward to seeing Jane and Sheldon. He liked them, he liked their conversation and their company. He experienced the unusual sensation of 'being at home' around them. In Jane he recognised common ground – in their backgrounds as much as in their worldviews. Alikeness. Sheldon carried with him the casual confidence of liberal Americans of a certain education and political stripe. Their appeal also lay in their newness. These were the first friends he had made outside his marriage, *beyond* his marriage; Jane and Sheldon were entirely his, his alone; 'my friends'.

Jane opened the door and stepped aside averting her gaze. The pale corridor ushered him into its calm. She took his wet coat, shook it out and threw it over a hook. He followed her into the ample resonant kitchen. The wood-burner emitted flames of hot welcome, the crisp aromas of a roasting chicken enveloped his body.

He has been here before: the capacious kitchen with its long stained wooden refectory table, the gleaming cabinets and integrated cooker; loose piles of papers and magazines waiting for attention scattered on surfaces; the family supper under way. This had been the setting of his life until fourteen months ago, the twin kitchen in Queens Park in west London, so like this in which he now stood, eerie with silence, the absent voices of teenage boys chattering in his head.

He sat on the sofa. Jane leant forward in the armchair, both hands resting on a tattered thick folder sitting on top of a copy of *Vogue* magazine. Two large glasses of wine shimmered ruby red. She changed her mind about something, took up her glass, drank and relaxed into her chair, eyes large with intent and nerves. Behind her on the expertly painted bleached lemon wall hung reproductions of Hogarth's prints *Beer Street* and *Gin Lane*. Next to it was a simple abstract in gouache, two figures discernible in the quick brush strokes. To the side on the dresser was a collage of photographs. He saw a lively Jane, windswept on a white beach. Jane, much younger, in a green sari. Sheldon and two young adults, beaming and clean-cut like him. A postcard, frayed at the edges, with 'Sarajevo' in bright red script across the top. Charlotte and Jane: heads touching in affection, waving at the photographer.

Jane allowed him a moment for these observations and followed his gaze from one object to the next. 'So tell me,' she started, 'how was Trieste?'

She wanted news about Charlotte. Trieste for her was Charlotte. Not yet. In his own time. His. He was still in the dark as to why she had summoned him here. Let it stay that way for a while longer. He launched into his subject against the grain of her impatient curiosity. He talked about the progress he had made on his book. There was mention of Motz und Sohn in an old newspaper clipping from 1912. Then there was the postcard sent by Theodor to his son

Stefan. He did not know what it meant. He discovered the names of several Italian families registered at that address. It was 1938, a year after the family firm had been sold. The year of the Anschluss, when Hitler annexed Austria. The year racial laws were introduced in Italy. So Theodor had made his way from Vienna to Trieste. He did not yet know why. He was moving from trouble to more trouble. Mussolini and his alliance with Germany. The Pact of Steel signed in 1939. What had Theodor been doing?

Jane gave her polite attention to his essayistic ramblings. Summoning up a courtesy that was not immediately automatic, she contributed: 'I found out all I needed to know about my father's first family from the old letters and then my mother filled in the rest. That was enough. I never wanted exact details of how they were killed. I've visited several times over the years, got to know the few remaining relatives. And of course I think I said my brother has fully embraced our Indian side. But why do you want to find out?' She was tracing shapes on the material of her chair as if writing a note.

'It's everything. How can we remember, how can we learn, unless we have the precise facts, the individual stories? We don't know anything without them.' He was now upright, making his case with a belief that masked the truth. He wanted to know because it was *his* story, *his* ancestor. The distinction he sought was not of the kind cannibalised by the media, commemorated in history books, rewarded by public gongs. He was after his own particularity, *sui generis*. Years ago he had slept with an American PhD student after an exhibition preview in New York. They had spent an evening in a bar in Hell's Kitchen near where she lived. She had the directness of her nationality and the certainty of her youth. She owned a cockatoo, who often came out with her. Why, he had asked, do you have a cockatoo? It's my gimmick, she said. We all need one. What's yours?

'And Charlotte?' She was unable any longer to contain her impatience. Head bent towards the fire, warm flames on lustrous hair. Hands a little clenched. The cold monotonous early spring wind hissed in the chimney.

He was humming now. It was an early Bob Dylan tune from his youth. His heyday. Bob: the man who replaced God for his generation of brainy young men yearning for the new. The song came into his head unbidden as if plugging a stream of uncontrolled feeling.

'Jacob?' Now she was turned to him again and in her deep green eyes he saw fierce animation.

'She's doing well.' He fell quiet; the clean white shutters creaked in harmony. Presently he continued: 'She's got things sorted at the maternity hospital. Met the consultant obstetrician. Next month they'll do some tests, standard stuff.'

'What did she tell them?' The words fell on him like balls of hail. He drained his glass, smacked his lips – smacked, he pondered the verb, wondered at its aggression.

'She told them she'd suffered from depression, that her baby had died, and that she'd had a breakdown. They seemed very on the case. Compassionate. I think she's in excellent hands.'

Jane waved all this aside. 'What about you two?' She looked at him severely.

He floundered. His mind skated over the myriad details of their lovemaking. He searched for the one that might address Jane's question. Were they, he and Charlotte, any kind of a two? He had thrown out titbits of his own life to Charlotte while they lay naked in the speculative peace after sex was done; it was like feeding a hungry bird intent only on the crumb. She wanted to know about his boys, only his boys. Mikey, he said, had red-blond hair like his mother. His mother's Irish forbears are all in Mikey, he had joked. Finn, light-haired like himself, same lean build. But a serious boy with a need for precision in all matters. She had wanted to know if they were kind, if they were clever, if they were happy. Was Kathleen a good mother? Yes, he conceded, wondering what that might mean. Kathleen was organised, attentive to the needs of their advancement through the world, and she could be funny. She had a short fuse, was often impatient. She was not a woman with many hugs. That was his role. They will like you, he whispered, holding her loose mane and perfect skull, slick with sweat, in the crook of his arm. Oh, yes, she'd answered mocking, me, a perfect mother.

Eventually he replied: 'I don't know, Jane. I'll be there for the birth. I want to be a father to our child.'

'Did she talk about Sylvie?'

'She didn't talk about the past.' She was emptied of stories, they had all been given to him here in Gloucester, in London, in one long scroll that had rolled out of her with the terror of an unending lizard's tongue. Trieste was not for the past, Trieste was the future.

Jane persisted: 'What about Sylvie's death? Did she mention that?'

'To the obstetrician, yes. In fact, I told him about the cot death.'

Jane tapped the large folder in front of her. 'It's all here.'

Obedient, he stared at the folder. Often he would wonder how things might have been had she left it where it belonged, forgotten in a hospital archive.

Jane continued, 'You see, I want to be helpful, to Charlotte, to you. I have experience. I was trained as a clinical psychologist and a forensic psychotherapist. I work all the time with psychiatrists.' She was allocating each word an equal weight, transmitting her credentials as if under interrogation before a committee. 'I'm Charlotte's next of kin. That's legal. She appointed me. And the lasting power of attorney. That and my professional position have allowed me to see her medical file. I've been in touch with her Italian psychiatrist.' She paused. 'I had to fudge a bit.'

He saw a crack on the ceiling, threaded down the wall under the cornicing, the only blemish in the room. He liked being here. Yes. He nodded again and adjusted his body to rest more comfortably in the sofa. He touched the soft material, a silken velour in a blue that conjured the luxuriant medieval robe of a well-born maiden. Sheldon was upstairs, the knight. He hoped Sheldon would come down soon. Sheldon would pour oil on troubled waters.

'Jacob?' Her forceful sense of purpose yanked him back. Irritation brought him to snap.

'Jane. I understand. I do. But maybe you can tell me more later. Tell me what you need to when we've had something to eat. She was ill. I know that. We've been through all this.' An enfolding weariness settled on him.

Heavy footfall on the stairs announced Sheldon's appearance.

The men embraced. Jane took the chicken from the oven and put it on the counter. Sheldon fetched a knife from the block. Jane drained broccoli which she poured into a ceramic white dish, squeezed lemon and sprinkled nuts. Roast potatoes crackled, fragrant with darkened rosemary stems. Sheldon carved. He loitered. When all was ready, they sat at table.

'Nice to see you Jacob,' said Sheldon, clinking glasses.

'So, Janie,' he continued, cutting up a piece of meat, and in American style put down his knife, changed hands for his fork and brought the chicken to his mouth. Jacob was a greedy eater, shovelling his food at twice the tempo of anyone else. Jane's chin was on her hands, elbows placed at either side of her plate, eyes fixed on her husband.

Sheldon cleared his mouth. 'Have you told Jacob everything you know?' Jane shook her head.

'Maybe not over dinner,' suggested Sheldon, mildly.

'Yes!' exclaimed Jane. She sprang from the table, strode to the ottoman on which lay the fat folder. Jacob continued eating quickly. He sensed their supper might be laid to the side at any minute.

Sheldon turned abruptly in his chair towards her. His movement thundered with mounting annoyance. Jane picked up the folder and hugged it to her breast.

'Put it down,' he ordered. 'Later.' Her head shook in a wild dance. Jacob ate and drank. 'OK,' calmed Sheldon. 'Honey, why don't you come back to the table?'

Jane returned to her seat, placed the folder next to her. More wine was poured.

'Don't see it makes any difference,' remarked Sheldon. Jane flashed, 'Of course it does! You big idiot.'

The inclusion of the word idiot led Jacob to believe that affection stirred in the brewing row, one that was veering and swaying towards his inexorable participation. His extensive experience of marital argument had given him a keen ear for the no-turning-back moment; Sheldon and Jane were not yet there.

That he was still in a state of ignorance about what information this folder contained and why it was so important allowed him a moment of respite. He understood, how could he not, that what was about to be revealed to him would complicate an already delicate set of circumstances. He silently agreed with Sheldon. Let them finish their dinner.

Sheldon: 'She's trouble.' Jane's tightened features were eloquent answer to his bald assertion.

Sheldon did not like trouble. His bonhomie was an effective block to the vagaries of human interference. Jane handled trouble and Sheldon handled her. He reduced her drama, he brought a cool calculating eye to her excesses and he most certainly did not like trouble. Jacob cleaved to Jane. How swiftly Sheldon's ease had become coarse. Where was the soothing oil?

His blood quickened. 'Charlotte's life has been full of violence and loneliness. She is deeply caring. She is grasping at some idea of happiness. Where's the harm in that?' His thoughts took shape as he spoke. He had not considered much before this moment about what it was exactly Charlotte was reaching towards. His words gave him comfort.

'She's cuckoo.' Sheldon's crudeness had a detached quality as if he were passing comment on a poor bottle of wine. In it was also contained a provocation to his dinner companions.

'Not fair!' barked Jacob. Beyond his irritation a bag of emotions stirred, not all disagreeable.

Jane reached out to her husband and stroked his face. The gesture was startling; Jacob was after all a newcomer to the elaborations of their couple's duet. Sheldon grasped her hand, kissed the palm and returned it to rest on the table. They all maintained a silence; the wind howled and a log broke and the ceiling above them juddered.

Then all at once the mood changed, each one sifting a desire for conviviality through ticklish nerves. He praised Jane on the meal, Jane said it was Sheldon's doing, Sheldon said it all came from an excellent organic farmer's shop. All in the quality of the produce, that's the secret, said Sheldon. Sheldon told a bad joke about a chicken crossing the road, and they all chuckled. Their cutlery clattered with the enjoyable business of cleaning plates. Sheldon asked him about the looming divorce.

'How're your boys managing the separation? I know my two found it real tough. They were both at college but might as well have been little kids. My ex and I didn't handle it well. We were sure we would, two grown-ups, all reasonable, we'd even paid some damned expensive mediator to help, but when it came to it we went for each other. She wanted everything. I didn't want to give her a penny. There you have it, it all gets worked out in the end, no wonder those lawyers are richer than Croesus. It doesn't matter now. And my kids are doing great. Thriving. My daughter has a great boyfriend, my son is married. All over. Clean plate.' His sympathetic punctuation was not reassuring.

'Now for the *pièce de résistance*,' promised Sheldon rising from his chair. 'I made it myself.' He took from the fridge a cake. 'New York cheesecake. My specialty.'

The dinner plates were cleared. The red folder was moved further down the table. The cheesecake was cut by Sheldon and dished into matching white dessert bowls.

Jane was biding time, participating in the conversation with a poised graciousness. They had eaten, they had chatted, they had laughed, they had exchanged sympathetic information about divorce. They could no longer delay. All thoughts returned to Charlotte.

'Jacob,' began Jane. She dragged the folder to her side. 'I've been through her notes again recently. I felt it was necessary. And it's persuaded me. I feel it's extremely important to bring Charlotte back here and get her set up for with the right kind of care for the birth. It's strictly confidential. I so want everything to be all right for her this time around.'

Sheldon bulldozed: 'Honey, none of that stuff before was your fault. Christ, the woman was crazy. It's a long time ago.'

Jane rolled back her head and snorted. Jacob could see that Sheldon wanted to protect Jane, and in so doing his pronouncements were awkward, releasing in her a wilful urge to patronise. Her insistence was fast approaching an edge of hysteria.

'What is in this folder – in all these lists of medication, the psychiatrist reports, group notes, nurses' notes, memos to staff – was that her psychiatrist at the time, the one I liaised with, believed her breakdown was part of, or consequent to, a condition known as puerperal psychosis. This is different to post-natal depression. It's rarer, more serious. It means a mother of a newborn can suffer delusions, hallucinations. Hear voices. She'll feel she's evil or that the child is. Have manic episodes. Her psychiatrist thought this is what might have happened to Charlotte.'

163

Sheldon thwacked the table with the palm of his hand in a gesture of 'so there'.

The smack of Sheldon's hand acted as a blow. Jacob recoiled sharply from this language of mental illness and its sinister nuances. He remembered how Kathleen had been a hormonal cauldron for many weeks after the birth of Finn. He had been warned about this in the numerous baby books Kath had instructed him to read. Hearing voices and seeing the devil seemed not that remote from the passions and fears expressed by Kathleen. 'Our baby will die!' she whimpered at him one day when he had left Finn in a low bouncy recliner for several minutes while he peed. 'He will bounce over and smash his head!' Then she would retreat in a daze as he rocked and cooed and fed and burped. 'I don't know who I am,' she said. Gradually life assumed its new rhythms and Kathleen was restored to herself, only more so. He felt unutterably changed by the depth of his love for his son. They distanced themselves from each other and drew deeply into their roles as parents.

'I believe Charlotte needs to come back to England for the birth,' continued Jane. 'She'll need full care and support. It's not certain whether the psychosis will return, if it was that, or if she'll suffer depression, but none of this is out of the question either. I'll assume responsibility for her, for her care, and will discuss this with her consultant and her health team when we've got her registered with a hospital here. You'll need to be completely committed to helping her and the baby.'

'Have you talked this over with Charlotte?' Jacob resisted the urge to launch into a speech about the vicissitudes of hormones. Another voice, a voice so faint and distant in him that he barely heard, wondered at Charlotte, wondered at Sylvie's death and these morbid tales of possession.

'I wanted to sound you out first. We've had a few email exchanges and she told me about the Trieste psychiatrist. But I want to make sure you and I are on the same page.' A coercive element had entered Jane's voice.

Sheldon harrumphed and discarded his napkin onto the table. He rose and gathered up dirty dishes. 'I've got work to finish,' he declared. 'I'll say goodnight.' He dumped the dishes on the counter and slapped Jacob on the back. 'Good to see you. You two have some talking to do. Not my business.'

Expertly Jane removed some pieces of paper from the folder and shuffled them across the table. He did not have his reading glasses to hand. He kept them hidden in his knapsack. Vanity was one of his many failings. Kathleen had liked the glasses, they suit you, she commented, they give you a serious look. He patted his jacket pockets, hoping Jane might retrieve these papers and give him a quick summary. Her voice would modulate the official words, render them conversational and personal. He continued patting then cast around for his bag, hopelessly vague.

'Oh sorry – let me. Anyway, you shouldn't see any of this stuff. I'm in breach of so many codes, I should at least respect the confidentiality bit.' She took them back, scanned, and began to read fragments.

'*Catatonic on admittance . . . unable to form sentences . . . dangerously thin . . . put on intravenous feed . . . Then . . .*'

She rifled through some papers, differing in size and colour. Most, Jacob could see, were handwritten, brought to life in looping lines of black, tiny scratches of blue; they carried authority, they conveyed experience. 'Here. Signs of life. *Talking, very confused. Doesn't remember how she got here.*' She looked back at him. 'She was on full suicide watch.' He nodded. She opened the folder and pulled out something from deeper in the pile. 'A nurses' note: *found her today with paperclip, don't know how she got hold of it, she was angrily cutting her arms –*'

Jane hesitated; he signalled for her to continue, the rough

texture of the scars on Charlotte's graceful upper arms vivid in his mind.

She continued: 'And then there's some from her psychiatrist and group therapist: *angry today, talks about Sylvie, says she was a vampire but no one but she knows it.* Then later – this note from the psychiatrist – *she remembered Sylvie is dead, couldn't talk about it, when I gently asked about Sylvie she drew up into small ball in corner of my office, I needed help to return her to her room ... revised her medication, more ECT ...* More from the psychiatrist: *great anger today, said Sylvie possessed her, that she was evil, said she hid this from Alex, said how clever she was. Large swings in lucidity and hallucinations.* Then, there was a change, a lasting change: *Hates herself, very strong, said she didn't look after Syvie, said she was a terrible mother. Repeats this again and again. Said she needs to die.*'

Jane put down the sheath of papers accumulated higgledy-piggledy in front of her.

'She was given electro-convulsive shock therapy. It helped bring her back to life. Doesn't always help. She was fortunate. She had an excellent psychiatrist who practised psychotherapy. She also participated in group sessions. It was an enlightened place. Of course no expense was spared. Alex at least did right by her there. Over the course of two years she'd begun to build an auto-biographical narrative. A coherent self. She is resilient.'

So many pieces of human life everywhere, like these bits of spilled food on the table, broken up, scattered around, no mess intended. Jacob brushed them into a pile.

'Her body is covered in scars,' he said in reply. Jane suppressed a startle. There are many routes to knowledge. Her belly, her wrist, her arms. The lasting marks on her temples from the electric nodes. This was the map of their lovemaking. A flush came over Jane as he held her gaze. His intimacy with Charlotte trumped this folder with its notes and reports.

The jealousy that stirred in Jane was remote, a feeling from childhood and adolescence; the clever girl who needed to win, who was not always liked, whose stapled confidence was alternately inspiring and intimidating. Charlotte had been her domain for so long she resisted the intrusion of another, even if this other she herself had so generously invited in. That he now had a privileged position, one from which she was excluded was disconcerting. This was his view. He had no wish to antagonise her and all he said was: 'I think I understand what you say. This might happen again?'

'Yes. But not necessarily. That's why I think she should be back here, close to me – and you of course if that's what you and she have decided.' She held his gaze, a blush suffusing her skin.

'She's been stable for years, is that right?' He understood about madness only as a biographical element in the lives of artists he knew something about: Van Gogh and his ear, Caravaggio and his passions, Jackson Pollock and his alcoholism. The links between childhood trauma and later instability were much written about, a fashionable approach in the last fifty years and one about which he was not sure exactly what to think. Amelioration to the point of full recovery was not part of the narrative. But Charlotte, with her intense strangeness and grief-stricken past, struck him as being quite sane. A strong resistance to Jane's alarming forecast was building in him. 'I don't think we should jump to any conclusions. It's up to Charlotte.'

Jane shifted awkwardly, paused, and continued: 'Puerperal psychosis, or post-partem psychosis, is unusual. Sufferers do recover. It's not like bipolar disorder or schizophrenia which afflicts you for life although those can be outcomes. But in some it subsides generally months after the birth. Longer in Charlotte's case, if indeed that is what she'd suffered from – her circumstances were –' Jane hovered over a long moment. He waited.

'Different,' she concluded.

'The grief,' he murmured. He felt curiously unafraid of what Jane was telling him. The multiple and various disturbances of the mind constituted her world. ECT, psychopharmacology, diagnostic labels, brain chemistry, neural imaging, psychotherapy. The fat folder lying between them was evidence of this, a place where science and emotion commingled. Evil, devil possession and vampires belonged to the grim stuff of fairy tales and the Bible, art and history; this was his world. He absorbed all this new information into himself with an efficient rationalism that superseded the reverberating small shocks he felt at Jane's stark language. Yes, he nodded smiling at Jane, yes I understand. Beyond this, a fierce need to protect her, Charlotte, and to care for his unborn child was asserting itself.

Abruptly, something occurred to him: 'Jane, why didn't you tell me this when we met? You talked about your suspicions of post-natal depression and then of course her complete breakdown, but you never linked her breakdown with this psychosis thing.'

He felt a refreshing uncompromised anger.

She took a long deep breath and considered his question. His anger was growing.

'I'm sorry. Maybe I should've. But, I don't know, I thought it was up to her to tell you I guess. I thought maybe she'd miscarry. It seemed better to just wait.'

'Wait. Fuck. And now. What the hell can I do?'

'She needs to be back here. Will you help?'

He remained silent.

'Jacob,' began Jane, 'I haven't asked, it's not really my business but, your wife, your sons … do they know about any of this?'

'They haven't a clue,' he said honestly, 'and I'll have to tell them. Kath and I have embarked on a divorce. I'll have to tell her before I say anything to Finn and Mikey. It'll be very confusing for them.'

'Will Kath take this on the chin?'

'No, she'll really go for me.' He spoke with repressed bitterness. 'She'll use it against me.' Jane clucked, though whether in sympathy or impatience was difficult for him to discern. 'One night.' One night. 'One night of sex, unintended, for me at least. It was wonderful – you see, I hadn't – in so long.' Pause. 'I was trying to reform,' he added. Did she believe him? In a moment of quick-passing the sensation of her rounded ampleness came back to him. One night in a hotel …

'In a way Charlotte's right. This is a miracle baby. She's what? Forty-three? And you're? Beyond fifty?' He shrugged and took the question as a rhetorical one. Jane reflected, 'One night as you say. You a stranger. A saviour of sorts.'

There were many ways to go with these explorations: towards recrimination and regret; or elation and wonder; or straight to the moral corner of rights and responsibilities, duties and restraint. It was not to his credit that he had not brought up the subject of contraception to Charlotte. Their sexual congress had happened in such an atmosphere of surrealism that the conscious reasoning of two middle-aged lovers about to embark on intercourse had been completely absent from their encounter.

Abruptly it came to him: 'She knew what she was after.' He had been foolish. That was it, how foolish he was!

Gently Jane remonstrated: 'No, no, she didn't. She slept with you as – as – a wonderful expression of life, of feeling alive. She told me that. Do you know you're her first lover since – god let me remember – since . . . well, years. A young doctor she'd had a fling with immediately after arriving in Bosnia. She said she felt almost on meeting you she could try again, something about your smile, she said, she trusted you, to be … what was it she said, to be gentle and light-hearted. She didn't want heaviness.'

If Jane's words were intended to comfort or appease, they provoked the opposite reaction: a fury of unexpected force broke through. He thumped the table and cried 'Fuck!' again. Jane's bright gaze remained steady on him. 'Fuck all this, it's a mess, a stupid stupid mess. I've tried so hard, done everything expected of me. What for? This is all going to come down on me like a big pile of shit. I'm going to lose Finn and Mikey. They'll hate me.' He sighed and heaved until finally tears came.

'I wondered when you might start to express something like this, it's only natural for you to feel this way. You've been so reasonable.'

Her hands were now folded on the assorted papers, her manner temperate. She waited, eyes roving from him to a distant point in the room and back to the folder. The agitation which had taken hold earlier had vanished and in its place her customary air of consideration and warmth had returned.

He dropped his head into his hands. Like the ebb of a wave his anger retreated back into the vastness of his emotional confusion. So many unanticipated and alien feelings had taken up residence in him over the past months that he rode each on the crest of the next. He longed for a stillness in which order would be restored to his inner self. He had no regrets, he felt no remorse but in these few moments raw despair shook him. I know nothing. I am nothing. Where would it end? How can I manage? He felt so very alone.

His tears fell and Jane kept him company. The room had grown colder, the fire now dead. The candles dripped wax onto silver holders. Many miles from here his sons prepared for bed, careless in their thoughts of him. He was not known to them, he was simply Dad. On the other side of Europe, his baby grew in the body of a woman who did not want him. His estranged wife would seek revenge, and across the table sat Jane, a fixer of human souls, with no balm nor remedy for his.

Presently she started up again.

'You've behaved with sensitivity, Jacob. I can well understand your fears, your frustration. I don't know anything about your life with Kathleen, but I see how caring a father you are. That's all Charlotte needs. Whatever help I can give you to make things easier for you with your family I'll give.'

'Ah, you have no idea. She wouldn't listen to you. You're either in or out with Kath. She'd see you as the enemy.'

Jane tried again. 'I do know the family courts and in my experience they take a far less biased view than you're assuming. She can't keep your sons from you.'

'It's not the courts, they're both almost beyond that anyway. It's Kath. She'll poison them against me.'

'Not for long,' said Jane decisively. 'She might try but I feel you love them profoundly, they'll come round in time.' Then she added in a more persuasive tone, 'But you must explain as best you can, how it happened, your feelings about the new baby, your unconditional love for them, your sons. They might feel displaced. They'll want to protect their mother. It's only normal. Don't short-change them, they're old enough to understand.'

How, how can they be when even he, their father, understands nothing?

He worked obsessively on a plan for his book proposal, sketching quickly the imagined life of Johanna and Theodor in secular bourgeois Vienna during the twilight years of the Hapsburg Empire. He conjured the atmosphere of the salons and the factory; the routine of young Stefan in the large apartment on top of a hill in a comfortable suburb. He used Google Earth to zoom in on the street, the block, the windows, and brought them into view. He walked the Ringstrasse, dragging along the little orange figure on the screen to stare at the magnificent architecture of the old mansions. He indulged his love of adjectives like 'dazzling', 'glittering', 'historic', 'unique'. Their well-worn usage brought comfort. No thinking required. Quick route to readers. His difficulties lay elsewhere. Money (idly: Charlotte, her wealth, how much?). Big holes. Alongside his sketching he composed a list of places and archives to be visited. An estimated budget. He would need to find the descendants of those who might have known his great-grand-parents in Vienna. Why did Johanna go to Prague from where she was deported to Theresienstadt? Many Viennese had relatives in Prague. Johanna's father had been a Christian Czech. Why had this not saved her? So his great-grandmother had gone north and his great-grandfather had gone south; both into the lap of trouble. He wondered how he might best contact all those names in the Trieste phone book. His mobile sat next door in the bedroom. Intermittent bleeps indicated messages were coming through. He ignored their summons. If Finn or Mikey needed him they had agreed a special code – to let it ring three times, end the call, repeat.

The stray sound from the street dented his concentration only at intervals. He worked with focus, with pleasure, with satis-faction. He emailed *Il Piccolo*, the Triestine newspaper, asking about how to place an ad for information about a missing person. He used Google Translate: 'I am searching for my great-grandfather who went missing in Trieste in 1938. I'd like to place an ad in your paper.' *Sto cercando il mio bisnonno scomparso a Trieste nel 1938. Vorrei mettere un annuncio nel vostro giornale.* He heard from them quickly. He could place an ad online and in the paper. Discounted rate over multiple weeks. He paid.

At lunchtime he stopped and munched on a couple of cold pizza slices. Later he would go to his cafe round the corner for tea and a sandwich. Tonight there was a reception for the preview in Shoreditch of a new exhibition. He would need his wits about him, at the ready with a Twitter stream that would feed straight onto the website of the paper he wrote for. Not for the first time he wondered at his place in this world. Come with me, he asked Finn. You can do the tweets, I'm too old. Finn had thought for a minute then shook his head. That wouldn't be right, he said. His son's moral probity always made him in his role of father feel a little renegade, their ages reversed.

He followed the contours of his living area twice round as if performing a ritual. On his third tour he stopped at the window and looked into the promising daylight. He felt there was space in this flat only when he looked out. Leafy twigs from a stalwart plane tree waved. The weather forecast trumpeted sun and warmth in the days ahead. He traced with his finger her name on the dirt-spattered pane, *Charlotte*. He stood back. Charlotte. He wondered if she was not a tantalising fantasy of what was unattainable to him. A chimera. Charlotte, lover. Charlotte, glamour girl. Charlotte, daughter. Charlotte, wife. Charlotte, charity worker. Charlotte, best friend. Charlotte, mother. Charlotte, mad. Charlotte, ghost. Charlotte, his. Her different selves had each a distinct flavour. When he was with her he grasped at one only to find her transformed into another. At times, an actual Charlotte materialised to him. Was he for her? For her, Charlotte, her character?

The intensity of his attraction was subsiding. Their future, the future of their baby, Jane and the folder; the tangle grew as his ardour dampened. He was worried about money. Last year the paper that had employed him for twenty-three years as an arts correspondent let him go. Fine turn of phrase. As if he had been prisoner for all those years and at last his freedom was restored to him. He did not feel free. He was adrift and anxious, unmoored from everything that had given his life a structure. He glanced at his computer, at the straggle of books on the floor and the notebook poised on the desk. This book, his book, might be a life-line to an economically viable future. That had been Kath's assessment, those had been her words – economically viable, as if he was a project whose budget and mission had a series of boxes and lines that could be adequately ordered and evaluated.

A hazy image of Johanna arose; her features resembled in his mind's eye Charlotte's. He had no picture of this distant relative. What had happened to her? He felt the pull of intrigue all over again and returned to the open file on his computer. The words struck him as garish. A dull flat screen covered in a march of signs. Who would pay for them? Someone, somewhere, he had to believe, would pay.

He picked up one of the papers from a pile at the back of the desk. It was from his lawyer. His ability to keep separate the new and complicated web of relationship that had arisen in Trieste from the shifting sands of his family life in London was fast diminishing. He had received from Kath's lawyer a proposal for the division of goods. She would keep the family house and her pension, all her own ISAs (more than he had); to compensate for his capital disadvantage, she would give him twenty per cent of the equity in the house in years to come when she came to sell it. He would pay twenty per cent of his income towards maintenance for the boys and share equally any expenses relating to travel or education. They could stay with him as much as they chose although she would maintain official custody. Finn would turn eighteen in several months. His lawyer thought this a rotten deal.

He sent an email to him:

This is all acceptable to me. What about status of Nisi? How long before full dissolution granted?

Time was running out.

Gloucester was neutral. Jane wanted Charlotte close to her. He agreed.

They had parted on a truce. She would email Charlotte. She would coax her into coming back to Britain. He would support her in this but would not put any pressure on Charlotte. I can't do that, he said, fidgeting on the doorstep, the taxi in wait. If she agrees to come I'll support you, but if she resists I'll respect her wishes.

Charlotte kept in regular touch. Small mails, affectionate in tone, about her changing body:

She's been kicking a lot these past days. My back is really beginning to ache!

Short anecdotes about the life in Sarajevo that she would soon leave behind:

I'll miss it. I think being here has saved me. The other night a group of us went out for supper, a doctor at the charity, an Italian from Trieste who introduced me to the city, he's a really lovely young man, and a great Scottish woman who runs a music therapy programme for the traumatised, and they all drank enormous amounts and toasted my baby. I could only sip on a little glass but felt as high as they were!

Sometimes she would mention Jane:

Jane sounds so incredibly busy, and is fussy mother hen in her mails to me. Are you two in touch?

He thought about the photograph on Jane's dresser: the two women's heads touching, a sheen of silver-blond on velvet brown; their lives animated through a set of blue and green eyes. He loved their closeness. He pondered their differences. He was outside their friendship. He would sit back now and follow.

At four o'clock he had a tuna panini and a large pot of tea at the Cafe Elena. These were served up by a young waitress with a bouncy manner who was an actress some of the time. At every visit she asked him what he would like and very occasionally he would change his order to honour her conscientiousness. The cafe was presided over by Elena, who had come originally from Greece in the 1970s and married an Irishman in Kensal Rise. She now found herself on the upward trend of a barista explosion. Alert to the nuances of consumer needs, she'd installed wi-fi, stripped back the floors to their original wood and offered a bewildering choice of fairtrade teas and coffees. There were other regulars, like himself laptops open, heads down, tapping away. And then a small group of older Greek men who came and went, flirting with Elena and downing small cups of her strong espresso. Elena would occasionally flirt with Jacob too and they would have a small conversation. He liked the recognition, the little courtesies and the absence of obligation these encounters entailed. He felt warmly towards them all, they were his familiars.

He drank his tea thirstily and gulped down his panini, eyes on the computer screen. Emails cascaded down the inbox. He scanned them, dealt with the immediate and moved the rest into appropriate folders. A new email had arrived from Charlotte. Jane was not copied in.

Jacob, Jane tells me you know about the condition I suffered with Sylvie. I'm so sorry I didn't say anything. So much of that period in my life is a fog. I remember little. I sometimes wonder whether all these labels make much sense. Do you think it's better for me to have our baby in England? I don't want to. I can't really explain why not because I'm not sure I understand myself. It feels much better to me to be in Trieste with her. I have my flat. I have friends. I'll go there very soon. I get six months maternity leave from my charity but I won't go back to Sarajevo. There is too much suffering. I know it would

*be much easier for you if I came back to England but it feels too soon
for me. Please let me know what you think. Charlotte x*

Across the room sat a young man with a full head of hair; he was
wearing stylish glasses and a leather jacket. His laptop bore the
apple icon. With the concentration of a precision sniper he stared
at his screen. That could have been me thirty years ago, thought
Jacob, and now I am old. Thirty years ago he'd had long hair and
wore flared jeans skintight at the crotch. He went on marches
in support of Nelson Mandela and the anti-apartheid movement in
South Africa. He was anti-war, anti-nuclear, anti-capital. Pro-sex,
pro-workers, pro-women. He had believed in the promise of an
egalitarian and fair future. By the time of his marriage to Kath in
the early 1990s the right-wing revolution had taken place without
many being aware of what had happened. Kath was pro-marriage,
pro-equality, pro-money. They both voted Labour. He had stuck
to his guns about high art.

'There is high,' he'd blaze, 'high, high, high, and then there's
proper low, what you call culture, shopping and street performance.'

'You're a snob,' she laughed.

He would not be deterred. 'Anyone can look at a painting, he'd
insisted, anyone, today, a decade ago, a century ago. You can walk
into a museum, or a church, or a gallery, just stand and experience
a picture. That's art. Not all the theory and the connoisseurship
and the money. That's just stuff.' Kath had almost agreed.

The young man felt his gaze and returned the look. He had
kindly eyes. There was pity in them too, unwitting, at the sight of
the ageing bloke across the room. You will be me, Jacob admon-
ished silently, even you, one day, you'll be old. A willowy young
woman carrying a baby bound to her front interrupted their silent
exchange. She kissed the man and undid the ties of her carrier.
He pulled the baby gently from the cloth and crooked it in his

177

arms. She swept back young hair from a fresh face and eyed the menu board.

His consciousness was filled with memories and prospects. That was him with Finn. That would be him with the new baby. He had sent Charlotte an email after his visit to Jane:

Never fear, Jane and I will be near!

It was a lame rhyme; he put an emoticon at the end: :)   Mikey liked emoticons and emojis; Finn was too literal for such signs. Both boys used words like 'lame', 'sad', 'pathetic', to describe naff music or geeky behaviour. When real distress came their way, they shrugged their shoulders and became monosyllabic. The introduction into their life of a new half-sibling would require from him patience and care, a maturity he had yet to demonstrate. It made him tremble.

> *Jane told me about your breakdown and that it might've been con-nected to a condition of post-partem psychosis. I'm so sorry for you. It must have been awful and to have everything made worse by Sylvie's death and that terrible trial. Jane says you're strong and resilient. She's explained it all to me. I told Jane I'd support whatever decision you made about where to have our baby. I'll do my best to be there. But I have obligations. My time will be limited. I count that there are not many weeks till the birth. I worry you will be too alone in Trieste. I have to trust that you know what's best for you and the baby. Jane has her ideas and I believe she really does know how to help. Please listen to her. This is after all part of her expertise. But that's between you and her. Please tell me when you arrive in Trieste. Jacob x*

He followed this with an email to Jane:

Dear Jane, I've received an email from Charlotte. She says she wants to have the baby in Trieste. I can't argue with her, it is her decision. She has her own flat, she knows people. The hospital is excellent. I believe you've been in touch with her psychiatrist there? Perhaps she'll then come back to England. I'll do what I can but my life is here in London. I'll keep in touch with you and with Charlotte of course. I still plan on being there for the birth. I have a lot of research to do for my book proposal and will be back in Trieste in the near future but I can't say how much. My sons' exams will begin soon and I must be here to support them. Ever Jacob

There pinged back to him within minutes a message from Jane.

This is not great. I feel such a sense of dread. I'll try to talk to her again. Our last conversation was not very productive. She then mailed me that she was in good hands, and that she trusts you, and that all will be ok this time. She wants me to be there for her. What can I do? I too have many obligations and commitments. Jx

As Jacob idled at Cafe Elena, Charlotte's voice from outside the cathedral came back to him as if from another world: 'This being growing inside me filled me with a sense of absolute power. She would love me as I never had been loved. I would be the perfect mother! She would be strong and clever, loving and kind, beautiful and sweet. Most, most of all, she would be mine, all mine!'

———

Jacob found out about Jane's trip to Sarajevo on her return. She spent two nights and a day. She stayed at the Hotel Europe. She helped clear out the small rental where Charlotte had spent the past five years. It reminded Jane of the time many years ago when on the eve of Charlotte's departure to Bosnia they had had a final supper together surrounded by boxes. Then, as now, Jane was over-come with anxiety. Then she felt sadness at the departure of her friend, now there boiled a mixture of alarm and urgency. That night years ago she had left her friend's place with a precious painting tucked under both arms, a painting whose value had now been transformed into a tidy sum from Alex, which Charlotte assured Jane would give her the means to buy a comfortable family place for her and the baby, perhaps in England.

'She told me I was making a drama.' Jane's call had interrupted Jacob during the PR launch of a new piece of digital software for artists. It was early evening and she had arrived back that afternoon.

He found a quiet corridor in the building where the reception was being held. A few workers straggled. The distant clatter of voices made hearing difficult. He made an effort; he switched to Jane's gear.

'Did you?'

'She told me she was OK. I doubt her self-sufficiency, it worries me. I know about this condition. She is being stubborn.'

'She's in good hands, I met the doctor, really, Jane, it's OK.'

What Jacob also discovered was that the friendship between the two women had experienced a rupture. They had said things to one another that had left them both with nowhere to turn – other than to him.

Hours after their conversation, he received a text from Charlotte:

I don't want Jane to help. I'll need as much time as you can give. love Charlotte.

Next morning, he received a further text from Jane:

Will be in London in three days. Can we have tea? Jx

He met her off the train at Paddington. Her panache, ever strong in her figure, marked her out from the travellers rushing towards the barriers. She was giving a talk at the Portman early evening, they had an hour. He steered her through the crowds out of the penumbral station and into the sunlight.

'Charlotte said talking to me removed all that kept her covered and safe,' she said. 'It's a terrible thing to hear for anyone in the therapeutic community. I should be the opposite for her. I didn't mean to make her feel that way.' He nodded and took her elbow.

They entered Hyde Park. The length of spacious green lawn opened around them. It was empty but for small groups of people – office workers dawdling in the late afternoon, lone older men and women on benches, the camera-toting tourist. Lured by the warming sun into fresh air, arms were thrown back, heads tipped up, coats unbuttoned. Traffic rumbled on Bayswater. Insistent birdsong lifted moods. Contentment reigned.

'Let's sit.' He pointed to a bench. 'Tea?' A kiosk was nearby.

'OK, thanks.' She shrugged off the fashionable coat and put on a pair of sunglasses.

A bulky man performed t'ai chi in the near distance.

'My approach was all wrong'. They sipped from steaming cups. Jane continued, softened: 'I kept insisting she come back to Gloucester. Move into our house. I rattled off lists of things to do, registering at the hospital, health visitors, medication. I was panicked. We don't have much time. Travelling on a plane, that kind of thing.'

'She's not coming, is she?'

'No.' He looked at the round dark glasses behind which she lowered her eyes. 'It'll be OK.'

She stood up, flexed her arms. She was thinking what to say next. She was wondering at him.

'Do you think the rich are different?'

He laughed, an easy release. Her question surprised him. She sat again and took off her glasses. He was reminded of their first meeting at the bar of the Excelsior. Her inviting intelligence, her attractive humour. Fleetingly she appeared to him in the hotel bedroom, close-up and sexual.

'Why do you ask?' He knew rich people. They crowded the arts. They were at the operas he reviewed, they bought art pieces he critiqued, they owned the houses whose architecture he championed.

'Charlotte lived that life. The life of the rich.'

'The thing about privilege is that those who have it have no idea they have it. I'd include both of us in the category. In fact, most people –' he waved his arm at the park – 'most if not all people I know are privileged. In a first-world sense. The rich, they exist on a different plane. They're the puppeteers.'

'I think the rich have God complexes.'

'What, all?'

'Yes!' She shouted this to the wide open space and raised her arm in a workers' salute, chuckled and patted his knee. He reached out to her and tugged a tendril of curl.

'Hadn't quite figured you for a revolutionary.'

'No, not in any Marxist sense, I suppose not. But of the psyche, yes, I think I am.'

'What happened with Charlotte?' The brightness diminished an infinitesimal notch as the planet turned. London sprawled and extended in all directions around them. He felt expansive like the city he inhabited. Trieste was different, a city whose fundamental purpose was intermittently being lost and renegotiated through history.

'She didn't want to hear me. My pleading just made her obstinate. It's as if she refuses to acknowledge what happened.'

'Not a bad thing is it? To look forward, to be optimistic about the future.'

She shook her head.

In her silence the ambient noise grew. The yap-yap of a cheerful terrier urging its owner to throw the ball overlay the constant hum of traffic from the perimeter. Up high the commanding throb of an aeroplane left its echo in the sky. Puffs of cloud hinted at a gentle gold sunset on the horizon.

He turned again to Jane. She was battling. She was here to say something to him. Something more about her stay in Sarajevo and her anxiety, the rupture in the friendship. Suddenly he did not want to know. He knew enough. He knew all he needed. This was their relationship, their problem.

She took a leather planner from her bag and held it in her hand. She scanned the sky as if searching for a signal. He looked again. The pellucid evanescent blue. Blue was Charlotte. Jane was green, the dancing vivid green of buds bursting through on trees in the park. She brought her eyes back to him. Now he saw a raw sadness, an unmasking that revealed a self that was new to him.

He was only two feet from her and pulled back. A stream of unhappiness was coming towards him. His being rebelled, no, not here, not now on this glorious spring day!

She collected herself and opened the diary in July. The week of the birth of Charlotte's baby. His child. The revolt in him grew.

'She says she doesn't want me around but I'll plan on going. I'll touch base with her psychiatrist again. I hope she'll change her mind. I'll need to ringfence the dates. We can alternate.' He saw large scribbles running across pages and blocks of time crossed out.

'I have to check about my sons and their exams. They'll be over by then but I'll need to be around. I'll email you.' He was aware his voice sounded dry and unsupportive. He had never been patient with being organised and now, just for these minutes, on this afternoon, he rejected Jane's conscientious intentions, he rejected the imminent role of responsible adult that he was being called on to play, the complicated and precarious future that drew closer with each passing day. Let them sort it. He would be there for the birth. That's all he knew.

The terrier's ball landed near them followed by the arrival of the scampering animal. He leapt up and ran to the dog. He wrestled the ball from the resistant creature's mouth and threw it back towards the owner, an older woman who looked disarmingly similar to her pet. Coming along the path was a child of about four, on a bicycle, intent on the arduous task of staying upright, behind her a proud mother. Where are the men? He looked far across the sloping green to the buildings rising up from the busy streets and the cars moving down below. There, he thought, they are all there, driving taxis, cleaning pavements, taking meetings, making noise. And over there, on the grass, jacket off, tie askew, snoozing in the late afternoon sun. And there, on the bench, reading a newspaper, old and alone.

The ball arrived again near him. He kicked it back. The terrier ran this way and that.

Jane stood before him. The coat was on, the glasses swept back her hair. 'I better go now, Jacob.' She hesitated. 'There's time. We'll be in touch. I understand this is asking a lot of you.' There was uncertainty and then determination on her face. Her long arm reached out and took hold of his. He looked away. No more. Not today. Enough. 'The thing is,' she started, 'the thing is, I suggested to Charlotte that she needed to think hard about whether she could be a mother. I said Sheldon and I could adopt the baby.'

He was shocked. All his life he had felt intimidated by the emotional zeal of women. His own mother, in her locked-down life, had brought vivid colour to the confines of their semi-detached. The wild experiments in cooking and the artful arrangements of furniture expressed a desire for so much more than the lot that befell her. She talked in bright eloquent tones, she laughed uproariously, and he as boy, laughed with her, unsure even then as to the joke. She cried with equal vigour, at a broken dish, a sentimental film. Her tears scared him. They excluded him.

Somewhere along the line of his life, he had simply detached, untethered himself; a helium balloon diving and swirling and rolling to the gusts of winds whose multiple and singular characteristics provided fresh impetus as the seasons rolled by.

He could continue floating, flying by. The aromatic spring breeze urged him to give a habitual shrug of the shoulder, a conciliatory smile and some gentle questions. But the revolt which stirred in him was gaining ground. Shock. He was shocked.

'Out of the question.'

Jane's eyes swam with tears but the set line of her lips indicated something more than distress.

'I've my reasons.' There was defiance and defensiveness in her tone. The shock grew to outrage.

'I know about those reasons. You wanted children, you couldn't, so you thought you'd just take Charlotte's.' Reckless. Satisfying cruel words. The look on her face told him he had hit very hard. She stepped back, and keeping her brimful eyes on him, shook her head from one side to the other in slow deliberate swings. 'No, no, not that, it's not like that. There are other things.' He had removed her protective layering. Momentarily he felt sorry, sorry for her, sorry for what he had said, but the churning rebellious anger was stronger than his compassion.

He moved away from her, then turned south and began to walk, then quicker, and then he was running at a fast exhilarating speed.

'Jacob, please! I'm sorry! Come back!' Her passionate plea lost volume with each stride that took him further from her. Across the soft grass and onto the narrow pavement he ran, and ran, until finally he stopped, out of breath, and collapsed onto the grass where he remained for some time while the sun lowered in the sky.

———

Her confession, if that is what it was intended to be, had the effect of bringing to a point of recognition the crisis approaching him. He sat at the window of his flat watching through dark branches life unfold behind lighted windows on the other side of the street. He registered an old woman in a recliner watching television in semi-darkness; a young professional on the floor below at a table working on a computer in a sitting room; and in the kitchen next door, another in exercise clothes prepared a meal. His eyes saw and his mind skipped along a range of thoughts that took him to people and places far from this street. Jane had texted him:

> *So sorry, terrible thing to blurt out like that. Not what it seems. Can we talk? x*

No.

There was something in what Jane had proposed that propelled him to think about the many questions that he had avoided.

It was not surprising Charlotte had reacted to Jane. But why had Jane suggested something so heartless? In the many months of knowing her he had never witnessed any expressions of cruelty from her. Is it possible Jane really believed adoption would be the best solution? She knew better than him the meaning Charlotte attached to this baby. A pang went through him. And he, did he not count at all, in either women's configurations? Mine too, he growled, my baby. His petulance was rekindled.

He opened the window to let in the sound of rustling branches on the street. His shirt billowed as he leant out. He could smell curry. A fox trotted across the street, its alert muzzle lifted pointedly to the possibilities of danger. It poised for an instant to take the measure of its surrounds. It would say he was a fool.

To have been so intimate with Charlotte had been a risk, uncontrollable and mysterious. Was it a mistake? Her beauty, her sorrow, her ungraspable nature had opened up in him a yawning, a place where the particles of his future might be reassembled. His falling for her had taken him by surprise. That she did not reciprocate left him with a sense of punching air. Soon they would have a baby together. His mind drifted to photographs of Sylvie, the trial, Charlotte's illness – and stopped short of death. The likelihood of cot death happening twice was tiny, almost unimaginable. But the psychosis? It would be OK. She would be OK. Jane did not think so.

And if Charlotte came back to England. Close to him. Where? He withdrew from the window ledge and cast about his flat. The couple next door were watching television. Upstairs was quiet. Finn and Mikey overwhelmed this room with lengthy limbs that extended octopus-like everywhere. Their presence reduced the flat to a doll's house. And to add a baby to this ... Where would she fit? He ran his hand along the wall to the bookcase. It was floor to ceiling. He had bought it from IKEA. His books were arranged in categories. He caressed spines. These were his selected, the rest remained scattered on shelves in the house several long streets from here. Moving along the wall, he came to the open door of his bedroom lit by the outside miasma of street and city glare. The double bed, an expensive purchase, had known only his body. Further along came an opening to his sons' bunk room. Thin like a railway carriage. The Venetian slats, clean and horizontal, filtered stripes onto the laminate floor. A neat pile of clothes sat on the high dresser, enough alternatives for them to spend two days here if they arrived with no extras. In the gleaming bathroom, recently modernised, their three electric toothbrushes were lined up on the glass shelf. Deodorant, razors, shaving cream, all shared. Mikey had only hints of fluff on his upper lip but wanted, had always wanted, to imitate his older brother.

Returning to the sitting room he appraised the small efficient kitchen area, the neat square table and standard sofa, his expensive eighteenth-century desk on which tilted the computer and piles of paper. Two pictures on the wall, costly buys. Objects calmed in the dark. Passably like a home.

He lay down on the sofa. The future that had so recently tantalised him with the prospect of wide vistas now seemed a thankless narrow place. He was helpless. Yet, he could hear the chorus of voices, Kath's, his boys'. Society had words for men like him.

He had decided not to tell his sons about the baby until they had finished their exams. There was no need. He would take them away for a week and do it when there was time to absorb the information without interference, without escape. There was a cottage they had rented in past years on the Norfolk coast. He had booked it last year before any of the recent events had veered his life off-course; he still held the booking. He would mail Kath from there. He did not want to have a confrontation, the script was too predictable, his culpability glaringly obvious. After a week with Finn and Mikey they might all discuss the event in a balanced manner. Briefly he wondered whether Jane might moderate. The baby would be born by then. She would have a name.

Jane's proposal returned to him. Adoption. Was it really so mad? He could slip into the nooks of this sprawling city, and one day, perhaps, when the terrain was safe again, re-emerge into the light. And Jane. She would have the child she'd always longed for.

He scratched away at his confusion and found further contradiction. Had he not hoped, a little, that she would miscarry? He had suppressed the feeling and gone straight to the naive hope that her pregnancy would draw her to him. A stirring in him brought a momentary light – perhaps, after all, it still might! She had not outright rejected him and his ideas about a life in England. I'll continue to woo her! Jane would help. A small arrogance allowed him to believe in the positive outcome of such a strategy. Yes, he could convince her of his better self, of the undeniable appeal of taking a risk on a life shared. She would meet Mikey and Finn, she would understand how good they might be all together. But, the voice of reason argued, but, you know, you do know, she doesn't really want you. Really? People change their minds, who can resist being loved? All she wants is the love of the baby. To love the baby. Heaviness set in again. The baby. How would she manage? If the psychosis returned Charlotte would be in a very vulnerable state. As would the child. His child too. Alarm returned his thoughts once again to Jane's proposal.

Jane knew things. She knew about fragile psychological states. She knew about Charlotte. She would be a good mother. Adoption? He could see it was an appealing proposition viewed from a certain angle. Why not? Yes, let her take the baby and provide a solid safe place … anger seized him all over again. No! No way. He understood he was in the grip of some force that existed between these two women. His will rose up against it. He went over his recent confrontation with Jane and buried his head in the soft fabric of the sofa. There were many things he did not, and had not, understood. This thought flashed through him with the illuminating strength of a Damascene moment.

He sat upright and grabbed a notebook. He had always solved thorny journalistic problems in the past by trusting in his intellectual intuition. He might be on his way to sixty – he stumbled and slumped back into the cheap foam of the sofa. Yes, I am old, too old for all this, for becoming a father all over again. He had back problems from a lifetime spent in front of a desk. His blood pressure yo-yoed. His leg muscles ached. His hair was falling out, he needed dental work, his testosterone was diminishing fast. What had Charlotte said to Jane? He could only imagine she had dealt Jane a resounding slap. He would write to Charlotte, he would talk to Jane. He would reconcile them to each other. And still there resurfaced in him the idea (was it hope, stupid hope?) that with time Charlotte would succumb to his persuasion. There was manoeuvring to be managed, positioning to be achieved, a renewed advance on her. When the baby came it would be much easier. He could show her how to be a family.

The next day he called Jane.

'Why did you suggest something so cruel to Charlotte?

'I felt pushed to it. She wouldn't listen. She's not taking seriously the probable return of the psychosis.'

'You don't even know for sure if it was post-partem psychosis. You know how important this baby is to her.'

'Of course. I thought pushing her to think the unthinkable would make her face the reality of her situation.

'She seems to be doing that very well.'

'Not if she doesn't accept the need for full psychiatric help.'

'You're assuming the worst. That's unlike you. Why should she?'

'Because it happened before. And I didn't see it back then, and, well, there.'

Dear Charlotte, Jane told me she said unforgivable things to you. I believe she's tried to call you and has written to you. I know it's awful what she suggested but perhaps let's move forward. She really wants to help. She is <u>very fond</u> of you. Please let her back in. Jacob x
    p.s. how is Trieste?

Dear Jacob, I'm enjoying being in Trieste without the stress of work. The charity gave me such a lovely send-off. The children sang a song and made me a special book of stories. I cried!
    I'm doing yoga and attending a pre-natal class. I've seen the

psychiatrist who is a sympathetic woman. I'm making friends with other expecting mothers. I feel wonderfully positive! A little uncomfortable of course. And sometimes if I'm honest, nervous, even quite scared. But the psychiatrist, her name is Martina, says that's natural and she's pleased I'm talking about it. She is ready to put me on an anti-depressant but I don't feel any need. She says we'll discuss it again when the baby is born. I don't want to pollute our baby with chemicals. I feel she is strong and so looking forward to being out in the world. C x

That's great news Charlotte. Sorry to bring it up again, but what about Jane? You know I'll be there to help as much as my time permits. I'd feel a lot better if Jane was around too. I gather she is after all your next of kin? x

I'm still cross Jacob. That doesn't really cover it. I was so hurt. And outraged. She's been the closest thing in my life to family ever since Alex and Sylvie. I know she can be a little controlling and sometimes goes too far but I always thought she was on my side. She scared me. I have answered her email, said we wouldn't talk of it again. And I'll leave it at that for now. Do you understand? x

I think so. x

PART FOUR

'There are moods in which we court suffering,
in the hope that here, at least, we shall find reality,
sharp peaks and edges of truth.'

Ralph Waldo Emerson, 'Experience', *Essays: Second Series*

HE REMEMBERS HER TALL FIGURE SHAPED IN A BACK-ward S outlined in the glow of a humid sun. He remembers the shriek as her waters broke and the joyfully chaotic trip to the hospital in the Italian ambulance. He remembers the intense concentration of the doctor and midwives. An emergency Caesarean, her fretful inchoate eyes. He remembers, most of all, the tiny red scrunched creature mewling in his arms where he crouched on the floor in the corner of the delivery room, protected, protecting, as the doctor sewed up Charlotte.

The mewling has become a strong cry. He picks her up from the cot beside his bed. Ashen light frames the closed curtains. The digital clock says 7 am. She is a good sleeper, unlike him. Her mouth is Charlotte's. He traces the tiny lips with his finger. She gurgles, her face crinkles with pleasure. He puts his finger in her mouth and she sucks hard, her eyes never leaving his. Her head is his, a long oval.

'I want to call her Mabel,' said Charlotte, drugged and breathless from her hospital bed. 'It was my father's mother's name.'

'Queen Mab!' He quoted: 'The fairies' midwife, and she come in shape no bigger than an agate stone.' He shared a smile with the midwife.

A small chuckle escaped Charlotte's spit-froth lips. 'God Jacob,' she said in a hoarse voice, 'start with a nursery rhyme why don't you!' The midwife was cleaning up Mabel, who declared her being in short cries like the call of a bird. Jacob leaned close to Charlotte and the two were one for a single short exaggerated second.

The pain is sharp, flint-edged. It is also blunt, it has no nuance. It is ever present and terrible.

He lifts himself, Mab nestled in his arm, and pads to the kitchen where he prepares a bottle of formula.

Their first night together he had latched her tiny mouth onto his dry insufficient nipple. She spat it out quickly, indignant. She was used to the bottle; Charlotte had found breastfeeding difficult. He had tried to help by lavishing calendula cream onto her breasts and nipples, cooing soft words into her unhearing ears. The midwife had latched Mabel onto the beckoning nipple over and again. The milk had come down but was not flowing. A device was attached to the breast, and this too made Charlotte wince. Several days later after his return to London Charlotte had said over the phone, it's too difficult, she's on the bottle, she's fine, she loves it; she took it immediately; she doesn't want me. Irritation surged in Jacob. For God's sakes, try a bit harder. He had had beaten into him the incomparable benefits of breast milk years ago when Finn came into the world. His reply was curt and banal, met by a sigh loaded with what he only now recognises as despair. What was he to do from his flat many miles away in Kensal Rise? She had not wanted him to stay with her. Go home, she had coaxed, you need to speak to Finn and Mikey. I understand. Jane'll be here next week, he said to reassure them both. When Jane arrived Mabel was on the bottle and Charlotte seemed relieved. She had handed both to Jane: you can feed her too. Jane had reported this to Jacob by text in answer to his anxious emails. Then Jane had left and Jacob had cancelled his next visit because he needed to stay close to the boys as they absorbed the news of this new sibling. Communication between him and Charlotte was as it had been, affectionate and limited, and for a period he felt calm.

Mabel guzzles and he sees she is contented. She does not yet know hurt. Finn and Mikey do. He saw it in their eyes last year when he and Kathleen told them he was leaving. He saw the same look again when he explained to them they had a baby sister. Finn's natural conservatism led him to judge his father severely; Mikey was emotionally shambolic, not knowing who to love or who to blame. Kathleen, perversely, had erupted into laughter, a kind of hilarity had characterised her response to the news that he was a father again, and it remained even now in her, three months later, a barely concealed glee. Mikey and Finn were settling into this new blend; a kind of docility prevailed.

He stumbles on a sucked lion. In the shadowy dawn his flat could easily be mistaken for the site of a break-in. Books, some no bigger than the size of a playing card, lie on the floor; clothes, tiny and large, drape the sofa, the radiator, hang off the bookshelf. Kitchen drawers, half-open. Stains on the carpet, smell of shit in the air.

Jane will come later this morning. She will take Mabel to Gloucester for several days. He will clean the flat, see Mikey, write a long email to Finn, now at university. He hates it when Jane has Mabel; a terrible fear that he will never see her again takes hold and then, as hours pass, it abates and he tentatively ushers back in his life as an ageing exhausted bachelor. He will meet his copy deadline. He will interview an artist. He might look at his book proposal, languishing somewhere on his desk, untouched since the arrival of Mabel. He is no longer so interested in writing the story of Theodor, there is too much work to be done, too much travel. He has no time for this kind of project. He needs more immediate ways to increase his income. His overdraft is growing, his credit card maxing out. The pay-off he got from the newspaper is paying the rent but will be gone soon.

He lives inside grief. His actions and words have become

exaggerated to himself, too loud or strange to exist alongside the pain. Incredulity is the current prompt. At first it was shock. Sometimes it is anger.

She planned it all. Her suicide was not a sudden act of folly. Only days before she had visited a Triestine lawyer who had drawn up her will with instructions for the guardianship of Mabel.

She was found by the health visitor only hours after she had taken the pills. Jane was due to arrive later that day for her second visit. Mabel was contentedly asleep. Everything had been arranged to minimise disorder. Aside from the act itself. She had left a note:

I leave the care of our beautiful daughter to you, Jacob, her loving father, and to you, Jane, my best friend. You will give her such a good life. You will be a far better mother than I ever could or deserve to be.

It had been a hot August. She had moved Mabel from her bedroom to the sitting room where a fan blew airy waves towards the cot. All her little items of clothing, her BabyGros and cotton tops, flowery dungarees and stripy dress, were freshly laundered. A new packet of nappies sat on the table, ready for use. Thought out.

Jacob arrived the next morning and for the following fortnight he and Jane sleepwalked through a flurry of nappy changing, bottle feeding, police, hospital, child protection services, lawyer, funeral director, bank and real estate agents. The scattering of her ashes to the sea from the far end of the Molo Audace, the pier stretching out into the Adriatic. Dog walkers, loners, exercise nuts, amorous couples, tourists, fishermen, all attended the funeral offering a genial ignorance to the small ritual taking place beside them.

The schedule they now operate skids all over the place. His life is the more adaptable and he tends to have Mabel during the week, though Jane sometimes takes her then when she is sure of Sheldon's presence (Sheldon is not adapting well to this change in his life with Jane, and Jacob wonders whether one day he will simply stay in the States and not return). That this interferes with Jacob's ability to earn a living presents a problem they have yet to solve. Both he and Jane are reluctant to find childminding help. That will come later. They are co-trustees of Mabel's inheritance, which Charlotte instructed be used for whatever Jacob and Jane felt was suitable for the care and comfort of Mabel's upbringing. Jane is inclined to think that the money from the sale of the flat in Trieste should be put towards buying a home for Jacob and Mabel. His little flat in Kensal Rise is too small, the rent high. He cannot afford to buy himself an adequate place with what is left to him from the divorce. A mortgage would cost him dearly if he were even to be granted one, which is unlikely. He is old. He has no stable income. A mortgage broker would not accept him. Jane wants them to come to Gloucester, or Cheltenham, if he prefers, the more elegant of the county cities with plenty of culture. Property is more affordable than in London. She is persuasive. She believes he would be happy there. She would be close-by. She is hopeful. Jacob agrees but for the moment he is resisting such a move. Until Mikey is at university he wants to stay where he is. He is acclimatising to – everything. His feelings lag behind the actuality of his life. He is catching up slowly with himself.

Sometimes he feels bewildered by the trust Charlotte has put in him. How could she know he would care properly for this little girl? What allowed her to imagine he and Jane would get on through the years in their joint role as parents? At other times, through dark angry hours in the night, he rages. *How could she?* Rationally he knows the answers. He and Jane have been over them many times with assorted people in Trieste, then with psychiatrist friends of Jane's who she turned to for consolation. The psychosis had returned, Charlotte became engulfed, no one was close enough to her to pick up on it. And so on.

He and Jane circle each other like hedgehogs. They are inarticulate against the power of their emotions. They feel dangerous to each other. They do not talk about Charlotte except to add a detail now and then to the facts of her death.

There have been moments between them in which a question has flashed up, unspoken and understood; and faded. It does not address Charlotte's suicide. It will be a long while before they might face the dull roar of guilt each carries within. The silent communication is of a different nature, it contains a possibility of an unformed future. It first glinted from Jacob last week when Jane sat on a chair in his flat waiting while he gathered up Mabel's bits and pieces. An autumn sun filtered through the russet leaves of the tree outside the window. Her hair glinted with copper and her face glowed bronze. In her green eyes a jumbled story was flowing. He started. He had never seen her look so beautiful nor so full of contradiction. She emitted a little laugh, then tilted her head and slowly shrugged one shoulder.

'Jane?'

She turned to him. Mabel was fast asleep in her cot next door. He sat on the arm of the chair and followed her earlier gaze to the dying leaves. She touched his thigh for a moment, sighed and leaned back into the chair.

'Sheldon.'

'You two.' The skittish leaves. 'Is it forever?'

'I'd hoped so. Now I don't know. He hates this huge change in our life together. He hates Charlotte for what she did. He's staying away longer and longer. He doesn't want Mabel.' He looked down at her and in that few seconds the question was asked. She accepted it and in her silent reply much was left wide open.

———

Kathleen has made several visits to the flat to meet Mabel. She is solicitous and merry in her dealings with Jacob. He thinks, 'She is being patronising, but I don't care.'

When Kathleen met Jane they were charming to each other.

'Mabel's gorgeous,' offered Kathleen, handing over the bundle to Jane. She lingered until the awkwardness brought on by her presence was palpable.

'Sorry,' explained Jacob, closing the door on Kath. 'She was dying to meet you. She's being quite supportive. Even if she has a tendency to giggle when she sees me. I thought she'd be out of her mind with anger.'

'It's because Charlotte's dead.' It was only the second time she had spoken these words in this blunt formation; the first was on the phone to Jacob after she arrived in Trieste and confirmed the identification of Charlotte's body.

'She doesn't have to be jealous. Her rival is gone.' The resignation in her voice carried humour too. She grinned apologetically: 'Sorry if that seems a little crude.' And then the question flashed up again, from him to her, and again she did not reject him in her silent reply.

Mabel is now six months old and the need to address the problem of his income has become urgent. It is time to act on the surprising outcome of his search for Theodor.

He visits Nicky at work. He brings Mabel. It is a brisk winter's day. She is bundled in a red down onesie. Nicky's ambitious assistant, a recent graduate of high intellect and earnest opinions, emits nervous clucks at the sight of the baby. Mabel regards her with interest and begins to grouch, hot in her swaddled cloth. He strips her off, asks for coffee and enters Nicky's generous office.

Jacob got out of his bag a print-off of an email in response to the classified advertisement he ran in *Il Piccolo* last spring. He had forgotten entirely about the ad. The paper must have continued to run it over months. His memory has for the moment ceased functioning. He remembers little about the weeks before Charlotte's death. The email came from a woman called Letizia Bonacchi.

Dear Jacob Bedford, I have seen your advertisement about your search for your great-grandfather. I can help you. I have been waiting for this day. Please send me your address and I will write to you. My English is not so good but my daughter helps me to write this. She has good English. Yours, Letizia Bonacchi.

Letizia is his great-aunt. The promised letter arrived enclosing a photograph of Theodor. Theodor is not how he expected him to look: he is tall and lean, like Jacob himself. The photograph though old and yellowed shows a man with sparse pale hair, light eyes, a clean-shaven face, high cheekbones. A refined wry expression gazes out. Jacob peers at the background: it is of an interior, some kind of a drawing room with a decorative upholstered chair and a heavy dark wood bookshelf. A stamp on the back reads *Wien* 1935. Theodor was 61 years old.

He fishes the letter out of his bag as well and gives it to Nicky to read. It is typed on a computer. The signature at the end is a grand black flourish.

The man you call Theodor was my father. I knew him by my family name. Bonacchi is my married name. He was known as Vincenzo. He died when I was little, 8 years old, just after the war. He was already an old man. I thought he was my grandfather. My mother was much younger than him. She did not marry again. I grew up with stories about this man very kind who had been my grandfather. She told me he was an agent for the big insurance company. Only when I was grown woman did my mother tell me the truth – that this man my grandfather was my father, and his real name was Theodor Motz, a Jew from Vienna. She said he came to Trieste to find her in 1938. They were lovers in the years after the First World War. She was a clerk in the shipping office, it exported his goods. She was very young. They laughed together a lot, they hit it off at once. He was the great love of my mother. Then after the First World War Trieste became Italian, Theodor's business was no longer good and he shut down his office. But he still came to see my mother. She says he loved Trieste, much more than the great capital Vienna. She says he was free in Trieste. She says she waited many years for him to come to her. He finally came when the Nazis entered Austria and he fled. My mother says that his wife, her name was Johanna, never knew about my mother. Johanna went to Prague to join her own father, a musician. My mother says Johanna was also musician. Her father was an Aryan and he thought she was safe. I don't know what happened to her. My mother says my father never knew. She knew he had a son, Stefan, in England. He was safe. After Italy passed the racial laws against Jews, my father and my mother panicked. They saw into the future. They thought he was going to be taken away. Now they committed their crime. This is where I'm sorry the story is not so pleasant. My mother lived with her sick father. Her mother died when she was a young girl. My grandfather was very sick. He was dying of cancer. My mother says he had not long to live. They could have waited but time was passing and Jews were fleeing Trieste or being put in prison and having jobs taken away. So one night they killed him with some morphine my mother got from a friend in the hospital. They buried his body in the dark of night with the help of my mother's priest. He was a good man. He kept her secret. My father became then my grandfather. He assumed his identity. They moved at once to a different part of Trieste, away from the suburb that is now by the industrial docks to the prosperous part of the city on the via di Scorcola. No one *knew who they were. They were very cautious. They made it through the war. My father even joined the Fascist Party for his disguise. Then he died in 1947. He was 73 years old. I would like to meet you. You have relatives in Trieste, cousins. I have a daughter and two sons. They have children. I have only recently told them about the truth about the grandfather they never knew.*

Nicky looks up from the letter and whistles. 'Quite a story!'

'Yes,' he says flatly. 'I'm working on a proposal. Letizia and I are in touch. I'm trying to track down descendants of those who knew Johanna and Theodor in Vienna. Needle in a haystack. Most of the Jewish families were killed or fled. I've been on ancestry.com and a few other websites but I can't find out much of value. I need to do a few research trips, work in the Vienna archives, but I can't afford that at the moment. I need money. Things are tight. Do you think an editor might be interested?'

'Maybe. Difficult to tell. You know advances have really dropped, I can't promise anything.' Nicky contemplates Jacob and then Mabel. His attention focuses on Mabel. Jacob has told him little about his daughter, only that he had a fling with the mother and the mother is now dead. Nicky's curiosity to know more is so strong he does not want to talk about Theodor and Letizia, the switched identity. He wants to find out more about what is in front of him. He probes: the mother? Charlotte? How did she die? Here Jacob hesitates, then, resigned, he says, 'Suicide.' Nicky's eyebrows raise. 'In Trieste,' continues Jacob. Now Nicky leans forward, all ears.

'Was she English? Does she know your relatives, this Letizia?'

'No, she didn't know them. That came after her death. Yes, she was English but she left Britain many years ago to work for a children's charity in Bosnia.

'Bosnia! Why there?'

'Her baby had died, she suffered a breakdown, her husband divorced her, when she came out of hospital she wanted a new life, a chance to –' Jacob hesitates again.

'Yes,' prods Nicky, 'a chance to . . . ?'

'A chance to recover, to heal.'

'And her suicide?'

Jacob explains about puerperal psychosis. Nicky is fascinated. He is clearly shocked too. There is a pause. Then something occurs to him. 'Jacob, I'm sorry, did you really care for her?'

Jacob nods, bewildered all over again by the startling power of pain. Mabel is fast asleep in her stroller. So beautiful. He rocks the buggy. It squeaks causing her eyes to flutter. Absently he thinks of Theodor, of Theodor's eyes, Polish blue, like Mabel's.

Nicky meditates on the information he has just been given. Jacob can see his brain whirring and clacking like an overworked machine. 'How did you meet?'

Jacob explains about his first visit to Trieste, about meeting Jane, about Jane's friendship with Charlotte. Nicky is again on the alert, a hunter in sight of prey.

'Jane? A psychotherapist you say? Are you two in touch?'

'She is Mabel's guardian. We co-parent. She lives in Gloucester.'

Nicky claps his hands once like a starting pistol. 'It's right there in front of you. Your story. This story. What's just happened. A memoir of sorts. Real life. I'll be able to sell this on a first chapter and summary. Place a long piece in one of the Sunday magazines. With this.' He grabs Letizia's letter and gestures wildly. The excitement spills out of him, little sparks in the air.

Jacob resists. The lines of books on shelves across two walls bear down on him. So many words. A sad sorry tale. He looks at Mabel and a fierce love shakes him up. She is not for public consumption. 'No,' he asserts and tears fall down his face.

'Think about it.' Nicky is calmer and says in a kindly manner:

'Look, you need money, don't you?'

He nods.

'Let's see if I can place a story about Theodor in a magazine. It's a start. Is that OK?'

He nods again.

'It might help you.'

Can he write this story, so fresh, so unclear to him? And whose story is it? He does not feel it is his. He simply happened to be present, neither amanuensis, nor bystander, nor witness. A bit part.

'Take your time,' encourages Nicky. 'Maybe jot down some notes. We'll take it slowly.'

———

Alex lifts Mabel high above his head and then lowers her quickly. She shrieks with excitement. He does this again twice and hands her back to Jacob, panting and smiling. Mabel is a pudgy cheerful little creature and now at nine months quite heavy.

This study, thinks Jacob, looking around him at the deck of computers and the soft sofa and the gallery of family photographs. Objects resist change better than humans.

He has come to retrieve the painting. Alex wants to give it to Mabel in memory of Charlotte. A gift. He has not yet sold it. Wrapped in brown paper, it remains where it was placed over a year ago when Jacob dropped it off. Has Alex looked at it every day and thought about Charlotte? Or has it become one of the many things in this room integrated into the quotidian and left unnoticed?

What is clear to Jacob is that Alex is captivated by Mabel. Her infant charm offers a route to amiability. He is kind towards Jacob, throwing him many ready smiles. He is pensive when Charlotte's name comes up. He wants to know exactly on what day Mabel was born and on what day Charlotte died.

'So it finally got the better of her', he murmurs, holding Mabel high above his head again such that her eyes open wide and she squeals in delight.

Jacob has to say something, so he says, 'Yes, the psychosis was finally too strong'.

Alex has a different answer: 'No, the guilt. It's the guilt, finally got too much for her.' Jacob understands what Alex is implying but it is for Alex to name.

'Perhaps finally this will bring an end to it, dear God. I know Jane has always hated me, blamed me for what happened all those years ago. But it wasn't –' and his voice begins to rumble – 'wasn't my fault.' His tone underlines the verb.

Jacob cares little about blame. He is turned to the future; he has to be. He knows little about Charlotte. He wants to find out more so that he can tell Mabel about her mother. This man lived with her as a husband. He knows many things. Like what it was like to have breakfast with in the early morning when she was fresh from sleep and how she danced and whether she liked pets and what it felt like to unbutton a party frock at night when she could not reach. Tears well up; he is so used to their presence that he no longer bothers to blink them away.

Alex hands Mabel back to Jacob, who settles her into her stroller. She wriggles and resists. She does not want to be strapped in, she wants to explore this small new world around her.

Alex crouches and stares intently into Mabel's eyes like a soothsayer. She holds his gaze for several seconds, then gives him the briefest of smiles and in that instant her infant features express a knowledge that far exceeds her capacity for thought.

Transfixed, Jacob wonders about reincarnation and the transmigration of souls, matter into matter. It is not a belief that has ever gripped his imagination. He prefers decisive new beginnings and conclusive ends. But the imagination can play funny tricks and in a momentary flash, Jacob sees Charlotte. Alex sees her too.

'What guilt?' Jacob picks up the threads of Alex's comments.

Alex views him with a look that is not without ironic sadness. It is difficult for Jacob to converse with this man. Signs of an active interior life are discouraging. The language of emotion brings Alex up against his own limitations. If he were to dig a bit deeper Jacob suspects he might find terror.

He is determined: 'The psychosis was not her fault. Why would she feel guilty?' The answer to his question starts to find its way into the forefront of his thoughts. But it is important to him that Alex tells him about Charlotte and her guilt. Mabel is now bored. Her strong eruptions have meaning. 'Dada!' Her one clear word. To Jane she says, 'Mmma!' He pulls her out of the stroller again.

'Does that nice woman, the one who gave us coffee when I was last here, look after children? Would she mind playing with Mabel for a bit?' Alex frowns. Unperturbed, Jacob persists. 'Or do you have a nanny?' It is a Friday late morning; as with his first visit, the house and garden are not disturbed by echoes of human voices.

Alex is reluctant to respond with any kind of action, but he sees that Jacob is insistent. He makes a decision and calls out to Angie. Mabel is taken off in a flurry of smiles and baby talk.

Jacob perches on the arm of the sofa, his focus directed with unwavering determination at Alex.

Alex stands in front of him, unwilling to settle into comfort, and asks, 'How much do you know about Charlotte's condition and what happened with Sylvie?' He is so tall that Jacob feels a slight crick in his neck when looking at him. He wishes the evasion and posturing would stop. He gestures to the sofa for Alex to sit. Alex obeys.

'I know little,' answers Jacob. 'I only found out about the puerperal psychosis from Jane a few months before Mabel was born. Jane had withheld from me what she believed was the true nature of Charlotte's breakdown. She'd found out during the time when she visited Charlotte at the hospital and became her next of kin. But I also understand that it's impossible to know for sure what she suffered from. The grief might have tipped Charlotte into the breakdown. You hadn't noticed her difficulties when Sylvie was born, whatever it was, Charlotte went untreated. And then there were Sylvie's respiratory problems and the cot death. She'd felt guilty for years for not having intervened. It may not have prevented Sylvie's death, but it would've helped Charlotte.'

'It would've.'

'Would've what?'

Alex now puts his hands over his eyes and exhales. Jacob is tensing up at what they are about to bring into words. He continues like a butcher with a knife hanging over the carcass of a pig. 'Would have prevented her death?' Alex nods, his eyes still covered.

'Sylvie's death?' Jacob utters this question with steadfast sharpness.

Alex removes his hands. In his eyes is written such sorrow and turmoil that Jacob relaxes his stance. Alex's gaze travels beyond Jacob to the photograph of Sylvie on the wall.

'If I'd known that she had this terrible condition, this psychosis, I'd have had her under psychiatric care. Sylvie would be alive today. How was I to know?' The question was rhetorical, tinged with anger and guilt.

The thoughts that flit through Jacob's mind follow patterns of accusation and compassion.

They go something like this: you know because you pay attention. You know because you love your wife. You know because you sleep naked with this amazing woman and make love to her. You know because you look. You know because you listen. Then as quickly as a film on fast-forward, moments from his own former marriage flicker by. No, you never know much at all. This poor man.

'I didn't even find out until she was in the hospital. Then it came out. They thought she had been suffering all along. The condition. Her –' Alex halts. He tries again: 'Her –'.

'She suffocated Sylvie.' Jacob announces this because Alex is unable to. The possibility came to him in a long moment of clarity on the drive to Gloucestershire this morning. The unease of the man last winter could not simply be explained away by a lingering passion for Charlotte. Then there were the newspaper clippings from the trial, followed by the big red folder that Jane appropriated. She kept things from him, he knows it. Her behaviour in light of Charlotte's past and the news of the pregnancy was too extreme to be put down to a mere former blip in her professional expertise. It is all there lined up in front of him. He chose not to see.

He is not shocked. A kind of peace descends. For the first time since meeting Jane and Charlotte in Trieste he feels back in charge of his life. There will be questions for Jane, gently put. Again into his unworded future there flashes a pairing: J & J. Perhaps that is what Charlotte intended all along. Perhaps in her craziness she was also clairvoyant; she saw how badly Sheldon would react and how much Jacob and Jane might love one another. Perhaps. He is running ahead of himself, way ahead.

Alex eventually says: 'When I found out, the psychiatrist told me, what could I do? I couldn't forgive her. I couldn't. All I could see was my baby – and that – her mad crazed arms squeezing the life out of her.' He pleads: 'Can you imagine such a thing?'

There are some sequences that are all too easy to put into pictures and words. Horror movies, melodramas and crime stories, tabloids, YouTube, cyberlife, the sensationalist depictions of such moments lavishly, ghoulishly, brutishly slathered over. Trauma writ large, written, represented, relayed, portrayed, filmed and photographed. It was everywhere. No, Jacob did not need to run this drama through his imagination. Charlotte's suffering, her violence if that is what it was, belonged to her, to her alone. What Jacob needed was unadorned fact. The very precise details that piled-up in consecutive order to tell the story of Charlotte and Sylvie. Would this lead to understanding? No, probably not, acts of violence are commonplace, only the circumstances of each one are singular. It is the singularity that precludes easy understanding. Better, he thinks, better than this horror movie that Alex torments himself with. He does not want to add further to Alex's distress.

'Yes, I can imagine.'

Later he and Mabel would drive to Jane in Gloucester. There he would sit with her and go over page by page the contents of the red folder. He would not interrogate Jane on her withholding of information. Had it been him in possession of such material he too would have kept it to himself. Some things are best left unsaid: once spoken they enter the real. Once in the world the words require action and reaction setting off an uncontrolled chain of events. He understands why Jane and Charlotte had had a fight in Bosnia and why Jane had been pushed to threaten Charlotte with adoption. Like a well-calibrated machine his logic leads him to put one thing after the other until it all slots nicely into place. On the surface.

There is always a 'but'.

'But,' reprises Jacob. 'How can you really know?' Alex is slumped next to him. Whatever envy Jacob might have felt for the man at his side has evaporated.

'It's all in the psychiatrist's notes. When Charlotte started remembering, it – she – it came back to her.' And why, thinks Jacob, would that be reliable, the mind of a demented tortured hallucinatory grief-stricken bereaved abandoned mother? Come, man, use your head!

'But how did they really know that what she was remembering actually happened? It's perfectly possible her grief and guilt created a false memory.'

Alex uncoiled from the sofa like a long crane opening into action. He took the photo of Sylvie from the wall. 'Because she's gone. A beautiful healthy little girl. My little girl. Dead.' Eyes gone savage. No tears. No more. Traces that remain.

———

Jacob arrives with Mabel, Finn and Mikey in Trieste. It is a sunny day in the clear promising month of June. The weather is pleasingly hot. They stay together in a family room at the Best Western Hotel near the maternity hospital. Jacob has mapped out the city in memory troves of family history. Finn is reluctantly interested: his history degree has awakened him to the vicissitudes of power and dislocation. Mikey shuns too much talk about these ghostly ancestors. He wants to shop and show-off his few Italian words.

They visit the apartment building where Theodor lived as Vincenzo on Via di Scorcola. They walk up and down the Via San Nicolò, where he ran his business as Motz und Sohn and where the Sohn, Stefan, bought books in the store above which Joyce taught English. He commemorates Charlotte's absence by showing them the Caffè San Marco and the hospital where Mabel was born. Mikey and Finn want to know about Theodor and Stefan, they do not want to know about Charlotte.

They have lunch with Letizia at a cafe near the old Jewish ghetto, a warren of streets filled with bric-a-brac shops. It only harboured Jews for a short period in the eighteenth century, explains Jacob. After the Edict of Tolerance everyone mingled and mixed. Why didn't people like the Jews? asks Mikey. Jacob shrugs, humans always need scapegoats, someone to blame for things that are wrong.

Letizia is a woman in her seventies. She is still sprightly. She is well-dressed in a floral skirt and white blouse; her hair is soft white and her eyes a pale blue-grey. She is warm and welcoming, eager to help. Finn takes a studious interest in the historical side, quizzing this distant and alien relative about the Nazi control of the city. Mikey prods and pokes Mabel, attending to her pizza slice, half an ear cocked to the conversation taking place. Jacob watches over him closely. He is only sixteen, still idealistic about the easy stories of his childhood in which romance and family evolve in a straightforward path to a hazy place called old age. This labyrinthine network of loves and lives, shocking deaths and pop-up relatives demand a lot from his teenage imagination. How to guide them, wonders Jacob, these children of mine into the uncertainties of adulthood where contingency and ambivalence haltingly meet? Finn wants facts, Mikey wants fables. Mabel wants fun.

Letizia has few papers relating to Theodor. All had to be destroyed by her mother when the identity switch took place. It was too dangerous. She hopes Jacob will pick up the threads and finish the story. Her English is broken and expressive. She waves her arms around a lot. Mabel's large eyes never leave the dance of hands. 'I show you Papi . . . Theodor. Ees in . . . chiesa – dare! Tomorroow.' And she points behind her to a part of the city. She has invited them to have dinner the next day at her daughter's; a strange kind of family reunion. They like her.

After lunch Jacob takes Finn, Mikey and Mabel to the end of the Molo Audace. The Castle Miramare is hazy on the other side of the bay. He sits Mabel on a bronze wind-rose hoisted on a plinth of white stone. She looks like an adorable elf atop a mushroom.

'This plaque,' he says, holding onto Mabel, 'tells only one part of a story.'

Finn looks closely: 'First World War.'

Mikey looks too: 'Audace, that's the word for audacious.' He is pleased with himself.

Jacob nods. It was the name of the first Italian destroyer that

213

docked here after the First World War and claimed Trieste for Italy, he says. Before that the pier was named after another ship, the *San Carlo*. The *San Carlo* sank here in the mid-eighteenth century. Out of the wreck they built this pier. It was first short then long as it is today. Many ships used to dock here, carrying people and goods from all over. 'This is when my grandfather was a boy, about your age Mikey. He walked all over this city, meeting Greeks and Italians, Arabs, Slavs and Jews like himself; he went to the theatre and the opera, he probably fell in love.'

Mikey grins, 'Hey, Dad, when are you going to take me to the opera?'

Finn shoves him, 'Loser, you hate that music, you think it's for old people.'

Mikey shoves him back, 'No I don't. Stupid. Dad why are the ships gone?'

Jacob explains about the war and Italy taking possession of Trieste, first after the First World War, then again after the Second World War. About the way in which cities, like families, like nations, like lovers are never only solid surfaces: beneath the stone, behind the story, lie more stone and more story. 'And now it's here for people like us to walk up and down, fish if we want to like those guys over there, or just enjoy the sea air.' He takes a deep breath.

Their insertion into the present function of the pier makes the boys stand up straighter and cast a keen eye into the distance. Mabel, aware of solemnity, pauses from her chatter. She too puts her head, abundant with Charlotte's blonde hair, to her shoulder and stares at the deep blue water.

The light breeze carries the smell of summer and sea in the gentle gusts that lick the stray tendrils of her curls. Absently Mikey lifts her and sits on the plaque settling her onto his lap. Finn, looking at a large trawler looming on the horizon, stuffs his hands into the pockets of his military jacket, and addresses his father: 'It's OK Dad. We can cope. It's all kinda interesting I guess.' Such simple words!

He pats his son on the back. 'I guess we will.'

There were many questions to be asked, trails to be followed, decisions made, none of which are very clear to Jacob as he stands at the end of the long *molo*. Particles cavort in the movement of the air and his thoughts turn to the great flight of Charlotte into this sky, to the tail of dark dust that flew about him and Jane, disappearing finally into the lapping waves below. Behind him, buried in a city graveyard lies what was once Theodor beneath the stone of someone called Vincenzo. Flying ash and buried mulch.

He remembers the wet ash and burnt leaves of the bonfire in the small garden of the house in Surbiton where every November he would stand with Grandad; smoke from the cigarette trailing smoke from the cinders. Grandad's bonfires never worked. He hated fire and noise, the onset of colder days.

These memories remain.

'Let's drink to Grandad, he's the reason we're here today.' He passes the bottle of water to Mikey who gulps, wipes his mouth, gives Mabel a sip.

'To the dude,' he says. Finn takes the bottle and pauses for a couple of seconds.

'To Stefan and Theodor.' As an afterthought he adds, 'And Johanna, murdered by the Nazis.'

Johanna, commemorated in a museum in a file in a town with millions of other pieces of human debris.

Jane awaits their return. Or is it his return? They have agreed to speak of Charlotte only when the potential for pain is outweighed by the possibility of repair. One day they will begin to tell Mabel about her mother. Over time a series of anecdotes and portraits will take shape. Only when Mabel is able to understand, when she has reached a certain maturity, will the darker shades begin to be filled in. They agree on this.

The five of them have planned a holiday together later in the summer. Jane has rented an eco-lodge in Cornwall. There they will celebrate Mabel's first birthday.

And Sheldon? Fading from the foreground of the future. Will he stick it out? Jane does not know. Neither does Sheldon. 'Time will tell,' said Jane.

'Do you want him to stay with you?' He had asked her this after they had gone through every piece of paper in Charlotte's medical files; after Sheldon had scattered the papers in all directions across the floor and slammed the door behind him to get into a taxi that would take him to the airport and then onto America. After Jane had wept for two hours straight in Jacob's arms. She had not answered. 'You do know,' she said to him, 'that just because Charlotte made a kind of confession doesn't mean she actually did this terrible thing.' Yes, said Jacob, he knew. He knew they would never know.

'So, what do you want for supper tonight?'

'Pizza! Pizza!' Finn and Mikey do a high five. Mabel wriggles. She wants off of Mikey's lap. Jacob picks her up and settles her in the stroller. Together they walk back down the length of the pier. Finn and Mikey chase each other, playing tag. An old fisherman scowls at them. Jacob yells: 'Hey, guys, watch where you're going!' The sun begins its imperceptible descent in the sky. Jacob takes a photo on his phone of the boys running down the pier and sends it to Jane: *All OK here! We miss you. Jx*